Leverage

*An Agent Jade Monroe FBI Crime Thriller
Book 4*

C. M. Sutter

Copyright © 2017
All Rights Reserved

AUTHOR'S NOTE

This book is a work of fiction by C. M. Sutter. Names, characters, places, and incidents are products of the author's imagination or are used solely for entertainment. Any resemblance to actual events or persons, living or dead, is entirely coincidental.

The scanning, uploading, and distribution of this book via the Internet or any other means without the permission of the publisher is illegal and punishable by law. Please purchase only authorized electronic editions, and do not participate in or encourage electronic piracy of copyrighted materials. Your support of the author's rights is appreciated.

ABOUT THE AUTHOR

C.M. Sutter is a crime fiction writer who resides in the Midwest, although she is originally from California.

She is a member of numerous writers' organizations, including Fiction for All, Fiction Factor, and Writers etc.

In addition to writing, she enjoys spending time with her family and dog. She is an art enthusiast and loves to create handmade objects. Gardening, hiking, bicycling, and traveling are a few of her favorite pastimes. Be the first to be notified of new releases and promotions at: http://cmsutter.com.

C.M. Sutter
http://cmsutter.com/

Leverage:
An Agent Jade Monroe FBI Crime Thriller, Book 4

FBI Agent Jade Monroe's partner, J.T. Harper, has abruptly disappeared. The entire Serial Crimes Division hands off its current cases to concentrate on finding one of their own. They soon learn that J.T.'s sister, Julie, is also missing. Since she has no connection to the FBI, they fear she has been kidnapped and is being used as leverage in a twisted vendetta against J.T. A video is delivered to the FBI with Julie as the unfortunate spokesperson, leading the team to believe that this mysterious kidnapper has more on his mind—and a deeper connection to J.T. Harper—than they could possibly know.
The mayhem worsens when J.T.'s former partner is murdered and dumped in front of the FBI headquarters as a sign of the kidnapper's intentions. Now J.T.'s life is in the crosshairs, and as the days tick by, Julie's life is in jeopardy too.

Stay abreast of each new book release by signing up for my VIP e-mail list at:
http://cmsutter.com/newsletter/

Find more books in the Jade Monroe Series here:
http://cmsutter.com/available-books/

Chapter 1

"Heads-up, the Fed is getting ready to leave. He just checked the balcony sliders and drew the curtains. I'm guessing he'll reach the parking garage in less than three minutes, so make damn sure you're ready."

The man calling out the commands lowered his binoculars and rearranged himself in the seat of the stolen champagne-colored Mercedes. From his location across the street from the stacked stone–accented condo in Whitefish Bay, he had the perfect vantage point, and the limousine tint on the windows afforded him a certain degree of anonymity. He didn't leave anything to fate or bad judgment. He hadn't gotten that far by being careless.

Carden Vetcher sat back low in the seat, thanks to the power seat adjuster at his left hand. He tipped his black felt fedora as he peered through the windshield at that second floor unit. A simple adjustment of the toggle switch on the side mirror gave him a crystal clear visual of the condo's driveway behind him.

His high-class appearance was nothing more than a ruse

that worked well in getting him through doors usually closed to Joe Q. Public. Having that powerful image also kept his subordinates in line. Truth be told, Carden had carved out a criminal enterprise for himself years back, and only his high IQ and a decent number of successes under his belt kept him in the black.

The earbud fit snuggly in his left ear, and his cell phone sat to his right on the empty passenger seat. "Where are you—exactly?"

"I'm lurking in the shadows. Where do you think I am?"

"Need I remind you who's calling the shots, Anthony? I'd be happy to personally get that point across to you if necessary."

"Okay, I hear the elevator coming down."

"His parking spot is the second one to the left. Can you see his car, plate number 379-NNF?"

"Yeah, yeah, I got it. The elevator just dinged."

"Make sure it's him first, then nail him with the Taser." Carden chuckled. "The idiot won't know what hit him. Go directly to the warehouse and take the route I outlined for you. Stay on the back roads. I'll be right behind you."

"I have to go. The doors are opening."

The phone call abruptly ended, telling Carden the attack had begun. The vehicle belonging to the agent would be leaving the underground parking garage at any minute, and the real fun would begin.

"Two down and one to go." Carden rubbed his hands with anticipation. He watched the garage's exit through his driver's side mirror, then he turned the key in the ignition and shifted into Drive as the agent's car came into view. A sinister smile lit up his face. "It's party time." He dialed the preset number on the burner phone. "Any problems, Anthony?"

"It was as easy as taking candy from a baby, Mr. Vetcher. He didn't even have a chance to react."

Carden laughed with pleasure. "Nice work." He clicked the blinker and pulled out into traffic. "I'm right behind you."

Chapter 2

I fidgeted as I waited in the booth next to the window at Café Central on Silver Spring Drive. J.T. was late, and that was unheard of. Our new Wednesday routine had been going well, and it gave us a nice morning distraction before our workday began. Whenever we were in town, we'd enjoy that weekday breakfast together before heading to the office. Our conversations centered around our siblings, pets, and current events. Shoptalk was shelved for fifty minutes once a week, and we'd enjoy good food and discuss everyday life.

I stared at my phone and willed a call or text to come in as it lay on the tabletop, but the phone remained silent. With a frustrated sigh, I looked over my shoulder through the wall of glass and peered down the street behind me. I did the same looking forward. The hustle and bustle of passersby going to work was evident on the sidewalk and street, yet J.T. was nowhere in sight.

"Agent Monroe?"

I glanced up and saw Amy, our usual waitress, holding the coffee carafe.

I forced a smile. "Hi, hon."

"Would you like a refill?"

I nodded then stared out the window again.

Amy tipped the carafe and poured. "You look worried. Do you want me to bring the check, or do you want to continue waiting?"

I glanced at the clock hanging on the back wall. J.T. was a half hour late and hadn't answered the ten calls I'd made to his phone. Each one went directly to voicemail. I was becoming more alarmed as the minutes ticked by. "Let's settle up."

"Sure thing. I hope everything is okay with Agent Harper."

I gulped the half cup of fresh coffee she'd poured. "Me too."

I tossed a buck on the table and followed Amy to the counter, where I paid for my coffee and left. I called Spelling as I climbed into my car and pulled out into traffic.

He picked up on the second ring. "Morning, Jade. What's so urgent that you're disrupting your Wednesday breakfast?"

"Sorry, sir, but are you at the office yet?"

"I'm pulling into the parking lot as we speak. Why?"

"Is J.T.'s car there?"

"Hold on while I get around to the back. I thought your Wednesday breakfasts were a standing thing?"

"I did too, but he didn't show and I can't reach him." I rubbed my forehead and said a quick prayer that his car was parked behind our building.

"No sign of him, Jade. You tried his phone how many times?"

"At least ten. Do you have Julie's contact information?"

"I do in my desk."

I turned left at the green light with two blocks to go. "I'll be there in five minutes." I clicked off and slipped into the far right lane. One more turn and I'd be at the driveway to our office in Glendale. I turned the last corner and pulled around to the rear of our building and parked. The void to my right, where J.T.'s car usually sat, felt like a bad omen. I rushed to the back entrance and swiped my badge then passed through the security door. Spelling's office was the largest, so it was located at the end of the corridor. Our conference room stood directly across from it, taking up half the length of the hallway. I knocked on Spelling's closed door. The rest of the team was due to show up within a half hour.

"Come in, Jade."

I entered and took a seat then placed my phone on the empty guest chair to my right. "I'm really getting worried, sir."

Agent Spelling pulled J.T.'s file out of the bottom drawer and lifted it to the desktop. He opened it, swiped his index finger across his tongue, and began flipping through sheets of paper. "Here we go. I have Julie's cell number and email address. What does she do for a living, again?"

"She works in radiology at Community Memorial Hospital in Mequon. I hope her phone isn't stashed in a locker during the day."

He held up his hand. "It's ringing."

I stared at Spelling as he waited, his brows furrowed with deep signs of concern. I heard the back door open and close—somebody had arrived. The two female voices in the hallway told me Val and Maria were headed in our direction. I rose and walked out before closing Spelling's door at my back.

"Morning, Jade." Val gave me a quick smile but seemed to realize something was the matter when she didn't get one in return. "What's wrong?"

"I'm not sure yet." I glanced back at Spelling through the glass. "We can't find J.T."

"What does that mean—exactly?" Maria asked with hesitation in her voice.

"I don't know, guys. I have to find out if Spelling got ahold of Julie." I turned and knocked.

Spelling called us in.

"Any news?"

"I didn't get through. Jade, you're coming with me. Delgado and Val, keep trying J.T.'s phone every five minutes and fill Cam in when he gets here. Other than that, stay busy and conduct the morning meeting as we normally would. We're heading to Community Memorial Hospital where Julie works."

Val gave us her best confident nod and squeezed my shoulder. "Keep us posted."

Spelling and I climbed into an available cruiser and took off. The fastest route was I-43 North. We'd reach the hospital in twenty minutes, maybe less with the lights and siren on.

"Jade, call the hospital and have them track down Julie. I want her waiting for us at the emergency entrance when we arrive. Time is of the essence."

"On it, sir." I made the call and was put on hold. I placed the phone in the cup holder and pressed the speakerphone icon. Soft jazz played on a loop in the background as we waited.

"Was there anything different when you parted ways yesterday? Did he seem sick, headachy, or worried about anything?"

"Not at all. The last thing he said to me was, 'See you at breakfast.'" I put up my hand. Somebody had returned to the phone. I picked it up and held the microphone near my mouth.

"Hello. This is Adam Beres, Julie Harper's supervisor. Who am I speaking with?"

"Mr. Beres, this is Agent Jade Monroe from the FBI."

"FBI? What is this in regards to?"

"I need to speak to Julie about her brother. Put her on the phone, please. It's urgent."

"I would if I could, Agent Monroe, but Julie didn't show up for work this morning. No show, no call, which is completely unlike her. Our department has tried her phone numerous times this morning, but she doesn't answer."

I mouthed the word *shit* then thanked the supervisor and hung up. Spelling exited the freeway at the next ramp and squealed to a stop at the shoulder. Dust and gravel sprayed out from under the car.

"J.T. owns that condo, right?"

"Yeah, and that means there isn't a manager with a key."

"We're heading back. Get Cam on the phone and have him pull up J.T.'s exact address. Tell him to call the Whitefish Bay Police Department and say we need a wellness check on that residence immediately. Make sure they're told there's a dog in the house and let Cam know we're on our way. Have them meet us there."

Chapter 3

The man popped the trunk lid and lifted it. He pointed his gun barrel at the dazed agent inside, stopping just inches away from the agent's face. The fierce looking man, much larger than J.T., stood over the trunk and waved his pistol. "Get out, tough guy."

J.T. squinted from the glaring ceiling lights thirty feet above then returned his focus to the thug standing a foot away and pointing a pistol at his head. He rolled from his side to his knees. Maneuvering was difficult with his hands cuffed behind his back.

"I said to get out—now! Don't try anything funny, either, or you'll get a bullet to the head."

"Yeah, I'm working on it. It's kind of awkward without the use of my hands."

"Figure it out."

J.T. lifted one leg out, balanced on that foot, then cleared the trunk and bumper with his other leg. He stepped to the ground and stared at the man pointing the gun at him. He smirked at the man's appearance. "Nice coveralls.

You the gardener or the not-so-Jolly Green Giant?"

The man didn't respond. J.T. jerked his head to his side and discovered that his gun and holster were missing.

The oversized stranger waved the pistol in J.T.'s face. "Look familiar?" His laughter echoed throughout the near empty building. "This is *your* gun, and it has a completely full magazine."

"No shit, genius. I was headed to work."

The man's laughter quickly soured into a sneer. "You'll regret your smart mouth in the end, and don't concern yourself with your ankle holster and gun, either. I have those too."

"What the hell do you want with me?"

"Shut up and start walking. There's someone here who wants to have a word with you."

The man pushed him forward, the barrel of J.T.'s own gun pressed deeply between his shoulder blades.

They reached a large steel garage door in the center of the building. The man stopped, tucked the pistol into his pocket, and pulled on a heavy chain that lifted the door. J.T. took the few precious seconds he had to scan the area and look for anything that could help him figure out where he was being held. He caught a glimpse of another huge man in the distance with his arms folded over his enormous chest, standing silently—like the typical hired muscle—next to an outer door. That man also wore a pair of green coveralls.

J.T. dismissed him and visually swept the room in a side-to-side fashion, trying to memorize everything he saw. The only thing he could tell for sure was that he was in an abandoned warehouse. Empty shelving units lined the outer walls three stories high, and broken window glass lay on the cracked cement floor with rocks nearby. Pallets stacked twenty feet high appeared as if they were about to tip over, and rickety metal stairs with broken handrails led to second-floor rooms that might have been offices years back.

As the overhead door inched up, something caught J.T.'s eye in the room on the other side. His heart began to race. "You son of a bitch! What did you do with her? Where's my sister?"

A voice from the back of the room spoke up. J.T. jerked his head in that direction but saw nobody.

"We'll discuss your sister later, Agent Harper. Right now, Anthony is going to escort you to a holding area that I'm sure you'll find to your liking."

"Who are you, and what do you want? Show your face, you coward!"

The room fell silent.

"Move it, Fed." Anthony gave J.T. a hard shove forward.

J.T. deliberately stumbled alongside the car's window, buying him a few seconds of precious time. He peered in, hoping to see a clue Julie had left behind, but her car was as immaculate as always. No purse, phone, or his sister lay inside. He sucked in a deep breath, thankful there weren't any visible signs of a struggle or blood within the car. Fifty feet farther into that second room stood a floor-to-ceiling holding area constructed of chain-link fencing. The makeshift prison cell was divided into two rooms, each with its own entry. The second side stood empty for now. Anthony pushed J.T. through the first open door and slammed the gate behind him. He snapped a heavy padlock over the latch and secured the door. He backed away from J.T.'s confinement, crossed through the garage door opening, and disappeared from sight.

"Where are you going? What's this about?" J.T. yelled as he kicked the fence.

"I need information, Agent Harper, but there's always a chance to exact revenge too. Everything going forward depends on your level of cooperation."

That voice had returned. The man hiding from view spoke up from the shadows somewhere at the back of the room. J.T. spun. His eyes darted back and forth, but he saw no one.

"Revenge? Revenge for what? I have no idea who you are or what you want, and why is my sister involved in something I might have done?"

"She isn't involved, but she could become a necessary tool I'd use to get information from you. For now, we'll call her leverage, but there is somebody else here you might enjoy getting reacquainted with. I don't believe you've worked with Agent Belmont lately."

J.T. heard footsteps heading in his direction. He looked across the room and saw Anthony reappear through the overhead door, this time escorted by that second man. They dragged a badly beaten and unconscious man by his wrists and headed toward J.T.

Chapter 4

We raced to Whitefish Bay after Cam called back with the exact address of J.T.'s condo. Spelling hit the brakes, and our cruiser squealed to a stop at the curb behind the police squad car that had arrived ahead of us. The main entry to the building led us into a small vestibule with a security door beyond that. On the wall next to the door was an intercom with buttons labeled with each resident's unit number. I pressed the button for J.T.'s unit and held it down, but no one answered. With my hands cupped on each side of my face, I peered through the glass into the building's lobby.

"The elevator is opening," I said.

The officer assigned to conduct the wellness check stepped out of the elevator and walked toward us. I held out my badge, and he nodded then opened the door and allowed us to pass through.

"Agents."

I checked his name tag before speaking, made the quick introductions, then asked Officer Carson what he had found upstairs.

"Nothing, ma'am. I knocked on the door of unit ten a number of times and heard a dog whimpering on the other side, but that was about it."

The outer door opened, and Cam, Val, and Maria entered the building. Spelling pulled the handle of the security door and let them pass through.

"What's the word?" Cam asked.

Spelling responded, "Does anyone know what Julie drives?"

We shrugged as we looked from face to face.

"I'll find out, sir," Maria said. She stepped away and called the tech department.

"Do you have a battering ram in your car, Officer Carson?" Spelling asked.

"I sure do, Agent Spelling."

"We may need it, and get your boss on the phone. We can use more officers out here since we have no idea what to expect."

"Yes, sir."

Spelling directed his focus back to us. "Okay, as soon as Maria has Julie's car type, I want"—he pointed—"Cam and Val to check every vehicle in the parking garage. You're looking for J.T.'s black Toyota Corolla and whatever Julie drives. It shouldn't take too long." Spelling turned and counted the number of units listed on the intercom. "There are only eighteen units in this complex."

Maria returned. "Julie drives a 2012 burgundy Fiesta."

"Okay, go. The rest of us are heading upstairs."

Officer Carson propped the door open with a decorative

stone from the flower bed along the sidewalk then left and got the ram from the trunk of his squad car. He said he'd make the call to his precinct and wait for the other unit to arrive.

Maria and I boarded the elevator to the second floor, and Spelling took the staircase. We reached the condo at the same time, and I dialed J.T.'s phone while Spelling dialed Julie's. The only sound that came from the other side of the door was the nasal bulldog whines from Ralph.

"Sir, there aren't any phones ringing in the unit, and how are we going to ram the door with Ralph whimpering on the other side?"

Spelling raked his hand through his hair as he paced. "All right. Call a locksmith, then, but he better be here in under ten minutes. We don't have time to wait around."

I made the call to the nearest locksmith. From the map on my phone, it looked as if his business was only a mile from the condo. He said he was on his way. I hung up and told Spelling we had only a few minutes to wait. The elevator dinged, and when the doors parted, Cam and Val stepped out.

"Anything?" Spelling asked.

Cam shook his head. "Neither vehicle is in the garage."

"Their phones didn't ring in the condo and their cars aren't in the garage, so where the hell are they?"

"I don't know, but maybe there's something inside the condo that could help," I said.

Spelling tipped his head at Maria. "Go downstairs and wait for the locksmith and check on Officer Carson. We're going to need somebody to start combing the grounds and knocking on doors. Somebody had to have seen something."

The locksmith, a Mr. Brian Joost from Locks "R" Us, arrived a few minutes later. Maria escorted him to the second floor, where she made the introductions.

"Okay," Mr. Joost said. "It looks like we have a doorknob lock as well as a dead bolt, but there's nothing unique about either one. They're run-of-the-mill locks anyone can buy from a big-box home improvement store."

Spelling gave him the eyeballs. "How long is this going to take?"

Mr. Joost knelt on the floor, eye level to the knob. He pulled several tools from his work case and inserted them in the key slot. With a few turns and jiggles, the door was unlocked. "Just about that long, sir." He repeated the process with the dead bolt, then he stood and turned the knob. "The door is open."

Spelling carefully turned the knob, covering his hand with the bottom of his sports coat. He jerked his chin at Val before continuing. "Settle up with Mr. Joost and get some gloves from Officer Carson."

"On it, boss." Val left with the locksmith at her side.

Spelling inched the door open carefully since Ralph waited on the other side. "We need to secure this dog."

Cam slipped his hand through Ralph's studded collar and allowed Spelling to squeeze past the door. Cam heaved the solid, fifty-pound dog up into his arms then looked helplessly toward me. I shrugged and pulled out my sidearm, following close at Spelling's back. Maria was directly behind me. It took only a few minutes to clear the two-bedroom, two-bath unit. I holstered my weapon.

"All good?" Cam asked as he waited in the hallway with Ralph in his arms.

"Yeah, come on in, and"—I pointed at the balcony—"put Ralph out there for now so he stays out of our way. He'll be fine. He's too fat to fall through the rungs, anyway."

I picked up the water bowl and cushion and set both outside in the shade. I closed the slider at Ralph's back with a dish towel in my hand. "Where are those gloves?"

Val walked in right as I finished my sentence. "Here, I have plenty. The officers' downstairs are walking the perimeter of the complex to see if anything looks out of place."

Spelling panned the space as we stood against the kitchen island. The unit was set up with a common center area consisting of a living room, casual dining room, kitchen, and a large balcony. The two bedrooms were on opposite ends of the unit, each with a full master bath. A powder room stood next to the louvered hallway doors where the stacked washer and dryer were located.

Spelling tried to roll the anxiety out of his neck. "Okay, let's do a slow and methodical search of this condo. From the way the unit looks, there wasn't a struggle here or a forced entry to get inside. It appears that they left on their own accord, but we still need to do a thorough search. We're looking for anything that might tell us where J.T. and Julie disappeared to. Look for day planners, wall calendars, and random notes. Val and Maria, knock on every door on this floor and see what the neighbors know."

Spelling, Cam, and I began going through every loose piece of paper, including mail stacked on the countertop next to the barstools as well as paperwork that sat alongside the home computer on the desk in J.T.'s bedroom.

It felt odd to be going through J.T.'s personal belongings, as if I were intruding on my partner's private property. But in that moment, I was an FBI agent and nothing more. Julie and J.T. needed to be found. We couldn't come up with a logical explanation for their disappearances or why neither of them answered their phones.

Thinking about the phones gave me an idea that I suggested to Spelling. "Why don't we ping their phones? Locating them or at least triangulating the general area they're in would tell us definitively if Julie and J.T. are somewhere together."

"Do it. Call Joe and give him the phone numbers. Get him started on that immediately and tell him to call me the minute he has something."

With a nod, I dialed our tech department and stepped out to the balcony to talk. Ralph lay on his cushion, fast asleep and snoring. His pink tongue rested against his paw. I smiled briefly and wondered whether I would make a good dog owner. They seemed like lovable pets.

"Tech department, Joe speaking."

"Joe, it's Jade."

"How's the search coming?"

"So far, we've got nothing. J.T.'s condo is empty with

no signs of foul play. We need you to ping their phones."

"Okay, shoot."

I rattled off J.T. and Julie's phone numbers. "Spelling wants you to call him directly as soon as you know something."

"Copy that. I'll be in touch."

I hung up and pocketed my phone then scanned the outdoor area. To my right, several officers walked the surface parking lot, their eyes to the ground. Below, I saw Officer Carson searching the shrubbery near the patio of a first-floor condo. I called out to him, "Anything look amiss?"

He shielded his eyes and looked up. "Nothing yet, Agent Monroe."

"Has anyone searched the parking garage?"

"That's the next place we're going to check, ma'am. We were waiting for the agents to clear it first."

"Okay, keep us posted." I stared across the street and took in the view. Several blocks of single-family homes faced the condo complex. I leaned over the balcony and looked to see where the driveway from the garage exited onto the street. A day care center stood on the next block to my right with two roof-mounted cameras facing in opposite directions down the street. I looked over the railing again then back to the camera that faced my way. From where that camera was placed, it would definitely catch every car going in and out of the parking garage. I opened the slider and called Spelling to come take a look.

Chapter 5

Horror overtook J.T.'s face as the men got closer.

The hidden man's voice called out again. "What's wrong, Agent Harper? I'd think in your line of work, you'd be numb to blood and acts of violence. Anyway, what's a little blood between friends?"

"Friends? That man is beyond recognition."

The men reached the cage and tossed the limp, nearly dead man into the second room. Anthony snapped the lock and gave it a shake, as if making sure it was secure.

"You do have a point, Agent Harper. I guess my guys went a bit overboard with your old pal, Agent Belmont. I can see how you wouldn't recognize his bloody swollen face." Laughter rang out and bounced off the walls of that empty, hollow room. "Oh, by the way, where are my manners? I forgot to introduce you to Antonio. Obviously, he and Anthony are brothers, but I'm sure you can see the resemblance."

J.T. knelt at the edge of his confinement. "Curt, is that you? Can you hear me? It's J.T. I'll get you out of here, man,

I promise. Everything is going to be okay. Just hang on."

A low-pitched moan sounded for a second, then silence.

J.T. yelled out in the direction he thought the man's voice came from. "Okay, you have my attention now, so what do you want, and where is my sister?"

"You'll be reunited with your sister in due time, Agent Harper, in due time. I want all of your security clearance information for the FBI. What that means is, I want your log-in and password, and then you're going to give me the name of every sensitive file in the system and how to access it. I want top-notch information—Secret Service, Pentagon type stuff."

"I'm not Secret Service, CIA, or anything closely related to the highest security clearances. I'm FBI, and there are at least thirty levels of security above me. Your request is impossible, and I don't have access to classified information like that."

"Get me what I want or suffer the consequences."

"I don't know what you want, and being vague isn't helping. You'll get nothing from me until I see that my sister is unharmed. Release Julie and Agent Belmont, and then I might work with you."

"You see, Agent Harper, Agent Belmont refused to get me what I asked for too, and look how that turned out. He's a bloody mess and barely breathing. The problem you agents have, and what will eventually be your downfall, is your damn arrogance. Even with your hands cuffed behind your back, even from the confines of a locked cage, you still think you're calling the shots." His laughter rang out again.

"The question is how badly do you want the information? Without my help, you get nothing."

"Then it looks like we're at a standstill, Agent Harper, but listen carefully to my words. You have two days to fulfill my requests. Meanwhile, I want you to envision what Anthony and Antonio are capable of. Those two men are in charge of keeping your sister entertained. My requests are simple. Give me your log-in information, and I want access to every case file you worked on with Agent Belmont in 2014."

"Why? What is so important about 2014? We aren't even in the same division anymore."

"Turn your focus to Anthony, Agent Harper."

J.T. turned toward the giant who stood on the opposite side of the cage, barely ten feet away. Anthony grasped J.T.'s Glock 22 and pulled it from his pocket, then he aimed it at Curt's head.

"Stop! I'll give you the information."

"Not yet. You need to stew on this a little longer. I want you to be sleepless for forty-eight hours, thinking of your sister and your old colleague lying there near death. The likelihood of Agent Belmont dying during that time will be considerably high."

"What?"

Anthony pulled the trigger, and a shot rang out. Curt's body jerked from the impact, and blood began pooling under his shoulder.

"No! You son of a bitch!"

Anthony and Antonio turned their backs and walked

away. Moments later, the lights went out, and a door slammed in the distance. J.T. sat on the floor five feet from his bleeding friend and stared through the links. He was at that madman's mercy, and there was nothing he could do to help Curt or Julie.

J.T. couldn't even help himself.

Chapter 6

"What have you got, Jade?" SSA Spelling stepped onto the balcony and closed the slider behind him.

I tipped my head toward the street. "Take a look. There are single-family homes directly across from us, but over there"—I pointed to my right—"is a day care center. Follow the roofline halfway up on each end."

"Uh-huh."

I glanced at Spelling. "See the cameras?"

"I sure do." He leaned over the railing and looked toward the driveway. "Yeah, the camera facing this way would catch every car pulling out of the garage. At least we'd know what direction they went. The question is, do J.T. and Julie take the same route to work? They both have to go north."

"I don't know for sure, sir, but it would seem logical that they'd both take I-43 to their respective exits. J.T. would get off the freeway first, but since Julie drives farther to work, I assume she'd leave the condo before him." I gave Spelling a hopeful glance. "We're going to be the unit handling this case, if that's what this turns out to be, right? J.T. is my partner, and I'm not going to take a backseat in finding him. I physically feel sick right now, but I can do this. We're going to find both of them, and they'll be okay."

"I know, and I'll make sure we're the lead investigators. If anything comes up out of state, we'll let another division take it. J.T. and Julie are our main focus right now."

"Thank you, sir."

Spelling tipped his head toward the day care center. "Get over there and see what they can pull from this morning. What's going on with the ground search?"

"Officer Carson said nothing has popped yet, but they're about to begin in the garage. Has Joe called you back?"

"Unfortunately, yes, and both of the phones are turned off."

I groaned. "Can this day get any worse?"

Spelling smirked. "Be careful, Jade. The day is still young."

"Roger that, boss." I pulled the slider open and crossed the living room to the front door then looked back at Spelling. "Call me if anything important surfaces."

Spelling gave me a look of concern. "You know I will."

I took the elevator down to the main level and exited the building. Officer Carson and two other policemen were walking toward the garage. I called them over.

"Those underground parking garages are dark. Keep your eyes peeled for anything out of the ordinary. Put a marker next to anything you see, no matter how insignificant you may think it is. Also, stretch some tape in front of the garage entrance and don't let anyone drive in or out until you've searched it thoroughly. When you're done, go upstairs and get SSA Spelling. Let him and the other agents take a look at everything you've marked. Any questions?"

"No, ma'am. I think we have it covered," Carson said.

"Okay, thanks. I'll be back soon." I raced down the sidewalk to the intersection and crossed the street at the green light. I approached the happy looking yellow building with red shutters. Written on a sign above the door was the name of the business—Kidz Rule Daycare. I entered the building and approached a young lady standing behind a counter.

She gave me a wide grin. "I don't think you're a mom I recognize. How can I help you?"

I pulled out the lanyard from inside my blouse and flashed her my badge. "For starters, I need to see your west-facing camera footage from this morning."

"Oh my goodness. Um, okay. Give me one second to get somebody out here to watch the counter. I'll be right back."

The young lady pulled off the stretchy band that hung from her wrist and unlocked a security door that likely led to the children's play area. She returned several minutes later with another employee who looked to be the same age—a twentysomething female.

"Okay, right this way, please." She stopped and introduced herself. "I'm Dee Dee Sanchez."

"It's nice to meet you. I'm Agent Monroe."

Dee Dee led me through the door of the secured area and down a short hallway. I heard the chatter, cries, and laughter of children coming from a room somewhere to our left.

"Our office is right here." She pointed straight ahead as she pulled off the stretchy band for the second time in five minutes and unlocked the door.

"I'm impressed with your security measures. If I ever have a kid, I'll bring them here."

She grinned. "Thank you, that means a lot. Okay, let me pull up the footage." She pointed at a guest chair. "Why don't you scoot in here next to me and the computer?"

I pulled a chair to her side of the desk and took a seat.

Dee Dee looked at me with her brows raised in question. "You said the west camera, right?"

"That's correct." I noticed the clock on her desk read 10:52. "I'll need you to begin at six thirty and go forward from there."

"Yes, ma'am."

I knew that was probably earlier than the time Julie normally left. From door to door, Julie might have had a forty-minute commute, but that would include parking and getting to her department in the hospital. I wanted to watch the entire complex for a bit to see whether anything had looked off before she left for the day. No one would likely be going into the building at that time of morning. Under normal circumstances, the only people leaving would be residents pulling out of the garage and heading off to their place of employment.

Dee Dee set up the camera footage and typed in the beginning time. The footage began playing at six thirty. I was thankful the day care center had newer cameras with modern technology. That made my job a lot easier. I sighed a deep breath, and Dee Dee gave me a quick glance.

I patted her shoulder. "Everything is okay. I'm just happy you have modern equipment."

Dee Dee pushed back her chair, stood, then walked around the desk. "Do you need me to stay, Agent Monroe?" She pointed at the door. "Otherwise I'm probably needed out front."

"I'm fine, and thank you. Hopefully I'll find what I need and be out of here in less than an hour. Do you have blank thumb drives in case I need to copy the tape?"

She returned to her chair and tapped a few keys to show me how to send the daily camera footage directly to my email address. "It opens up in Media Player like any other attachment."

"Awesome." I gave her a nod, and she left the room. Young adults were far more advanced in computer technology than I was. I reminded myself to have my sister Amber show me the ropes when we both had time.

I tapped the forward arrow and continued watching that morning's footage. Several people passed the camera as they walked their dogs. Cars buzzed by, and joggers made occasional appearances. City buses stopped and picked up people waiting on benches in the covered structures. I glanced at the lower right corner of the computer and nothing unusual had surfaced yet. It was closing in on seven o'clock. I was beginning to fidget. Julie should be pulling out any second, and J.T. would be close behind given that it was the morning of our scheduled breakfast together. Any other day, J.T. wouldn't leave the condo until seven forty-five. He lived only ten minutes from our Glendale office. An idea came to mind, and I quickly jotted it in my notepad before it faded away. I'd check to see whether either vehicle had been picked up by the plate readers on the interstate. That could speed up the search process considerably, yet we still had to rule out any foul play at the condo. I paused the tape and called Joe in Tech again.

"Joe, I need to know if any plate reader got a hit on J.T. and Julie's plates on I-43. Yes, call me back as soon as you find out."

I hung up and leaned forward with my elbows on the desk and my face in my hands. I continued to stare at the screen. Several minutes later, what appeared to be two men from the gardening crew crossed the front lawn. They stopped briefly, said a few words to each other, then parted ways and disappeared off screen. I watched the garage exit and barely dared to blink. The garage door rose several minutes later and a burgundy Fiesta pulled out. I stopped the tape and checked the exact time—7:07 a.m. I began the tape again. Julie turned right at the end of the driveway.

Where the hell is she going? The freeway is to her left.

I jotted down the time she pulled out and the direction she went—east. I continued the tape. If J.T. had had any intention of meeting me at seven twenty, he'd be pulling out in the next five minutes. I watched and waited, then I waited some more. Every second seemed like an eternity. I checked the time, heaved a sigh, and stared at the screen again. The door rose at seven thirteen, but it was a false alarm—the car was white. I let out a slow breath and settled in. A flash of movement at J.T.'s balcony caught my eye.

What the hell was that?

I backed up the tape and saw it again but couldn't make out what I was looking at. It seemed as if the drapes fluttered for a second, and then it was over. I wrote down the time. At seven twenty-one, the overhead garage door began to lift. I sat up straight with my eyes laser focused on the garage. It had to be him, or my timing was completely wrong. The door reached the top, and a black Corolla pulled out. I nearly jumped from my chair to pause the video. I stopped the footage at exactly 7:22 a.m. It was definitely J.T.'s car, and he turned right at the end of the driveway, just as Julie had.

Where the hell are they going, and why didn't he call to say he wasn't showing up for breakfast?

There was nothing else I needed to watch at that moment. I knew what time each of them left the condo and what direction they headed, although I'd email a copy of the footage to myself. I wanted the tech department to look it over. Even the smallest detail could be significant.

I thanked Dee Dee, told her I'd forwarded a copy of the footage to my email, and left the day care center. My pace quickened, I got back to the condo in less than five minutes. With the door still propped open, I passed through and gave the officer watching the entrance a thank-you nod. I took the stairway, not wanting to wait for the elevator doors to part.

Val and Maria had returned from their knock and talks. Because it was a small complex and most people were at work during the day, Spelling had the officers speak to every tenant who was home.

"Get anything?" I asked as I entered the condo.

Everyone turned toward me. "Yeah," Val said, "a complex consisting of six people who answered their doors and didn't see or hear anything unusual."

Spelling slid out a chair and took a seat at the dining room table. "I finally got ahold of Mr. and Mrs. Harper. They haven't spoken to J.T. or Julie and said there weren't any family emergencies. I hated to worry them, but we had to know." He took a deep breath. "What did you learn, Jade?"

"First off, I forwarded the day care center tape to my email. We can all go through it again back at the office."

Spelling nodded. "That could help—the more eyes the better."

"That's what I thought too, sir. Anyway, I saw both cars leave. The condo doesn't seem to be related to their disappearances since they left on their own accord."

"We're thinking the same, that there's nothing unusual here," Maria said. "So can I make a quick pot of coffee while Jade goes over her findings with us?"

Spelling waved her off. "Yeah, go ahead. This unit is clean." He turned his focus back to me. "Okay, tell us what you learned."

I let out a deep breath to clear my thoughts, then I pulled out my notepad and flipped to the last used page. "Okay,

Julie drove out of the garage at seven minutes after seven. The timing is within range given the fact that she starts work at eight o'clock. That would give her time to park, go inside, grab a coffee, and have a few minutes before she reports to her department."

"I agree. Then what?" Spelling asked.

Maria brought five cups and the carafe of coffee to the table. She poured a cup for everyone and sat down.

"Then she turned right."

"The opposite way of the freeway?" Cam asked.

I nodded. "My exact thoughts, but what's even stranger is that J.T.'s car exited at seven twenty-two, and he made a right-hand turn as well. He's never late for our Wednesday breakfast, but if he didn't intend to show up, which seems obvious by the direction he turned, then why didn't he call me?"

"And you tried his phone numerous times while you waited."

I turned toward Spelling. "That's correct, and he never picked up. Something is definitely off."

A knock sounded on the front door. Val got up and opened it. Standing in the hallway were Officer Carson and two other officers. Val ushered them in.

"Carson," Spelling said, "have you finished searching the garage?"

"Yes, sir, and I'm sure you'll want to see the areas we've marked."

"Then let's go." Spelling stood, guzzled the coffee, and followed Officer Carson out the door. We fell in line at his back.

Chapter 7

The eight of us piled into the elevator and stood against the walls. Val pushed the button for the garage level, and the doors closed. With a slight jerk, the elevator began its descent two more floors to the garage. Once the elevator settled at the bottom floor, the doors opened, and we exited into the darkened parking space. Even with the lights on, the garage was dim, and anything could be missed.

"We used our flashlights, Agent Spelling, and did a thorough search. We even looked under the few cars that are still parked inside."

"Understood, Officer Carson. Show us what you found."

"Sure thing, sir." Carson took several steps to the left of the elevator and pointed at the ground. "We found an earbud where that marker is."

"An earbud?"

Carson shined the beam of light to the small orange marker on the floor. An earbud lay on its side next to it. The parking space was indicated by a large number three in white paint.

Every spot in the garage was marked by a number.

Spelling turned to Val. "Go back upstairs and open that file cabinet in J.T.'s bedroom. One of the folders inside that cabinet had *Deed* typed across the tab. See if there are parking spaces indicated with the paperwork that goes to his unit."

"On it, boss." Val entered the elevator, and the doors closed at her back.

I knelt down and took several pictures of the earbud and where it sat within that parking spot.

"We found a few stomped cigarette butts scattered throughout the garage. Don't know if they're related to each other since they're different brands, but we marked all of them, anyway," Officer Rankin said.

Cam tipped his head, and with the officers, we walked to each marker. I snapped pictures of each cigarette and its location within the garage.

"Anything else?" Spelling asked.

"You bet, sir, and this one is substantial."

I gave Cam a concerned sideways glance as he scratched his chin.

Carson knelt at the last marker and pointed. "Take a look at that."

Each of us knelt down at the rectangular, two-inch-long pin on the floor. The backside had the typical pin clasp attached to it. We took two steps to the front and knelt again. *Julie H.— Radiology Department* was embossed across the face of the pin.

"Son of a bitch, this garage is probably a crime scene," I

said. "If that was J.T.'s earbud on the floor, then maybe his phone is missing too. That could be why he didn't pick up and probably why we can't get through to either of them. The likelihood of J.T. and Julie having possession of their phones anymore is slim."

Spelling began calling out orders. "Cam, organize things with the Whitefish Bay Police Department. Get this garage sealed off. Nobody except the crime lab comes in or out, and get them here immediately."

"I'm on it, sir."

"Carson, get your superior out here. We need officers on-site to keep the residents out and to usher them through the front doors only. Until further notice, everyone has to park in the surface lot."

"What about the cars inside the garage?" Maria asked.

"Too late. They aren't getting moved until this garage has been gone over with a fine-toothed comb." Spelling pointed at the dumpsters at the far end of the garage. "For all we know, the phones may be in there. Everything is getting searched again and printed, and somebody is going dumpster diving today too." Spelling hollered to Carson before he was out of earshot. "Get somebody to bring portable floodlights."

Val returned from the condo and approached us. "J.T.'s parking spot is number three, and Julie's"—she looked down at the marker in front of us—"is number twelve."

"Something falling from both of them right as they reached their cars is far from coincidental. It sounds like an ambush to me. Jade?"

"Yes, sir."

"Go downtown and get Joe started on that videotape. There has to be something on it that you missed. Call him and let him know you're on your way."

"I'm on it." Spelling handed me the keys to the cruiser, and I took off.

The drive to our downtown FBI headquarters would normally take fifteen minutes, but since it was lunchtime, I knew that it could be closer to a half hour. I called Joe as I drove.

"Hey, Joe, it's Jade. I bet you were about to take your lunch break, weren't you?"

He chuckled. "Something is telling me I may have other plans."

"Sorry, it's urgent. We think the parking garage is a crime scene, and I have video footage from a day care center across the street that aims right at the complex. There has to be some kind of clue on it that I've missed. Even zooming the images in closer would be a huge help."

"Sure, no sweat. I'll just grab a sandwich and a soda out of the vending machine. Want anything?"

"Whatever you're getting for yourself is fine with me too. I'll be there in fifteen minutes as long as the traffic doesn't back up." I clicked off and thought about J.T.

Where the hell are you, partner, and why has somebody kidnapped you and Julie?

I thought back to the clues in the garage and the video footage. Julie was taken first and J.T. only a few minutes later. That told me there had to be more than one assailant.

It was an organized, planned attack that somebody pulled off without a hitch. Chances were, they didn't even realize items were dropped. They would have surely picked them up otherwise. The attack had to have been done quickly and efficiently given that other residents could have come down to the garage and caught them in the act. It was a blind side, a blitz attack, and well planned. J.T. and Julie's daily habits had to have been monitored for a while, but why?

I reached the downtown headquarters on East Kilbourn Street at twelve thirty and slid my badge into the slot for the security gate. I drove to the third floor parking area designated for our FBI personnel and pulled into the first empty space I could find. Once inside the building, I took several hallways to the tech department, where a thumbprint ID pad was mounted next to the door. Luckily, the last time I had been in that facility, my thumbprint was entered and stored at all of the areas that needed security clearance. I pressed my thumb against the pad and waited for the scan and beep. The lock clicked, and I passed through.

Joe waved as he saw me enter his department. He sat at the last row of computers, wolfing down his lunch. A cellophane-wrapped sandwich, bag of chips, and a can of iced tea sat on the table to his right.

"Thanks for the food, Joe. I appreciate it."

He waved my comment away then wiped his mouth with the napkin and pitched his wrappers in the garbage can at his back.

"Okay, agent, what do we have?" He gave me a quick

smile, but I knew Joe was all about business. He was an expert at his job.

"Log in to my FBI email address, and the attachment will be from Kidz Rule Daycare." I ate as Joe tapped away at the keyboard.

"Okay, I'm in."

I pointed. "Right there. It's the fifth email down."

Joe opened the email and clicked on the attachment. He tapped more keys, replicated the attachment, and dropped it into his software program. He closed out my email and slapped his hands together.

I took a gulp of tea to wash down my sandwich. "Are we ready to go?"

"One second. I want to tweak the video a bit first to get the best resolution. That way I can zoom in if necessary without a pixelation issue."

"Thank God for tech-savvy people like you."

Joe smiled. "Why do you think the FBI hired me? Plus, it helps to have a clean record and a lot of training under my belt. How much footage is there?"

"I copied everything from six thirty this morning until about eleven o'clock. The actual amount I needed was less than an hour long."

He smirked. "That's what you think."

"Meaning?"

"We're considering this an abduction, correct?"

"Yes, of course we are. Half of Milwaukee's finest is probably headed to the condo right now." I felt my throat tighten with anxiety and heard my voice crack. Joe gave me a concerned look and squeezed my shoulder. I could barely hold back my tears.

"Jade, we're FBI, remember? We're experts at our jobs. Everything on that tape is going to be considered suspect until proven otherwise. We may even need more footage, who knows. One way or another, we're going to solve this case because of that tape." Joe drummed the tabletop with his fingertips and gave me a nod. "People don't disappear into thin air. If their vehicles were driven out of that parking garage like you say they were, then we've got something to work with. We'll get J.T. and his sister back safely. Now come on, let's buck up and dig in."

I wiped my eyes with the back of my hand and sat up a little prouder. I shook off my doubts. "You're right. Let's figure this out. J.T. is counting on us."

Joe hit the tab to start the video, and we watched the early morning scene play out again. Things I hadn't noticed earlier, because I had been so focused on the garage, now caught my attention.

"I guess I put all my energy into staring at the garage earlier, but now I'm noticing even more." I saw people walking their pets, sitting at the bus stop, joggers here and there, school buses, and cars pulling out of the garage. "That's about it. Julie pulled out and then J.T. did fifteen minutes later. They both turned the wrong way, though, opposite the freeway. Oh, wait, I did see a split second of movement at the balcony after Julie left but before J.T. did."

"Which unit is theirs?"

"It's the third set of balcony doors on the second floor, right above the main entrance."

"And what time was that?"

I checked my notes. "The flash of movement I saw was at the seven seventeen mark. It looked like the curtains fluttered. I even backed up the footage but couldn't tell what caused it. For all I know, Ralph might have bumped the drapes."

"Sure, but I'll forward the footage to that time and freeze it. Maybe we can make out an image if it's zoomed in a bit. Because we're watching the complex from an angle and a block away, we aren't going to see everything as clearly as we'd like."

I watched as Joe tapped a few keys and framed the balcony at the seven seventeen mark. With each click of the mouse, he enlarged the image on the screen.

"This is about as big as I'm going to get the image without it pixeling on us."

We both leaned in and stared at the screen.

"Okay, Julie had already left, so that would leave Ralph and J.T. in the condo. The movement was about halfway up, so that would rule out the dog. I think it's J.T.'s hand. Maybe he's making sure the slider was locked before he left." I checked my notes again. "The timing would make sense considering his car pulled out of the garage five minutes later."

"I have to agree with you, Jade. So likely it's saying that all was well inside the condo five minutes before J.T.'s car left the complex. Unfortunately, that lends to the theory of a blitz attack from someone waiting in the garage, hence the items on the floor at both of their parking spots."

Joe rubbed his chin while his eyes were glued to the computer screen. "Has anyone checked for camera surveillance on buildings behind the complex or to the west?"

"I only saw the day care center and ran over there, but I should call Spelling and get somebody checking for other tapes. We need to see what's going on from all angles."

Joe nodded. "Get on that, agent. I'll keep watching the footage."

Chapter 8

"Curt, can you hear me? Tell me you're still alive. You can't die on me, man. You need to hang on."

A moan sounded on the other side of the enclosure. "Who's there?"

"It's me—J.T. Look to your left. I'm over here."

The blood loss had weakened Curt, and he could barely turn his head. "J.T.?"

"Yeah, it's me, and you need to listen closely. Take off your belt and cinch it above your shoulder. You have to slow down that bleeding, or you won't make it. I can't help you. I'm locked up on this side and handcuffed."

J.T. watched as his former colleague tried to pull his belt off. Every movement caused him to cry out in pain.

"Come on, Curt. You have to do this."

"I don't have the strength."

"Yes you do. You're the toughest agent I know, now do it!"

"They have Julie, J.T."

"You saw her?"

Curt groaned with each word. "She was in a small room, and I only saw her for a second before they slammed the door." Curt fell quiet.

J.T. turned around and grasped the links with his hands. He shook them violently. "Wake up!"

"What? I'm fading, bro."

"No you aren't. Get that belt around your arm and stop the bleeding. Don't you dare give up on me. You have friends and family who care about you, so fight to stay alive. What do these people want with us?"

"I don't know. They said they wanted my FBI log-in information, but I wouldn't give it to them."

"Do you have any idea who they are?"

"Hang on, I'm cinching the belt."

"Do it tight."

Curt cried out as he pulled the belt and tightened it around his shoulder.

"Make sure you buckle it so it holds. Who are those men?"

"I have no idea, but there were three of them in the room with Julie."

"Yeah, and the two I saw were enormous."

"There was blood on her."

"They hurt my sister?" J.T. ran into the wall of fencing as hard as he could but bounced back and fell to the cement. He yelled, "Son of a bitch, I have to get out of here! How long have they been holding you?" He waited for a response. "Curt? Curt!" J.T. knelt on the floor and stared through the links at his friend. Even in the dim lighting, he could see that Curt had passed out again. J.T. yelled with everything he had. "What do you maniacs want with us?"

The warehouse remained silent.

Chapter 9

I paced the tech department's tiled floor as Spelling updated me over the phone on the events taking place at the condo.

"The PD had the waste management company come out and tip the dumpsters over in the parking lot. Several officers are going through things as we speak."

"That sounds like an awful job."

"Well, it will be time consuming since they'll have to dump out every garbage bag. Meanwhile, Forensics is printing the areas near the markers as well as the earbud and pin. All of the evidence is going back to the crime lab as soon as they're done."

"They're printing every doorknob and the elevator too, right?"

"Yep, no stone will be left unturned. This is one of our own and his sister, Jade. Forensics is being very thorough. I'm not sure how optimistic I am about the dumpsters, though. I'm not confident even a stupid criminal would deliberately leave evidence at the scene of the crime."

"Right. Anyway, we're going to need some people

scouring the neighborhood for more cameras. To get the entire complex, we need the west and back views of the building. The day care center camera wouldn't pick up somebody entering from areas out of their range."

"Sure. I'll put somebody on that right away."

"Thanks, boss. I'm going to get back to watching the footage." I hung up and told Joe that Spelling was having the Whitefish Bay PD send officers to the neighborhood to look for more cameras.

"That should help." Joe waved me over. "Take a look. What's your take on these two grounds crew guys?"

I shrugged and leaned in close to the computer screen. "I guess the time of day is right. Most gardening and landscape crews start their workday early. Those guys probably have a bunch of apartment and condo complexes to maintain."

"Yeah, maybe, but where is their equipment and work truck?"

"They could be scoping out what needs to be addressed before grabbing their clippers and weed whackers. The camera doesn't capture the entire block. Their truck could be parked farther down and out of the camera's view. Does something seem off about them?"

"Not yet, but like I said before, everything is suspect until it isn't."

Joe tapped a few keys to zoom in on the image of the two men standing together on the lawn.

"Are you looking for something specific?"

"A company logo on their coveralls, but I don't see one.

They aren't facing the camera at the right angle, though."

"The management company for the complex shouldn't be tough to track down. I'll find out who runs the HOA too. I'm sure they can direct me to the right place."

"It's too bad the camera only caught the cars as they came out of the garage and turned. You can't even see who's driving."

Joe's statement startled me. "Are you thinking somebody else was behind the wheel in both cars?"

"We're considering this an abduction, so yeah, unless there's someone in the backseat, calling out orders. Two vehicles mean two abductors."

"And there were two men with no lawn care equipment talking among themselves in the front yard."

Joe nodded. "Looks like the agent might be on to something."

I stood and gave Joe a grateful hug. "I've got to find the person in charge of the lawn services. Thanks, bud."

"You guys did rule out a family emergency first, right?"

"Yeah, Spelling did that right away. There wasn't any, but that still doesn't explain the lack of communication and the items we found on the garage floor." I headed for the door. "I'll keep you posted." I power walked through the two hallways that took me to the parking structure exit then raced through the garage to the cruiser. I descended the three floors to the street level and sped off on my way to the condo.

After turning onto J.T.'s street, I found the entire complex wrapped in yellow police tape. Squad cars, cruisers, and the forensics van were parked at the curb directly in front of the building. I continued on until I found a spot to pull in a half block away. With the engine killed and the doors locked, I took the sidewalk back to the activity going on behind me.

Four officers rummaged through mountains of garbage on the far left side of the parking lot. The disgusting odor of days-old trash filled the air. The overhead garage door was open, likely to get more light in that underground space. In the distance, I saw officers walking the neighborhood. I hoped they would find more cameras mounted somewhere, but since this was a residential area, they would be looking at every house on each block that surrounded the complex.

The front door was still propped open when I entered. A half dozen officers milled about, searching nooks, crannies, and maintenance closets. I pushed through the stairwell door and nodded a hello to the officers searching the stairway.

Halfway down the hall on the second floor, the door to J.T.'s condo was guarded by an officer standing at the doorframe, his hands clutched in front of him. Spelling, Val, Maria, and Cam sat inside and filled the chairs at the dining room table. They looked to be engaged in a brainstorming session.

Spelling peeked over the top of his reading glasses when I entered. "Anything new on the video?"

"Possibly." I took a seat. "There are several things I need to follow up on, but first Joe was able to enlarge and zoom in on an image I saw on the tape. It was after Julie left but before J.T. did. It looked like he was checking to make sure the balcony door was locked. I saw a short movement right at the handle height, which would make sense if he was ready to leave for the day—locking up before he walked out."

"Meaning nothing was wrong inside. He was getting ready to head out and meet you for breakfast."

"That's the way I see it, sir, otherwise he wouldn't have left for another half hour."

"It would be too risky to ambush him in the hallway, and with the earbud on the ground near his car, the perp must have been waiting just outside the elevator. Unless the guy was wearing gloves, there has to be some prints or biological evidence from a struggle near the car." Spelling jerked his head at Maria. "Run downstairs and tell Forensics to be especially thorough at the elevator, the walls, and the support pillars right by J.T.'s parking spot. My question is how did the perps get into the garage?"

Cam spoke up. "With all of the people heading off to work at that time, they could have slipped in on foot right after someone pulled out. The garage door is on a sensor, which probably keeps it up for a good ten seconds or more after the driver pulls away. We can test that easily enough."

Spelling rubbed his brows. "Yeah, these types of places give people a false sense of security just because you have to use a card to get into the garage. There's probably five different ways to enter the building undetected. Anyway, write that down, Cam, so we don't forget to test it."

"Speaking of security, sir, I may have something

interesting. I noticed this when I was at the day care center, and Joe commented on it as well. Granted, the angle of the camera from a block away doesn't capture everything, but we saw two large men dressed in grounds maintenance coveralls, talking with each other on the front lawn. They parted ways and disappeared off camera after a few short minutes."

"That makes no sense at all. If they were going to do groundwork, then why wouldn't they go get their equipment?" Val asked rhetorically.

"Exactly our thoughts too. Unfortunately, the camera couldn't reach the entire curb along the front of the building, so we didn't see a work truck."

Cam whistled and raked his hands through his hair. "What time was that, Jade?"

I flipped to the last page of my notepad. "They were standing in front of the building at six forty-seven a.m., which was twenty minutes before Julie left and a good half hour before J.T. did."

"And when did Carson arrive on site?"

Spelling picked up his phone and dialed. "Maria, find Officer Carson and ask him what time he arrived for the wellness check on the unit. Call me back right away." Spelling clicked off.

"So, if Carson didn't see a work truck or anyone grooming the grounds when he arrived, well—"

I interrupted. "Well, that in itself is telling us a lot. This complex has to take up at least five or six acres if you take into consideration the pool and clubhouse areas. There are a lot of bushes to trim, lawns to cut, and sidewalks to blow off. There's no way they wouldn't still be here, even when we arrived. We need to find out who the grounds maintenance provider is. Has anyone talked to the management company yet, and do we even know who they are?"

Spelling pointed toward J.T.'s bedroom. "Val, grab that folder with the deed out of the filing cabinet again. I'm sure the management company has to be listed in there."

Val rose and headed to J.T.'s room. Seconds later, she was back with the folder and began browsing through it. As soon as she returned, Spelling's phone rang.

"Yes, Maria, he's sure? Okay, good enough. Check on everyone's progress as long as you're down there." Spelling clicked off. "Carson arrived at ten after eight."

I wrote that in my notepad along with the time we arrived. "And we got here at eight twenty. I'd assume under normal conditions, it would take a crew about three hours at a minimum to groom these grounds. That's probably with a few more people too."

"Got it." We turned to Val as she pulled out a sheet of paper and closed the folder. "The management company is Meadowbrook Management. Don't know if they're still the ones running the HOA here, but there's one way to find out." Val pulled the phone from her pants pocket and dialed the number listed on the sheet. Then she tapped the icon for speakerphone and placed her phone in the center of the table.

"Meadowbrook Management, Bea speaking. How may I help you?"

"Hello, Bea. This is Special Agent Valerie Moore from the FBI calling."

"FBI? Oh my word, what is this about?"

"I'm at the Summerset Commons Condominiums. Does your company still manage this complex?"

"Yes, we certainly do. Is there a problem with an owner?"

"No, ma'am. What we need to know is the name of the grounds maintenance company you use here."

"Of course. We use the same company for all of the complexes we manage. It's called Green Space Landscape Services. We've used them for seven years now. Have they done something illegal?"

"Not to my knowledge, Bea, but where do the funds come from for the work they provide?"

"From the HOA fees everyone pays quarterly."

"And you keep records of every visit, the type of work they do, and how long they're at each complex?"

"Yes, indeed. We have to know how much to pay them."

"Ma'am, will you please look to see when they're scheduled to go to Summerset Commons and how long they're usually there?"

"Sure. It'll take a minute to pull it up on the computer."

"No problem."

We heard the tapping of computer keys as we waited for Bea to find that information.

"Here we go. They're set at a ten-day schedule for Summerset Commons, and it looks like tomorrow is when they show up. The average amount of time they spend there is between three and four hours."

"And they're scheduled for tomorrow?"

"Yes, ma'am."

Val gave us a thumbs-up. "And can you tell me, Bea, what kind of work uniform they wear?"

"I believe they wear khaki shorts and green polo shirts with the company name embroidered on the chest area."

Val grinned at the rest of us listening in. "Very good. Thanks so much for the information."

I had already found the name of the company and their location on my cell phone. It looked as though their main office was fifteen minutes west of the condo.

"I'd like to interview the people who run that business. I can have Joe send a still shot of those guys to my cell phone. We need to verify if those two men are employees or not, but my gut says they aren't."

Spelling stood. "I'll go with you,"

Maria walked through the open door and took a seat. "Forensics has dozens of prints to put into the system so they can run a comparison on any known felons. They said they did find prints at the back wall behind J.T.'s parking space. They'll check those first."

"Good to hear," I said.

"What about more cameras?" Spelling asked.

Impatience was written on Maria's face. "The officers are still out, sir, and I haven't heard any updates."

"All right. Why don't the rest of you head back to the office? It sounds like Forensics will be leaving soon, and there's no reason to stick around here. I guess we'll have to lock this place up for now."

"Sir?"

"Yep?" Spelling turned to Cam.

Cam tipped his head toward the sliders. "What about Ralph?"

"Shit, I forgot about the dog."

"I'll take him home until J.T. gets back. He'll be the household entertainment for a while. Kaden and Liza will love him."

Spelling slapped Cam's back. "You're a good agent, Cam, and a good friend. I just hope you don't have the dog for too long. Go ahead and pack up Ralph and his gear and take him home. Get back to the office as soon as you can, though. We have a lot of work ahead of us."

Chapter 10

"Move to the back wall, sit down, and put your legs straight out."

J.T. spat his anguish. "Where's my sister?"

Anthony smirked. "She's the least of your worries, Fed. Now do what I said unless you want a few broken ribs." He looked to the right and chuckled. "Guess your pal isn't hungry."

"He's unconscious, moron. He's lost a lot of blood and needs a doctor."

Anthony laughed. "Like that's going to happen."

"So, you and that other thug are the hired guns for that coward who hides in the shadows, right? Who is he?"

Anthony remained silent.

"How am I supposed to eat when my hands are cuffed behind my back?"

"Figure it out, genius. Dogs can eat without using their paws."

"That was almost funny. You really got me back on that one. Did my genius comment hurt your feelings this morning, big guy?"

"I told you to sit down by the wall." Anthony placed the tray on the floor, cracked his knuckles in his balled-up fist, and waited.

J.T. took a seat at the wall.

"Put your legs straight out like I said before."

"Why? Are you afraid of me?"

"I have a hundred pounds on you and both of your guns. I think I'll be fine." Anthony unlocked the gate and slid the tray inside. Then he closed the gate and snapped the padlock over the latch. He clicked it and gave it a tug.

"I need to piss."

"Sucks for you." Anthony turned around and left the room.

J.T. yelled, "I want to see my sister!"

It took a few minutes to get his legs back under him in order to stand. J.T. got up, crossed the enclosure to the tray of food, and knelt next to it. He had to eat to keep up his strength. If there was any chance of escape, he'd need all the energy he could muster. He leaned over the tray and ate.

Chapter 11

Spelling pulled into the single-story, stand-alone building that housed Green Space Landscape Services. With the cruiser parked, we crossed the lot to the side fence and peeked over the railing. Work trucks in all sizes—some equipped with plastic barrels containing liquid fertilizer—filled the space behind the six-foot-high security fence, along with self-propelled and riding lawn mowers and cabinets of trimming equipment.

After a scan of the area, we headed to the front door. Inside the building and just beyond three mismatched chairs pushed against the chair rail, a counter spread out in front of us. A sign hanging from two hooks on the back wall described the services Green Space offered along with the daily rates for renting equipment.

The man behind the counter looked up from his computer screen and lowered his glasses. "Can I help you folks?"

I gave him a thoughtful smile. "I sure hope so." I pulled out my badge and showed it to the man. "We have a few questions for the manager."

"You're looking at him, ma'am."

"Great, that was easy. So, to begin, I understand your company does the landscape services at Summerset Commons Condominiums. Is that correct?"

"We sure do. Was there a problem with our work that needed the FBI's assistance?" He shot me a quick grin.

I chuckled. "I wouldn't know that specifically, but what I do need to know is if your crew rotates their locations, or do the same people always work at the same places?"

"Each crew is assigned their locations, and that's where they work throughout the season. That way they know what needs to be done and what equipment to take with them."

Spelling spoke up. "Who usually works at Summerset Commons?"

"Give me a second to check the schedule." He stuck out his hand. "By the way, I'm Rick Dobbs."

We shook his hand, then he went back to tapping the computer's keyboard.

"Here we go. Manny Gomez, Lance Johnson, and Phil Hardy work on that side of town. Actually, they're scheduled to do Summerset Commons right after lunch tomorrow. They have two of the larger complexes on Thursdays. In the morning it's Blueberry Woods, and the afternoon is Summerset Commons."

I pulled out my cell phone from my pants pocket. "Would you mind taking a look at this picture and tell me if you know these men?"

"Sure, no problem."

I brought up the picture from the text Joe had sent me,

enlarged it on the screen, then turned my phone toward Rick. "Do these men work for you?"

"Do you mind?" He reached for my phone.

"Go ahead. Give it a long look, please."

Rick spread the picture with his fingers. "Well first off, if these are supposed to be workers from our company, they're dressed completely wrong. Our guys don't wear coveralls. They're too hot, especially in summer. Maybe in fall during yard cleanup, but that would be the only time." He enlarged the picture as wide as he could and stared at the men's faces. "Hard to identify them from the side, but they don't look like anybody I know."

Spelling took his turn. "And your crew never goes to Summerset Commons first, and never on Wednesdays?"

"No, sir, they have a regular schedule they stick to."

Spelling pulled out his card and slid it across the counter. We shook Rick's hand, thanked him for his time, and left.

Back in the cruiser, Spelling asked me to call the day care center. We needed to search through their videos, going back several days.

"Ask the young lady you spoke with if she'll forward the footage to you from the camera that faces the condo. We need to go back a week."

"Not a problem. Those men had to be watching Julie and J.T. for a while to know what time they leave for work. I'm guessing those landscaping coveralls were just a ruse so they wouldn't attract attention."

Spelling switched lanes and merged onto the freeway.

"Call Joe too and see if he can capture facial recognition of those men with the image he has. If not, we'll have a week of tapes to go through in hopes of getting those men to look directly at the camera."

I called Dee Dee, told her what we needed, and gave her my email address. She said I should see the footage in my in-box by the time we got back to our office. Joe said he would let us know whether he had any luck getting a match with the FBI's facial recognition software.

Spelling pulled into the back parking lot of our office, and we exited the car. Inside the building, our group of agents were hard at work trying to come up with reasons Julie or J.T. might have been kidnapped. Val spoke with Adam Beres, Julie's boss, and asked whether any disgruntled patients or staff members had a reason to be angry with Julie. According to Val, Mr. Beres said everyone loved Julie, and no complaint had been filed against her from the hospital staff or radiology patients.

We took our seats in the conference room, and Spelling led the meeting.

"J.T. has to be the target. We just have to figure out why. An FBI agent is far more likely to have enemies than a radiology technician. If it was about Julie, then why take J.T. too?"

I sighed. "Okay, then let's focus our energy on anybody who's had a beef with J.T. The question is how far back do we go? Our current branch has only been in operation for a year. Prior to that, all of you were located at the downtown headquarters. J.T. was in the violent crimes division, wasn't he?"

Spelling leaned back in his chair and sucked in a deep breath. "Do you have any idea how many cases he worked on in the five years he was in that department?"

"Boss?"

"Go ahead, Jade. You've got the floor."

"Apparently these men, or somebody they work for, wants J.T. but took Julie along too for leverage. That says J.T. either knows, or has, something they want and they'll get it through Julie. She's in as much danger or even more than J.T. is."

Cam spoke up. "J.T. has been in our current division for a year, so what has changed, and why now?"

Spelling rubbed his chin with a deep groan. "Okay, guys, let's focus on one thing at a time. We have plenty of video footage to go through." He jerked his chin toward me. "Jade, you want to see if the videos have arrived?"

"Sure thing. I'll be right back."

I took a right out the door and entered the second office on the left. Our division branch held only four offices for agents and the conference room. The remainder of the building consisted of common areas used by everyone. I turned in to the office that I shared with J.T. and stared at his empty desk.

Where are you, partner? I hope to God we get you and Julie home safely.

I jiggled the mouse and woke my computer. The newest email in my in-box was from Dee Dee. I opened it and saw a week of videos, each in its own Media Player folder.

Thank you, Dee Dee. That's exactly how we needed them sent.

I forwarded a folder to each agent, starting with the first folder from last Wednesday morning. We'd have seven tapes to go through, and hopefully we'd see these men again on the footage, sooner rather than later.

I tapped the print button and headed to the next room to retrieve copies of the still shots of the men in question. When I returned to the conference room, I passed a copy to each agent. "These are the men to watch for on the videos. I just sent a video link to each of your in-boxes."

Spelling pushed back his chair and rounded the conference table. "Okay, people, we have work to do. Once we find out who these thugs are in the green coveralls, we'll be able to start putting the puzzle pieces together." He smacked the doorframe and crossed the hallway to his office.

Chapter 12

"Nothing has popped up on the facial recognition of those guys, Jade. I'm not saying they aren't in the database, but the software can't hit enough markers to make an ID."

"Because of the side view?" I tapped my pen against my desk calendar.

"That's exactly why. You said you have a week of footage to go through?"

"Yeah, we're all working on that now. If any of us get a hit, you'll be the first to know."

"Okay, good luck. If you need anything else, let me know."

I clicked off the call with Joe and glanced at the time on the bottom corner of my computer monitor. J.T. and Julie had been missing for more than eight hours. I couldn't let my mind go to that dark place. I had to focus on the video in front of me. Each of us started our tapes at the same time—daybreak—which was five thirty. We had been reviewing the footage for over an hour, and nobody had mentioned seeing those men yet.

I leaned in when I noticed a gold Mercedes drive by the complex slower than most of the other traffic. I was sure I had seen it earlier, near the beginning of the tape. I jotted down the time that the vehicle passed the condo then moved the scrubber bar to the far left and started over. I hit Pause when I saw the same car at the forty-seven-minute mark. The black-tinted windows made it impossible to see anybody inside. I rose from my desk and went to inform my colleagues. Maria and Val were stationed in the office next to mine.

I walked in. "See those thugs yet?"

They both shook their heads.

"I might have something, and I think we should all watch for it." I turned and saw Cam behind me.

He pointed over his shoulder as he walked in. "My office door was open. What do you have?"

"Not sure if it's related or not, but a gold Mercedes passed by the condo several times on the tape I'm viewing. It drove by slowly both times."

"Could you see the occupants?" Cam asked.

"Blackout windows, so I couldn't see a damn thing. I couldn't pull the plates, either, since it was too far away. I wanted to give everyone a heads-up in case it comes across on your tapes."

Spelling walked in. "What day are you looking at?"

"I have last Friday."

"That would give them plenty of time to case the complex. Let's have a look at that vehicle so everyone knows what to watch for."

We entered my office and crowded around my computer. I hit the play button, and the Mercedes passed by in front of us. I pointed at the screen and paused the video. "That's it right there. It passed at the forty-seven-minute mark and again a half hour later."

"Okay, people, we're looking for two men with dark hair and large frames, both exceeding two hundred fifty pounds and well over six foot. They could be of Italian or Spanish descent. I'm leaning toward Italians, only because they're normally taller than Mexicans. There's a suspicious champagne-colored four-door Mercedes sedan, possibly an E-Class, trolling the neighborhood. Jade, go back to the video from this morning and see if that vehicle enters the footage at any time before Julie's abduction. The rest of you watch for that car and keep searching for those two men."

Everyone returned to their offices to dig in, and I went back to my in-box. I scrolled down to the earlier email I had sent myself from the day care center and opened the video attachment again. I began the footage at daybreak, just like the others we had been watching. At six forty-seven, I hit the pause button and jumped from my chair. I yelled out into the hallway, "I have it. I've got that Mercedes on today's video!"

Spelling was the first one through the door. "Show me."

Everyone joined in and peered over my shoulder. "See, there it is again. It can't be a coincidence, but we also can't see where it went or if it parked."

Cam spoke up. "What happened to looking for more cameras? If anyone got out of that vehicle farther up the street and doubled back, we're missing the west half of the complex. The camera from the day care center doesn't reach that far."

"I'll check with Carson," Maria said. She walked out into the hallway to make the call.

"The complex has a main front entrance, the garage overhead, and a back door at the center of the building that lines up with the front door. The back door only opens from the inside," Spelling said.

"That's correct, sir. If one of those men sneaked in through the garage door before the overhead went down, he could have opened the back door for his partner."

"Did anyone from the police station test the overhead to see how long it stays open after a car pulls out?" Spelling asked.

"They sure did. It stays open for seven seconds once the car passes the electronic eye. That would give anyone ample time to slip inside," Cam said. "Oh, and a quick side note, the officers who went through the dumpsters said they didn't find anything inside them except trash."

Spelling groaned. "Back to square one."

Moments later, Maria returned to my office. "Carson just got word that a three-story office building two blocks to the rear of the condo has security cameras around the perimeter of their entire structure. They're reviewing the video from this morning and will call you as soon as they know something."

"Okay, good." Spelling slapped his hands together. "Maybe we'll get something after all. Let's get back to work.

I want these thugs identified before the sun goes down."

We continued reviewing the videos. By four thirty, we had come up with two more sightings of that Mercedes. Val had the best image of the blurry license plate and sent it over to Joe. With any luck, he'd be able to sharpen it and get us a legible number.

At five o'clock, we broke for fifteen minutes to revive ourselves. I rose from my desk, rolled my neck, and stretched. My eyes burned from staring at the computer screen so intently. Tonight's dinner would consist of a cellophane-wrapped sandwich from the vending machine, a bag of chips, and strong coffee. I started a fresh twelve-cup pot, knowing we would all be drinking it. While the coffee brewed, I made a quick call to my sister, Amber. She was probably on her way home.

Amber picked up immediately. "Hey, Jade. Will you be home for dinner?"

Her question reminded me that I hadn't informed her of J.T. and Julie's disappearance. The day had been so hectic and nonstop, it hadn't even occurred to me to let her know.

"I'm so sorry I didn't text you, Amber. We've barely taken a breath today."

"That sounds ominous. What happened?"

"It's bad. J.T. and his sister, Julie, are missing. Kidnapped, actually, and we've been on this all day with no substantial leads."

"Oh my God, that's horrible. You said you have nothing to go on?"

"Nothing that can identify the individuals who did this.

There aren't any ransom demands or that type of thing and I can't even begin to imagine what they're going through."

"Don't go there, Sis. Is there anything I can do to help?"

"Nah, but thanks. I'm sure I'll be here most of the night. Just feed Polly and Porky, please. Give them each a kiss for me." I exhaled a deep sigh.

"You know I will, and you sound exhausted."

"I am, but this isn't about me. We have to find J.T. and Julie as soon as humanly possible. Time isn't on their side." I hung up and poured myself a cup of coffee. I took the coffee, sandwich, and chips back to my office and plopped down at my desk.

A knock sounded on my door just as I tossed the sandwich wrapper in the trash. It was Spelling. He peeked in and jerked his head toward the hallway. "Conference room. We have an update."

Chapter 13

J.T. opened his groggy eyes. The loud sound of the outer door opening and closing woke him. That large empty warehouse was dark—too dark to see his former partner's condition. He scooted to the left side of the pen and whispered. His voice was dry and cracked when he spoke. "Curt, wake up. Come on, buddy. I have to know if you're okay."

Bright lights suddenly illuminated the building, and a fuzzy image headed J.T.'s way from across that wide-open space. The clip-clop of footsteps got closer, but J.T. still couldn't make out the face.

The deep voice spoke from fifty feet away. "I have a message for you."

J.T. squinted and rubbed his eyes against his bent knees. Something was wrong. He rubbed his eyes again and squeezed them open and closed. The blurred vision was still there, and the fact that he slept at all made no sense. He tried to focus upward and out beyond the broken windows, but the sun had long passed that side of the building. It had to be late in the day, meaning he had slept for hours.

Those assholes put something in my food.

He craned his neck toward Curt, who was balled up in a fetal position, his back facing J.T.

J.T. whispered again, but this time with urgency. "Curt, wake up, man. Are you okay? Just move your hand if you can hear me."

A slight movement from Curt's right index finger was enough to tell J.T. he was still hanging on.

The man reached the enclosure, grasped the links, then gave them a hard shake. That time it wasn't Anthony, it was Antonio, and he was likely trying to instill fear in them.

J.T. stood and smirked at the man on the other side of the cage. "I see you've changed out of your Jolly Green Giant suit. So, what's the message, goon, and why did you drug me?"

"I didn't—Anthony did—and the message is from Mr. Vetcher. He's changed his mind and decided not to be so generous. He wants your log-in and password information by morning."

"Tell him to go to hell. I'm still waiting to see my sister."

"He was certain you'd say that too. He told me to do this so you'd realize just how serious he is."

"Yeah, what's that, big guy?"

The ear-piercing sound of bullets firing echoed off the walls. In an instant, Antonio pulled out J.T.'s Glock 22 from under his suit jacket and shot off two rounds—one, a direct hit to the back of Curt's head.

"No, no, no! You son of a bitch! I'll kill you—I'll kill all of you! Tell that coward boss of yours to face me, that piece of shit!"

Antonio turned and walked away. J.T. kicked the links of the enclosure and cursed the man who disappeared from sight. He yelled out his intentions for all of them, but his threats went unanswered.

Chapter 14

We filed into the conference room and took our seats. Spelling stood at the head of the table and began with the latest update.

"I've just gotten word from Captain Groves of the Whitefish Bay PD that his officers did see a few seconds of activity at the back of the condo complex from the office building's security tape. Apparently, one man in green coveralls stood at the back door for a minute before it opened outward and he disappeared into the building."

I added my two cents. "And according to what you said earlier, that door only opens from the inside. The man was waiting for his partner to let him in just like we thought."

"True enough, but they didn't see the second man on the tape. He stayed within the doorway and was hidden by the shadows. They're sending a copy of the video to us and one to Joe. It should be landing in my in-box any minute. The good thing is, the captain said his officers saw the man look straight back, only for a second, but that may be enough for Joe to get a hit with the facial recognition software." Spelling jerked his head toward Val. "Would you mind grabbing my laptop off my desk?"

"Not at all, sir. I'll be right back."

We waited only a minute and Val returned with the laptop cradled in the crook of her arm. She set it on the table, and Spelling logged in. We gathered behind him and looked over his shoulder.

"Okay, here's the footage." He hit the play button, and we watched as a man rounded the west side of the building and stood at the back door. In a minute's time, the door pushed outward, and he crossed over the threshold. Within that minute, he scanned the horizon from left to right. The camera caught his entire face when he looked straight back.

"There! Gotcha!" I pointed, and Spelling paused the footage. "If Joe can't get enough markers to hit on that guy's face, nobody can."

"Give him a call, Jade, and see if he got the file yet. We need a rush on that man's identity and the plate number for that Mercedes."

I pushed back my chair and stood. "Got it, boss." I walked out into the hallway and made the call.

"Joe, it's Jade. What's the word on the plate number?"

"Yeah, no luck there. That license plate is registered to a 2005 Nissan Sentra—a far cry from a late model Mercedes sedan."

"Crap. So it's stolen and we have no idea who really owns that Mercedes, which is most likely stolen too."

"I'd have to agree with you on that. It looks like a video file just came in, though. You want to walk me through that one?"

"Yep, that's why I'm calling. The tape is from an office building's rooftop camera, and it catches the back of the condo complex. One of the two guys who posed as the landscape crew shows up on the footage and waits at the back door. We're assuming the other man sneaked in through the overhead when somebody pulled out since the back door can only be opened from the inside." I paced the hallway as I talked. "There's a split second where the guy at the back looks directly at the camera, even though he certainly didn't realize it. We need you to do your magic with the facial recognition software and see if you come up with a hit. Even though there's only one person we can see, it's a start. If that guy has a record, then maybe the other one will show up as one of his known associates."

"Sounds good, and I'll get started right away. I'll call as soon as I have a yes or no for you."

"Thanks, Joe. I'll keep my fingers crossed." I clicked off and rejoined everyone in the conference room. I spoke as I took my seat. "I gave Joe a brief rundown of the footage and told him he'd see the guy looking straight back toward the camera about a minute and a half into the video. Joe also said the plates on the Mercedes are stolen. They don't belong to that car."

An audible groan filled the room.

"I knew this wasn't going to be easy," Cam said.

"All right, until we hear back from Joe, let's continue searching the tapes for more sightings of those two men. It's the only thing we have to work with for now. I want to see them and that car in the same frame. One of them drove it there, or there's a third mystery person involved." Spelling closed the laptop and took it back to his office.

I was restless as I sat at my computer and searched the footage. I didn't find anything more from that morning. I glanced at the time—7:18. My phone hadn't rung yet, and my optimism was fading.

"I got one of them!" Val's voice rang out into the hallway.

I leapt out of my chair and rounded the doorway to the next office. The rest of the group was on their way in.

"Here"—she pointed—"it's Monday morning, and he just stepped into the frame."

"Check it out," I said. "He's wearing a suit this time and an expensive looking one, I might add."

Cam knelt to Val's right and maximized her computer screen with the mouse. "Funny how these guys always stare at the ground or look to the side. It's like they're mindful of possible cameras in the area, plus the sunglasses help hide their identities."

"Well, they didn't wear sunglasses this morning. I wonder if—" The ringing phone on my desk interrupted me. I bolted out the door to answer it. The caller ID showed it was Joe. I said a quick prayer in hopes that he had something useful.

"I have news, Jade. I have a hit on the man at the back door."

"Hang on, I need to get everyone into the conference room. Call back on my cell so I can put you on speakerphone." I hung up and gathered everyone into the conference room for the second time that evening. Each of us had paper and a pen handy. My cell rang just as Spelling entered and walked to the head of the table. He gave me a nod as he took his seat. "Hello. Yep, I'm putting you on speakerphone, Joe. Okay, we're all here. Go ahead."

Joe began by telling us he got a positive facial recognition hit on the man at the back door of the complex. His name was Antonio Pirelli, and he had an extensive rap sheet.

Spelling nodded. "Italian, just like I thought."

"That's correct, sir," Joe said. "Apparently, the Pirellis are a well-known Chicago-based crime family that works for hire. They'll do anything, really, depending on how much money they're offered. Antonio was recently released from Stateville Prison after doing a nickel term for aggravated assault."

"What do we have on his known associates and family members?"

"He has three sisters and two brothers. The one I find interesting is Anthony, his elder brother by two years. Based on the video of the two men in green coveralls standing on the front lawn, I'd venture to say the other could very well be Anthony. He has a similar rap sheet and is built very much like Antonio—large, stocky, and capable of brute force."

"Good work, Joe. What age are we talking about? Could the old man or uncles be involved?"

"Possibly, sir, but I doubt if it's on the grunt work end of things. The old man, Giancarlo, and his brothers, Leo and Mauricio, are all in their late sixties. Anthony is forty, and Antonio, thirty-eight."

"Okay. Tell Forensics to put a rush on those prints. From the way it sounds, if they belong to anyone in the Pirelli family, they'll be on file." Spelling dug his fists into his eyes. "Now all we need to know is why they were hired to go after J.T. and by whom."

We ended the call, and Joe forwarded Anthony and Antonio's rap sheets to each of our computers.

"Jade, get on the horn with the Chicago PD and find out everything you can on that family. Tell them to get to the Pirelli compound and start hauling in family members. Somebody better start talking and fast."

Chapter 15

The lights blasted J.T. in the face again. He looked up and stared at the men approaching. Anthony and Antonio headed toward the enclosure where Curt's dead body lay. A body bag, draped over Antonio's shoulder, swayed with his stride. Neither man acknowledged J.T. or even looked his way. Antonio stood a few feet back as Anthony unlocked the gate and stepped inside. After rolling Curt over, Anthony cocked his head toward Antonio.

"Come on. Let's put him in the bag. He's already getting stiff."

Antonio pulled the gate completely open and entered. He spread the black bag out onto the floor and unzipped it.

With a smirk, he addressed J.T. "See what happens when you won't cooperate? Remember what I told you earlier, Fed. You have until morning or your sister gets plugged in the head too."

"Let that piece of shit Mr. Vetcher know I'll give him the information he wants, but I have to see my sister first. I need his word that he'll release her after I tell him what he wants to hear."

Anthony and Antonio chuckled as they dropped Curt's rigid body into the bag and zipped it. With their hands slipped through the looped handles, they dragged the bag out of the cage.

Anthony looked back at J.T. and grinned. "Get some sleep, Fed. Tomorrow may be your worst day yet."

Antonio stopped and reached into his coat pocket. He pulled out a bag of crackers and tossed it through the links. "Eat your supper. You won't see us again until tomorrow."

"How about taking these cuffs off, then? What harm is one night going to do? You can put them back on me in the morning, and your boss won't be the wiser. There's no way I can get out of here, anyway."

Anthony gave Antonio a nod.

"Turn around and put your hands against the fence."

J.T. did as he was told and backed up with his wrists against the links. Antonio fished through his pants pocket for the handcuff key and pulled it out. He unsnapped the cuffs and pulled them through the opening next to the gate, then he dropped them to the floor.

"Don't make me regret this." He turned his back to J.T., grabbed the handle of the body bag, and disappeared around the corner with Anthony.

Moments later, the lights went out, and J.T. was left alone in the blackened room. He sat in the corner and ate the crackers as he waited for his eyes to adjust to the dark. He rubbed his torn, aching wrists, then stood and paced.

I've got to get out of this damn cage and find Julie. Tomorrow might be too late to save either of us.

Finally able to see shadows in the dimly lit warehouse, J.T. caught a glimpse of the handcuffs lying on the floor just outside his enclosure. He pulled off his belt and tried to snag the cuffs with the belt buckle. Somehow, between the cuffs and the belt, he was sure he could figure a way out of the cage.

Chapter 16

The sounds of pounding startled me, but when the loud cursing began, I was sure Spelling had news—and it couldn't be good. I jumped from my chair and met with the rest of our team in the corridor. We headed to Spelling's office at the end of the hall.

Through the half-cracked-open door we saw him, his head buried in his hands and his elbows on the desk.

"Sir?" I pushed the door open wider. "What happened?"

"It's Curt—Curt Belmont."

I turned to the group for help. I didn't know who Curt Belmont was.

Cam scooted around me and entered Spelling's office. "What happened to Curt, boss?"

Spelling palmed his eye sockets and looked up. "It's bad, guys—really bad. A motorist called it in. They were driving a few car lengths behind a dark-colored van when suddenly the back doors flew open and a body bag was pushed out. They had to slam on their brakes so they wouldn't run over it. The van disappeared into the night. Whoever those sons of bitches are dumped his body right in front of the parking garage to our downtown headquarters."

Cam raked his hair with both hands. "You're saying it was Curt? Curt is dead?"

Spelling nodded. I was sure he was overwhelmed with grief and anxiety. "Shot nearly point blank in the head and chest. Somebody is making a statement, and it's probably the same person who has J.T. and Julie."

I turned to Val and pulled her out into the hallway. "Who is Curt?"

Val was visibly shaken, and tears pooled in her eyes. "Curt used to be J.T.'s partner in the Violent Crimes unit downtown. He decided to stay in that unit when we opened the Serial Crimes Division here. He wasn't one who wanted to be gone often. His mom lives in the northern Chicago suburbs, and he goes there every weekend to check on her."

"Then why wasn't a red flag raised? Today is Wednesday." When the tears began rolling down Val's cheeks, I put my arm around her shoulder.

"I don't know, Jade. Maybe he took a personal day." Val wiped her eyes with the back of her sleeve. "Curt was such a nice, fun-loving guy. Who could have done this, and why?"

Spelling cleared his throat and pushed back his chair. "Let's go. We've got work to do downtown. The local agents and the PD have that street and the scene blocked off. Forensics and the ME just arrived, according to SSA Hopkins. I want everyone in the parking structure in five minutes."

I rushed back to my office and shot off a quick text to Amber saying not to worry, I had to work late. I secured my shoulder holster, slipped my badge on the lanyard over my neck, made sure I had a notepad and pen, and grabbed my purse. I looked back at my desk before I turned off the light—I was good to go. I waited in the hallway for the rest of the team, and we left together.

"We're taking two cruisers, lights and sirens engaged." Spelling jerked his head at Cam. "You're driving that one"—he pointed to his left—"and I'll take this one. Jade, jump in with me."

"Yes, sir." I climbed into the passenger seat, slammed the door, and secured my belt. Within seconds, the cruisers hit the street, and we were on our way to the scene.

I turned toward Spelling. "What can you tell me about J.T. and Curt's relationship?"

He shook his head as if to clear his thoughts for a minute. "They were partners between 2011 and early 2016 when we moved our office to Glendale. Curt has"—he paused—"or had a brother in Omaha and his mom in Waukegan, Illinois. Why his missing work today didn't alarm anyone, I don't know. I'm sure we'll get more details after talking to his immediate supervisor."

"Is that SSA Hopkins?"

Spelling nodded. "He was notified the second the agents realized who was in the body bag. He's at the downtown office along with most of the crew and the city police."

"Do you think the Pirelli family is involved?"

"I don't think they have a personal issue with anyone,

they're just hired killers. But did they commit the act? I'd say there's a good chance of it. There's a reason they've been canvassing the area around the condo, and then the getups they wore this morning? You know that was a ruse so they wouldn't attract attention while they kidnapped J.T. and Julie. Why any of our people were targeted is yet to be known, but I'm sure Curt's death and the fact that he and J.T. used to be partners isn't a coincidence."

"And Julie is the leverage for whatever they want from J.T. and didn't get from Curt?"

"I'd say so, one hundred percent."

Spelling hit the freeway with Cam on his rear bumper. The drive to the downtown headquarters would take us only ten minutes at the speed we were going. Every car to our front and sides parted ways and pulled to the shoulder, giving us a clear path to Milwaukee.

We arrived at the blocked off street and parked at the intersection. Police tape, as well as wooden sawhorse type barricades, shut down two city blocks. We climbed out of our cruisers and headed toward the flashing lights a block ahead. From the location of the medical examiner and the forensic team's vans, we knew where Curt's body lay.

We approached the group, and Spelling shook SSA Hopkins's outstretched hand. They patted each other on the back and began discussing the situation. Hopkins waved Agent Bill Lewis over and invited him to take part in the conversation. Bill had been working closely with Curt on several recent cases.

Hopkins picked up where he had left off. "Bill and Curt

were working together on something else, but I'll assign another agent to that case for the time being. We need everyone on board who knew Curt and J.T."

Spelling turned toward me. "Jade, I want you and Cam to go inside and talk to the people who called in the incident. They were interviewed briefly when the police showed up at the scene, but I want every detail. Leave no stone unturned."

"Got it, boss." Cam and I took the elevator to the third floor and signed in at the registration counter. We showed our badges to Maureen, the night agent in charge of signing people in and out. She pointed to her left, toward the visitors' lounge.

"Just a heads-up, guys," she said with a concerned look.

Cam nodded.

"It's a family in there. A husband, wife, and two kids under ten. They're pretty distraught, and the kids are overly tired. They've been here for nearly an hour and have been talked to once already."

I groaned and hoped the children hadn't actually witnessed the event. I was sure Cam felt their anxiety since he had a young child too.

"We'll be easy on them, but we're talking about one of our own. We need to know everything they can remember," Cam said.

"Has anyone checked the street cameras for that van?" I asked.

"I believe the tech department is working on that," Maureen said.

I smacked the counter and jerked my head toward the visitors' lounge. "Come on. Let's talk to these folks so they can get their kids home and put to bed."

Cam and I entered the comfortably decorated lounge where two love seats faced each other with a coffee table between them. Several round tables filled the rest of the space, with four chairs at each one. A TV played quietly in the background.

The parents looked up from their cell phones when we entered the room. Both kids slept soundly on the love seats. I was thankful for that and took in a slow, calming breath. I hadn't realized how late it was until I glanced at the clock above the coffee station—10:38. Cam and I approached the mom and dad and introduced ourselves. They responded with a tired handshake and their names—Richard and Amy Lawrence.

We pulled out the two empty chairs next to them at the table and sat down. Cam explained that Curt was a former colleague and we needed every bit of information they could remember in order to apprehend those violent killers.

I reached in my pocket and pulled out my notepad. I would write down the information. Since Cam knew Curt personally, it was better that he lead the questioning.

"Okay, folks, we're going to try to get you on your way as soon as possible. We know the police department questioned you already, but since the individual in the body bag was an FBI agent, we need to ask questions of our own. Why don't you just begin with the way the event played out in front of you, and we'll ask questions as we go along."

"Yeah, sure," Richard said. He began by telling how they had just left a friend's high-rise condo after a birthday party. They were taking Kilbourn Street to the freeway entrance so they could head south on Interstate 94 toward their home in Caledonia. He said he didn't know where the van came from or how long it had been in front of them. It wasn't anything they were paying attention to until Amy yelled out that the back doors were opening.

"I thought the doors accidentally swung open until I saw somebody in the back shove the body bag out. It rolled for about fifteen feet, and the van sped off. I had to slam on my brakes—"

Amy patted her husband's hand and took over the conversation. "It was terrible," she said. "I mean, we weren't even sure what we saw was real. We nearly hit the bag, and of course by the shape—well, you know—there had to be a body inside." She paused and took a sip of water from her Styrofoam cup. "That's when Richard squealed to a stop and called the police. I swear he didn't touch anything. Richard stood by the bag until law enforcement arrived and I stayed in the car with the kids. We had no idea we were in front of the FBI building until the agents poured out onto the street, probably because they heard the sirens. I guess when they looked inside the bag, they realized the poor man was one of their own."

I nodded and wrote as fast as I could.

"Can you tell us anything about the van or the man you said pushed the bag out?"

Richard spoke up. "The van was a dark color, either dark

blue or black. I couldn't tell you anything else about it because we only saw it from behind."

"Were there windows in the back, or were they solid doors?" Cam asked.

"Solid, that much I'm positive of."

"Anything else like bumper stickers, dents, taillights out?"

"Not that I noticed." Richard wiped the perspiration off his forehead with the back of his hand.

"You're doing fine," Cam said. "Now, what about the person who pushed the bag out?"

"I can't tell you anything about him. It was more like we saw a shape and movement than an actual person. Obviously, somebody pushed him out, but it happened so fast. It wasn't like there was eye contact between us, and the side streets aren't well lit around here. It was just a shape moving inside, then a push, nothing else. It was over and done with in a matter of seconds, then the van was gone."

Cam exhaled a deep breath. "Were there any numbers on the license plate you remember seeing?"

"I never even noticed the plate. Like I said, it happened so fast. My main concern was to avoid hitting the bag."

"Okay, I think we have everything we need." Cam reached inside his sport coat and pulled out two cards. He handed one to each parent. "Please don't hesitate to call if you think of anything else. Even a small detail could help. If you want to gather your kids, we'll escort you out."

Once outside, we watched as the barricades were moved long enough for Richard Lawrence to drive out. Cam and I crossed over to the sidewalk where Spelling, SSA Hopkins, Val, Maria, and a group of other agents stood.

"Anything on the Pirelli family from the Chicago PD yet?" I asked.

"According to the police department that hauled a few of them in for questioning, they were told nobody has seen Anthony or Antonio for months."

Cam smirked. "That's convenient."

SSA Hopkins spoke up. "That group is tight-lipped. We may have to reopen old charges filed against the family before we can get any of them to sing. Meanwhile, let's get a warrant to tap their phone lines. They may be tight-lipped with us, but I bet they say plenty to each other."

I cleared my throat and waited my turn. "If you don't mind me asking, sir, why didn't Curt's absence from work raise a red flag today?"

"Actually, he took several personal days off, so we weren't even aware that he was missing."

Val asked whether Curt mentioned why he needed a few days off.

"He said he had to take care of some legal matters for his mom's estate."

I gave Spelling a dubious glance. Chances were, the Pirellis had kidnapped Curt yesterday and killed him after he wouldn't tell them what it was they were hired to find out. Just the thought of that made me shudder. I wondered whether that was J.T.'s fate as well if he didn't talk. And what would they, or had they, done to Julie?

Dave Mann, the county ME, approached us. "Bob and

I are going to head out, guys. We'll have a detailed report for you in twenty-four hours. Sorry for your loss."

Spelling and SSA Hopkins shook their hands, and we watched as Curt's body was loaded into the back of the ME's van. Hopkins called out to Butch Martin and Hal Friedman, who were packing up their forensic equipment.

"Anything stand out, guys?"

"Not yet. Chances are the assailants were gloved. Dave transferred Curt into one of his own bags. We're taking the original back to the crime lab to go over it thoroughly. It's all we have to work with."

Hopkins jammed his hands into his pockets and nodded. Frustration was written all over his face.

Spelling spoke up. "Got the results from those prints in the condo's garage yet?"

"They weren't a match to anyone in the Pirelli family who has prints on file, but we're still searching."

Spelling let out a few choice curse words and walked away.

Hopkins nodded. "Keep us in the loop, guys."

"You got it, sir." Butch and Hal climbed into the forensics van and drove away.

Chapter 17

After finally snagging the handcuffs with the belt, J.T. secured them to the chain links of the enclosure on one end and through the belt buckle on the other. He pulled and jerked the fence inward. He was making slow progress and needed only a few links to weaken enough for him to snap away from the framework. If he could manage that, he'd bend and twist enough of the fence to fold over and out of his way. With any luck, he could slip through the opening and out into the warehouse. He wrapped the end of the belt around his arm for leverage and pressed his feet against the bottom of the fence to brace himself.

After several hours of effort, the fence had bent inward considerably. It wouldn't take much longer.

I need to get out of this damn cage, find Julie, and make our escape before morning since I know what these monsters are capable of.

J.T. watched as the links began to pull away from the cross bar at the top of the fence.

Just a little more and it should come loose.

With every ounce of strength he could muster, J.T. wrenched on the belt, wrapped it around his forearm, and pulled again. One by one, the links bent away from the top bar as he continued to pull. They finally broke free.

He dropped the belt, wrapped his fingers through the links, and pulled that section toward him. The opening he created was four feet from the ground but wide enough to get out. He climbed the fence, reached around the opening, and pulled himself through.

The skin on his arms was torn and bleeding from the sharp edges, but even that didn't deter J.T.—he needed to find Julie, and the sooner the better. First, he had to be certain the oversized thugs and the mystery man calling the shots weren't anywhere in the building.

J.T. slunk through the shadows, trying to stay as quiet and inconspicuous as possible while passing under the interior overhead garage door. He looked left and right for movement before continuing on. Julie's car stood directly in front of him. He approached cautiously and peered through the window with hopes of seeing her keys in the ignition. He knew that was only wishful thinking as he grasped the driver's door and slowly opened it. He dropped down into the seat and patted the floor beneath him. Then he checked the console, under the floor mats, in the glove box, and behind the visor. The keys weren't there. He held his breath as he popped the trunk. It opened silently. J.T. sucked in a deep breath of relief and searched the trunk with no results. He needed to move on and find his sister—and a way out of the building. He remembered Curt saying he saw Julie for a split second as he was pushed through the open door of the room she was in.

It was time to search the entire structure. J.T.'s ears were perked for sounds of anyone else in the building. He needed to be alert and careful as he pressed along the walls of the second floor and crept forward inch by inch. He'd clear the second level then search every room, closet, and alcove on the first floor. Julie had to be somewhere in that building.

He'd gone through all five offices on the second floor, and they were all vacant. J.T. retraced his steps down the stairs to the lower level and began at the west wall. Four rooms with closed doors lined that side of the warehouse. He pressed his ear against the first door—dead silence. With a careful twist of the knob, he opened the door and peeked in. The room was small, likely a storage area back in the day. Mice scurried at the disturbance from the door opening. J.T. didn't see anything inside except an upended shelving unit on the floor. He pulled the door closed and moved on. He crept to the second room and listened. He pressed his ear against the door. He was sure he heard something on the other side, possibly muffled sobs. He turned the knob and pushed. The door opened, and inside lay a few pieces of strewn office furniture but nothing else.

My mind is playing tricks on me. I swear I heard Julie.

Only two rooms were left on that side of the building. He'd clear them and continue on to the bathrooms while making his way across the warehouse. He went to the third door and turned the knob, but it didn't budge. He put his shoulder into it and pushed. The door was locked from the outside. He touched the center of the knob and felt a slot where a key would be inserted. That door was locked for some reason.

He whispered her name. "Julie? Sis, are you in there? It's J.T. Answer me if you can." He listened and heard the sobs again. "Julie, is that you?"

"J.T., you're alive? Help me, please. I'm bound to a bed. We need to get out of here before they get back." Her sobs became more urgent.

"Shh, I'll get you out. Just stay calm."

J.T. turned around and panned the darkened warehouse. His mind was going in a hundred different directions. Speed was necessary, but so was silence until he was sure the building was empty. He needed to find something he could use to pry open the door, but first he had to make sure the other rooms were empty.

"I'll be right back, Julie, but please don't make any noise."

J.T. moved on to the next door and turned the knob. He peered in and saw a small room with a table, two chairs, and a twin bed. The blankets had been tossed back, and the room appeared to have been recently used.

I bet that's where the thugs sleep when they're here.

Only one room remained. J.T. inhaled a deep breath and took three steps. He stood outside the last door and listened. All was quiet. He grasped the knob and gave it a turn.

Chapter 18

At least a dozen agents gathered in the large conference room in our downtown headquarters. The air in that room was heavy with solemn silence. We had to figure out the connection between Curt, J.T., and the psychos who'd murdered Curt and were still holding J.T. and Julie hostage. We had sleepless nights and busy days ahead of us, and we didn't know what state of mind those individuals were in. Would they lose their patience, and would J.T. and his sister endure the same fate as Curt? There had to be something important going on that caused them to spring into action at that particular time.

Spelling and SSA Hopkins each took a corner at the head of the table nearest the back wall.

Agent Hopkins stood and held his closed fist against his mouth. He cleared his throat and began. "Most of you at this table knew Curt personally and, in one way or another, treated him like family. He worked at this location for nine years, and four years prior to that at the North Chicago field office. I can only thank God he wasn't married and didn't have children." Hopkins smiled thoughtfully and took a second to compose himself. "No encumbrances, Curt and J.T. always said. It was a standing joke between them. That's why those two made such good partners, and now one is dead and the other is missing."

I wiped my eyes, which were beginning to blur. I remembered our team joking about that on the first day I met them. That was the reason Spelling assigned me to J.T. Neither of us had encumbrances. I glanced up, and Cam, Maria, and Val were staring at me.

Hopkins sighed deeply before continuing. "He had a mother who depended greatly on him. She hasn't been told yet, but in all probability, I'll be taking a drive to Waukegan tomorrow to tell her face-to-face that her son is dead. We need to find the connection. Somebody wants something that Curt and J.T. knew about or worked on together. There would be no other reason to kidnap both of them. Apparently, Curt wouldn't give them whatever they wanted, and he died because of it."

Spelling took over. "What we need is every case that Curt and J.T. worked on together. I realize that's a daunting task and it's going to take time, but we need to start at the beginning. Curt and J.T. were partners between 2011 and early 2016 when our team split off and moved the Serial Crimes Unit to Glendale. Curt stayed behind because of his mom, and J.T. gained a new unencumbered partner in Jade." Spelling gave me a weak smile.

My voice caught in my throat. "May I say something?"

"Go ahead," Spelling said.

"I think that because five years of working together is a lot of case files to go through, we should focus on the most notorious criminals, the ones with an ax to grind and who likely ended up dead due to a gun fight or who are in prison. The families could be seeking revenge."

"True," Cam added, "but J.T. and Curt haven't been partners for a year. There had to be a trigger for the person calling the shots to suddenly come out of the shadows."

Hopkins took his turn. "Okay, let's begin with the cases that Curt and J.T. were primaries on. They led the investigation and most likely made the arrest themselves. Also, focus on anybody who was personally shot or sent to prison by either of them. Those files should hold us over until morning." He jerked his head at Agent Lewis. "Bill, start making calls. I want every agent who doesn't need eight hours of sleep to get down here immediately. Let's get started. Agent Pearson?"

"Yes, sir?"

"Show Agent Monroe where we keep the files that Curt and J.T. worked on between 2011 and 2016. Bring all of them in here, and we'll begin. I'll get Maureen to start a few pots of coffee. We have a long night ahead."

Joe from the tech department knocked on the door. I was shocked to see him still at work.

"Sirs?"

"Go ahead, Joe," Hopkins said.

"I was able to pick up camera footage of the van for three blocks, and then it disappeared into a residential area. There aren't any cameras along the streets in that quadrant."

"Anything that stood out?"

"Nothing that will help us. I didn't get the driver in any frames, and I didn't see the plate number since the view was always from the side. All I can say with certainty is that it was a panel van, likely five to eight years old. Nothing else stood out, and I can't even tell you the make or model. Every other streetlight leading out of downtown was shut off, and still is, due to the energy saving initiative Milwaukee has in place. Also, at that hour, the only places lit up on a weeknight are the bars, which are few and far between in this area of downtown."

"Let's get that information on the news, anyway. Somebody's neighbor may have a black or dark blue panel van. The more eyes helping us look for that vehicle, the better. We find the van, we'll likely find the people responsible for Curt's death and J.T. and Julie's kidnapping," Hopkins said.

I entered the file room behind Agent Pearson. As we worked our way through the cabinets of archived cases, she explained that she was a recent graduate of the FBI training course in Quantico and hoped one day to be a profiler. I told her about Amber's aspirations too as we filled a cart with every file folder with J.T. and Curt's cases between 2011 and 2016. I pushed the cart out of the room and waited as Agent Pearson—or Sandra, as she liked to be called—locked the door at our backs. I wheeled the cart down the hallway and snugged it against the wall just outside the conference room door, then we began placing folders on the table.

"We have five and a half years' worth of cases. How should we divide these up?" I asked.

Spelling scratched his chin as if in thought. "Let's go year by year and pull out the folders where serious consequences took place. Don't forget, agents, these men worked in the Violent Crimes Division. All of the crimes were serious, but not all led to death or a lengthy imprisonment for the offender. Let's begin with any criminal who died in gunfire then see what their crime was. Maybe we can link that to something current, like an anniversary of their death, if you get my drift. There has to be a trigger. Cam, pull up anyone who was released from prison this year who was incarcerated directly because of an arrest made by J.T., Curt, or both of them."

We gathered around the table in a somewhat organized state of chaos. Each agent paged through, and stacked, the folders that contained the most violent cases and placed the other folders to the side.

With a pot of coffee at the center of the table and twelve agents digging into the folders, we spent two hours perusing case files. We narrowed the stack, concentrating on only the worst offenders in eleven archived cases. There were three in 2011, two in 2012, one in 2013, three in 2014, two in 2015, and none in 2016.

We would spend the rest of the night trying to connect the dots and figure out how the Pirelli brothers were involved—and who was calling the shots.

Chapter 19

"Open your eyes, Fed. You wanted to see your sister? Well, here she is." Anthony kicked J.T.'s leg with enough force to break his kneecaps.

"Please, leave him alone. You've already beaten him to a pulp. He's unconscious, for God's sake!"

Anthony laughed. "Religious are you? I'd leave God out of this because there isn't a damn thing he or you can do. We're getting information out of your brother come hell or high water." His laughter echoed off the walls. "Get it, hell? If you think God is going to save his sorry ass, think again. The only thing that's going to save your brother is him giving us the information our boss wants." Anthony kicked J.T. in the shoulder. "Wake up, pussy!"

J.T. writhed in pain as he began to regain consciousness. Even lifting his head off his chest took every ounce of strength he had. His body had endured a severe beating over the course of the last few hours.

"Who do you think you are, anyway—MacGyver?" Antonio shouldered Anthony and jerked his head toward the mangled enclosure. "Nice work getting out of there. Let's see how you do being chained to these support posts. Have fun trying to eat when your arms are stretched so far apart they're nearly ready to snap. I bet that's pretty uncomfortable. Right, Fed?"

A voice at the back of the building spoke up. "Nice to see you survived the night, Agent Harper. Your sister may not be so lucky if you don't wake up and answer my questions coherently. I want your log-in and password to the archived case files you and Agent Belmont worked on in 2014, and I want it right now. You have one minute to provide that information correctly or the beating will begin."

"Beat me all you want. I don't care. I think your goons already started that hours ago."

"That's apparent, Agent Harper, but I wasn't talking about you. I was talking about Julie."

J.T. wrenched against the chains. "Leave her out of this. She works at a hospital, for God's sake."

"Here we go again bringing God into the mix," the voice from the back said. "Anyway, your minute begins now."

J.T. lifted his head and squinted. Julie sat on a chair twenty feet in front of him. Anthony and Antonio stood to either side of her like matching bookends. Dried blood coated her face and matted her hair. She had already been beaten.

"Sis, are you—"

"I'm okay. I'm sure I look worse than it really is. Head wounds bleed easily."

"Stop the chitchat. You have twenty-seven seconds before she gets a severe blow to the face, and believe me, it will be more than a simple flesh wound."

"Fine, I'll tell you what you want to know. Just leave her alone."

"Wise decision, Agent Harper. Anthony, go get the laptop."

Anthony crossed the open expanse to the other side of the warehouse. J.T. watched as he entered the fourth room on that side. That was the final room, the one where J.T. remembered touching the doorknob before everything went black.

That must have been the room they were waiting in. They ambushed me the second I turned the knob.

Anthony returned minutes later with a laptop tucked under his arm.

"Go ahead, Agent Harper. Tell Anthony your FBI log-in information, and do it now!"

J.T. told them his login information and said his password was "untouchable." He smirked at their expressions. "Yeah, I'm sure that's funny to all of you thugs."

"Actually, it's quite amusing. Thank you for that bit of humor in an otherwise gloomy day. Anthony, make sure the log-in is working properly."

Anthony jerked his head at Antonio, and Julie was swiftly pushed off the chair.

"Hey!"

"It's okay, J.T. Don't piss them off." Julie brushed off her scraped knees and remained on the floor.

Anthony took a seat and tapped at the keyboard. "I'm logged in to the FBI's site, Mr. Vetcher."

The low chuckle increased in volume until the sound filled the room. "That's wonderful. Now how do we access the cases from 2014?"

J.T. panned the room from left to right without a visual on the voice. The man didn't want to be seen, and there had to be a good reason.

"Who are you hiding from, mystery man? Do I know you? Is there something that will stir a memory for me if I catch sight of you? Why don't you show yourself?"

"In due time, Agent Harper, in due time. Antonio, lock up his sister for now. She may come in handy later if he decides to stop cooperating."

Without warning, Antonio grabbed Julie by the hair and violently jerked her across the room. She screamed, her hands clinging to her head as he dragged her away.

"You son of a bitch, leave her alone!" J.T. stomped the floor with his heels.

"Let's continue, Agent Harper. We can certainly take care of your sister if she becomes too much of a distraction for you. Do we understand each other?"

J.T. hung his head. "Yes."

"I didn't hear you. Please repeat that."

"I said YES!"

"Good, now continue on. How do we access the case files that you and Agent Belmont worked on together in 2014?"

"What's so special about 2014?"

"Not your concern. Now go ahead and don't make me ask you again."

"On the left sidebar is a tab that says archived case files. Click on that, and the drop-down menu will show each year. Click on 2014, and the page will open with a list of cases Agent Belmont and I worked on."

"Are the full reports, including every detail, contained in each case file?"

"Yes."

"Perfect. Anthony, follow his instructions and bring me the laptop."

"I'm pulling up 2014 right now." Anthony nodded. "It's all there, sir."

"Exactly what I wanted to hear. Let's take a look."

Anthony walked to the back of the room and disappeared around a stack of crates.

"Why are you afraid to show yourself? You're nothing but a coward."

"Antonio, make Agent Harper shut up."

J.T. received a melon-sized fist to the face and slumped over into unconsciousness.

Chapter 20

Cam reentered the conference room with his findings and glanced at the clock. The hour hand had just hit six a.m. He had been working alone in the computer lab, searching the database for any recently released criminals from federal lockup who might have a connection to J.T. and Curt.

"I have a few names but nobody who would seem to pose a serious threat to Curt or J.T.," he said.

Spelling perched his reading glasses on top of his head, pinched the bridge of his nose, and gave Cam a nod. "Go ahead. Let's hear what you have." He poured tepid coffee into his cup.

We all leaned back, stretched, and regrouped as Cam read his report.

"Of course, we already know that Antonio Pirelli was released a few months ago, but he never had a direct connection with anyone at the Milwaukee field office. He's just a hired gun. There's Brad Derringer, who served fifty months for five ATM thefts. He got lucky and was released two years early because of prison overcrowding. Vaughn

Moss robbed two check-cashing stores in 2011 and was just released in April, minimal take. Then there's Pedro Martinez, who with his brother, Marco, held up two liquor stores and pistol-whipped the owners. They were released after serving five years each. The only reason they didn't get more time is that the robberies netted them under three hundred dollars. That's it as far as the recently released cons. Nobody stands out as somebody who would go to the extreme of murdering and kidnapping federal agents."

Hopkins fisted his long yawn then added his opinion. "Okay, let's set the released prisoners aside for now. What else do we have?"

Bill Lewis took the lead. He had been with the FBI for fifteen years and had seniority. He also had been working with Curt on nationwide internet predator cases during the past year, according to Hopkins. They had been close friends. We sat back and listened.

"Out of the eleven most violent cases, three resulted in our agents killing several of the individuals, and five involved life imprisonments. Now, any of those could be cause for retaliation from family members for whatever reason. We need to check for anniversary dates that came up in the last two days. They could be the dates of the crime, of a death, of a conviction, or even the date the individual began their prison sentence. Let's look through those files for June, with the dates of the second, third, or fourth being noted."

We took a five-minute break and dug back in. Several agents took half-hour nap rotations.

Spelling gave me the eyebrows. "Jade, you good to go? Don't feel bad if you need a quick nap."

"I'm fine, sir, but I could use some strong coffee. I'll make a fresh pot." I rose and took the carafe back to the lunchroom, washed it out, and started a new pot. I leaned against the wall and closed my eyes. I began to drift off and had to force myself to stay awake. The twenty-four-hour mark was almost here, and we had nothing other than a dead agent who was thrown out of the back of a moving van. I pressed my fingertips against my temples and rubbed.

"Anxiety or overly tired?"

The voice made me jump. I hadn't noticed Cam entering the lunchroom. I shrugged with discouragement. "Both, I guess. Do you think we'll figure out something today? The hours are ticking by. Isn't time our enemy?"

Cam squeezed my shoulder. "We're trying, Jade, and I'll be the first one to admit, this isn't going to be easy. We aren't working on an ongoing case. Hell, Curt and J.T. haven't been in the same division for a year. We don't know who committed the crime, so there isn't a motive to expand on. We're going in blind. We have an APB on the dark-colored van, and it's on the Crime Stoppers segment of the news. Let me talk to Spelling. I think we ought to do the same with the gold Mercedes. We'll talk to the person who owns the car the plates were stolen off of. Maybe the Mercedes will flip a switch with them, or maybe it was stolen randomly."

I heard the coffeemaker beep. "Mind giving me a hand? Grab a stack of Styrofoam cups and the packaged creamer and sugar. I'll take the carafe and some napkins."

We returned to the conference room, and Cam suggested putting the description of the Mercedes on the news as well. Spelling agreed and shook his head. "We've been so focused on trying to figure out who kidnapped our agents and Julie, we completely overlooked that yesterday." He turned to Val. "Get that description on the news right away along with the stolen plate number. Make sure the FBI's 800 tip line phone number shows up on the screen."

Cam called the tech department and got the name and address of the person whose plates happened to be on that Mercedes sedan. We needed to know why the plates for a 2005 Nissan Sentra had never been reported stolen. He turned to me. "Maybe a drive will wake you up. Looks like the person who owns those plates lives in New Berlin. We need to have a talk with them now."

"Give me five minutes to freshen up." I took my cup of coffee and headed to the ladies' room.

Ten minutes later, we were out the door and on our way to the western suburbs. We passed the city limits sign for New Berlin a few minutes after seven. I pulled up the address and led Cam to the front door of an eight-unit apartment building. I craned my neck to see the numbers above the front entrance. I nodded. "This is the place."

Cam parked along the curb, and we took the sidewalk to the glass doors. Inside the vestibule, a wall-mounted intercom contained every resident's name and apartment number. I pressed the buzzer for apartment five.

After I pressed the buzzer a second time, a man's

agitated, groggy voice answered. "Yeah, who's there?"

"FBI agents, Mr. Hadley, and we need to speak with you."

"Real funny. I'm not in the mood for pranksters. Who the hell is this?"

I gave Cam an eye roll. "Either buzz us in or come down and see for yourself. We have identification, and we need to speak to you immediately."

"Give me a minute."

He clicked off the intercom, and we waited in the vestibule for several minutes. The arrow above the elevator illuminated, and the doors parted. A young man wearing only sleep pants headed toward us. His bed hair told us he had just awakened. We pressed our badges against the glass, and he opened the security door.

"Mr. Hadley?"

"Yeah"—he rubbed his eyes—"that's me. What's going on?" He held the door open, and we passed through.

I pointed toward the elevator then looked over his attire. "May we go upstairs where we can speak more freely?"

"You sure you have the right Dan Hadley?"

"Yes, we're sure."

He scratched his head. "Okay, I guess. Come on up."

We rode the elevator up a short flight then walked the hallway to apartment five. Dan opened the door, ushered us in, and told us to have a seat at the kitchen table.

Cam spoke up. "Live alone?"

"Yeah. So, what is this all about?"

I took over the questioning. "Do you own a 2005 Nissan Sentra?"

"Yeah, except I haven't had it for a while. Why?"

"Then who does?" Cam asked.

"My little sis. She just got a new job, and until she can afford her own car, she's using mine. I work four blocks away from here and can walk. I told Deb she can use my car for another month and then I want it back."

"Has she mentioned that the license plates are gone?"

"Gone? Not at all. You mean fallen off?" Dan placed a cup of water in the microwave and set the timer for two minutes. "All I have is instant coffee. Would you like some?"

I politely declined. "No, thanks. Your license plates were stolen off your car, Dan. Do you know anyone who owns a late model, gold Mercedes sedan with blacked-out windows?"

He smirked. "Hell no, I'm a simple guy. I've never even sat in a Mercedes. I am curious, though, why that's an FBI matter."

"Your plates are on that Mercedes. It's been connected to some very serious crimes."

"Wow, Deb hasn't said a word about the plates being gone. She's an eighteen-year-old kid and probably didn't even notice."

"We need to know where she lives."

Dan pulled the steaming water out of the microwave and dropped a teaspoon of instant coffee into the cup. He gave it a stir and took a seat across from me.

"Sure, here's her address. She lives in an apartment with four other kids. Maybe I should get my car back, and what do I do about plates now?" Dan rattled off Deb's address, and we thanked him.

After jotting his sister's address in my notepad, I handed him a card. "Go to the DMV and tell them your plates were stolen. They'll issue replacements for you. We'll be in touch."

Cam and I left and headed to the address for Debbie Hadley.

Chapter 21

J.T. sputtered and gasped as water hit him in the face. That ice-cold wake-up call did the trick. He coughed and opened his eyes. Sitting twenty feet away in the dimmed room was a man wearing a fedora tipped low on his forehead and a pair of mirrored aviator sunglasses were perched on the bridge of his nose.

"Done napping, Agent Harper?"

J.T. spat a mouthful of blood from his earlier beating out onto the floor. "Where is my sister?"

"Please stop talking about your sister. Your constant pleading has become tiresome. Julie is alive. That's all you need to know at the moment."

J.T. cursed the man in the shadows.

"Is there something you'd like to say, Mr. Hotshot Federal Agent?"

An angry smirk sounded from J.T. "So, you're the all-important Mr. Vetcher, Carden Vetcher, I believe I heard them say. You're the guy those thugs in the monkey suits work for? What makes you so special? You're obviously too scared to show yourself."

"Not scared, Agent Harper, just smart. Timing is everything. You're an educated man, I assume, and understand the concept of payback, correct?"

"Meaning?"

"Meaning we have a history whether you realize it or not. You see, I'm much smarter than you, and I've bided my time, but now I need your help."

"And why would I help you? You're a low-life criminal who has kidnapped one civilian and two federal agents. Did I mention that one agent is dead because of you?"

"My hands are clean, and you'll help me even if you don't want to."

"Why would I?"

"Leverage. Did you forget that I'm holding your sister hostage and won't think twice about torturing her to death right in front of you?"

J.T. pulled at his restraints. "You sick bastard."

"No need for name-calling. I'll be in touch, but right now I have your FBI files to look through. I want to know who fired the shot that killed my brother. Was it you or Agent Belmont?"

"How would I know when you haven't told me the case you're talking about? Either way, neither of us has ever shot anybody with Vetcher as their last name."

Well, I guess Agent Belmont already paid his dues with his life, so it's up to you. It's time to pay your penance. Either help me or watch your sister die. My plan is set to take place in two days. Anthony, kill the lights."

The room went black. J.T. heard footsteps walk

away, then an outer door creaked open and slammed closed. He sat alone once more with nothing but his thoughts.

Chapter 22

Cam parked in front of the older two-story house that had been converted into a duplex. The clapboard siding was in dire need of paint, and the neighborhood was sketchy at best. Now I understood why Dan let his sister borrow his car. Even sitting at the nearby bus stop to catch a ride to work could be a dangerous endeavor, especially for a young female.

We rang the bell for the lower unit, and a pimply faced man who appeared barely old enough to shave answered the door. Our badges were already out and exposed when he opened it.

"Whoa, dude, check this out," he said. A wry grin spread across his face and exposed the tartar on his teeth.

A second male and one female peeked around the corner. The air was thick with the scent of marijuana.

"We need to speak to Debbie Hadley right now." I wasn't in the mood to deal with that young punk.

He cocked his head toward the arched doorway that led into the living room. "Yo, Debbie, you have company." He laughed and walked away. He scratched the back of his leg as he retreated to another room.

The blond-haired girl who had peeked around the corner stepped out and into the kitchen. "What did I do wrong?"

"Are you guilty of something other than possession of an illegal substance?"

She looked mortified.

Cam spoke up. "We aren't here to bust your chops. We just need to ask you a few questions."

"Oh, okay." Relief swept across her face. "Want to sit down?"

"Sure." I pulled out a chair, and Cam did the same. "Let's cut to the chase. We have a very busy day ahead of us. How long have you been using Dan's Nissan, and have you loaned it to anyone else?"

"Um, um."

I groaned. "Real words, please."

"Oh, um, I've had it since April. I've let Tommy use it once in a while."

"Were you aware of the missing license plates?"

"No. When did that happen?"

I stared at her. "Well, there isn't a way we'd know that. Do you or your friends know anyone with a gold Mercedes sedan?"

"Hang on." Debbie rose from the table and disappeared around the doorway.

I glanced at Cam. "Seriously?"

A few seconds later the other roommates entered the kitchen.

Deb nudged Tommy. "Well, say something."

"I don't know anyone with a Mercedes."

"How about the rest of you?" Cam asked.

Each person crossed their arms over their chest, shrugged, and shook their head. I tossed a few of my contact cards on the table before we left.

"Get your acts together, will you, and lay off the weed." I looked at Debbie and shook my head. "Your brother said he's taking his car back."

Cam and I walked out with nothing more to go on than when we left the office an hour earlier.

We reentered the FBI's downtown headquarters at nine thirty and followed the third floor hallway to the conference room. Cam and I had been up for over twenty-four hours. I wasn't sure about the rest of the team. Spelling sat at the head of the table, his face propped between his open palms.

He turned toward us when we walked in. "Anything?"

"Dead end, boss. The owner of the vehicle loaned the car to his younger sister. She's about as ditzy as they come. She had no idea the plates were missing, and nobody knows anyone who owns a gold Mercedes."

Val entered the room. "The tip line got a hit on the Mercedes."

Hopkins perked up. "Yeah, let's hear it."

"A man called in from Sheboygan County saying he had a 2012 champagne-colored Mercedes that was stolen eight months ago. It was never recovered. He did mention that the windows weren't tinted, though."

"Okay, get on the horn to the local places that do vehicle

window tinting. Have them pull up any light gold Mercedes that had limousine tint put on less than a year ago. Get every available agent on those calls. Cover Sheboygan, Washburn, Ozaukee, and Milwaukee Counties."

"Right away, sir." Val turned and disappeared out the door.

"Where are we with information on those eleven most violent cases? Anything hit with anniversary dates?" I asked.

"Unfortunately not," Maria said. "I do have an idea, though. How about we dig a little deeper into each specific case? Were J.T. and Curt called to testify in the cases where somebody went to prison? Those are usually conducted in open court. Anyone with a grudge could have sat in on those hearings."

"True, but if there aren't any anniversary dates of someone being sentenced this week, then what's the connection?" I poured myself a cup of coffee and took a seat. "I'll go over the three cases where somebody was killed during gunfire and see if anything pops."

Spelling jerked his head at Cam. "Give her a hand. I'm going to catch a thirty-minute nap. You two are after me. No back talk, either. I need everyone fully alert and on their game."

"Yes, sir." Cam slid one of the folders across the table to me. "Here, read everything over twice and don't fall asleep."

I smirked. "Yeah, back at ya."

The conference room phone rang, and SSA Hopkins picked it up. "Yes, okay, and it's addressed to me? Bring it here, please." He hung up.

"Is something wrong?" I asked.

"We'll know in a few minutes, but my gut is saying absolutely. Get Spelling back in here and call the forensics team. A padded envelope just arrived in the mail, and it's addressed to me. There isn't a return address on it, either."

I pushed back my chair and stood. "Oh, shit."

Chapter 23

Lynette from the first floor reception counter brought the sealed manila envelope upstairs and placed it on the table. We were all in attendance, including Spelling, who'd barely had a second to close his eyes.

I pulled out the box of gloves from the cabinet at my back. Spelling nodded.

"Yeah, let's all glove up. No sense in adding more fingerprints for the crime lab to check out. That envelope is probably filled with dozens of prints already."

Cam spoke up. "Yeah, but I bet none are from our perps."

Hopkins slipped on a pair of latex gloves as he picked up the envelope. "What's the ETA on Forensics?"

"They'll be here in five minutes, sir," I said.

The Milwaukee County Crime Lab was the local forensics agency that serviced the downtown police headquarters and our FBI division. Luckily, their main facility was located only a few blocks from our building. Minutes later, the ding of the elevator doors opening alerted us to their arrival.

I tipped my head toward the hallway. "Sounds like the boys are here. Mind if I snap off a few quick pics, boss?"

"Go ahead. It can't hurt," Spelling said.

I pulled out my phone from my pocket and leaned over the envelope on the table. I closed in on the front side and took three pictures of the address, postmark, and stamp. Then I flipped the envelope over and looked at the back. Nothing stood out on that side, but I snapped a few pics, anyway.

Leah Jasper and Terry Franklin entered the conference room. I took my seat and watched with the rest of our group.

"What have we got, sir?" Leah asked.

"A suspicious padded envelope addressed to me. It was sent USPS, so there has to be dozens of prints on it," Hopkins said.

"Sure thing. Let's get a few shots of it, then we'll open it up and see what we've got." Leah used her digital camera to zoom in on the writing and postmark.

With his hands gloved, Terry carefully lifted the envelope, checked the seal for anything that appeared unusual, and straightened the metal clasps. Leah handed him a long, flat blade from their kit, and he slipped it under the crease at the seal. It cut through the envelope like butter. We sat forward and alert, our eyes focused on whatever came out of the package. Terry looked in before dumping the envelope on the table.

"We're going to need a laptop. Looks like we have a thumb drive here."

I groaned with understanding—nothing good ever came from looking at a video—and I expected the worst.

Bill Lewis rose. "I'll get mine." He left the room, and Terry slid the thumb drive out of the padded pouch.

I snapped several pictures of the ordinary looking black thumb drive as we waited. Leah pulled an evidence bag out of her kit, dropped the envelope inside, and closed it. She wrote the time and date on the red seal.

"Nothing unusual about the thumb drive?" Spelling asked.

She shrugged. "We aren't going to get that lucky right out of the gate, sir. It's as common as it gets, likely from any big-box store nationwide."

Bill Lewis was back within minutes with his laptop cradled in his arms. He placed it in front of Leah and sat down. "It's good to go."

Leah nodded a thank-you and checked all of our faces. "You guys ready to see whatever is on this drive?"

Hopkins heaved a deep sigh. "As ready as we'll ever be."

Leah pushed the drive into the port on the side of the computer and clicked the control panel icon. She rolled her neck, gave each of us another glance, and clicked the cursor over the new file. With the laptop turned to the group, we simultaneously held our breath.

A close-up of Julie appeared on the screen. Tears stained her cheeks, and fear clouded her features. Dried blood matted her hair and coated her forehead.

"Those sons of bitches," Cam said as he pressed his temples.

I had met Julie only once, but the rest of the team knew

her slightly better. No matter what, she was an innocent victim. Other than using her as leverage, the kidnappers had no reason to include her in their quest for revenge against the FBI, J.T., or Curt.

Her mouth was covered with a piece of cloth tied behind her head. She was unable to talk. A hand moved into the screen and placed that day's newspaper on her lap to indicate the tape was current and filmed that very morning.

Spelling sucked in a long breath. "Okay, that's this morning's paper. It comes out at six thirty. At least we know she was alive and breathing then."

"Right, but there's no sign of J.T.," Maria said.

Hopkins spoke up. "The camera is so close to her we can't see anything in the background."

"I'm sure that's deliberate," I said. "They aren't going to give up their location that easily."

We watched as the newspaper was taken away and replaced with notecards. All we saw was a large male hand moving in and out of the video. In short, the notecards told us that Julie's condition would only get worse if we interfered. They had a job to do, Agent Harper was going to assist, and if things didn't go smoothly, J.T. would witness his sister slowly being tortured to death. Rants written on the cards spoke of an eye for an eye, revenge, family being everything, and a long-overdue payback.

An unexpected familiar voice yelled out in the background, and the tape was quickly cut short.

"That was J.T., I know it was! At least they're being held at the same place."

Spelling agreed. "Play that last part again, Leah."

Leah backed up the scrubber bar then clicked the forward arrow. We listened, our ears perked for any word or background sounds that could give us something to work with.

"It sounds like he's yelling Carden."

Hopkins shook his head. "I think he said something about the cards. He probably wants us to focus on the notecards they're placing on Julie's lap. Maybe there's hidden clues within those rants."

"Yeah, probably," Cam said. "Did anyone catch a sound of background noise? Trains, airplanes, heavy machinery, traffic?"

I listened carefully. "No, but don't you think his voice echoed a bit? Let's take another listen."

Hopkins nodded at Leah, and she backed up the tape again.

Val agreed that J.T.'s voice did seem to echo.

"Okay, what is that telling us?" Spelling said. "Throw out your opinions, people. Everything is fair game."

I dug deep into my training and rubbed my forehead as I thought. "The building they're in is empty, large, or both. There's no carpet to muffle the sounds or rooms to deaden the echoes."

"A large warehouse or almost any empty building would fit that description," Hopkins said, "and unfortunately there are plenty of them in a fifty-mile radius. Actually, we have no idea if they're in the area at all."

Spelling took his turn. "We have no other options. Get

Joe to pull up every vacated building over three thousand square feet in a twenty-mile radius. Have him search foreclosed properties, bank-owned buildings, and abandoned industrial sites. Someplace remote would make the most sense. I doubt if they'd be coming in and out where there's a lot of people. No one who's up to no good wants an audience. Keep in mind, Curt was shot several times. That sound is going to be loud, especially in an empty building. Tell Joe to look for places off the beaten path first."

Maria walked out and headed to the tech department.

I glanced at the pad of paper in front of me. I had written down every message on the notecards. "I'm going to try to decipher these messages for a bit."

"Nope, not until you take an hour-long nap. Don't argue with me, either. Get going now. Cam will do the same once you're back out here. I'll send Val in to get you at lunchtime. Leave that cell phone behind too."

I opened my mouth to protest, but the look on Spelling's face was unwavering. I wouldn't win. It was useless to argue with him, and truth be told, I was exhausted. A fresh set of eyes and a clear mind would benefit the investigation in the long run. With my cell phone left behind, I headed to our private lounge and snuggled up on one of the three couches and closed my eyes.

Chapter 24

I woke and felt somebody shaking my shoulder. I cracked open my eyes and saw a blurry shape of a person sitting on the edge of the couch. I squinted several times.

"Jade, it's time to wake up. We're going to order lunch and eat in the conference room, then we'll get back to work."

I remained in place and stared up at her. My mind hadn't yet comprehended what that person was saying.

She chuckled. "Man, you're still out of it."

"What?" I sat up and rubbed my eyes then took in my surroundings.

"Yeah, this is the FBI lounge. Don't you remember coming in here to take a nap?"

"I do now. Sorry, Val. I'm out to lunch, literally."

"It sure seems that way. Why don't you go splash some cold water on your face? That might help. After we eat, Cam gets his turn at a nap."

"Okay, thanks." I placed my feet on the floor and rubbed my temples. I needed a minute to regroup.

Val cocked her head. "You good?"

I nodded and stood up.

"Okay, we've got a dozen sub sandwiches in the conference room. Maria just made a fresh pot of coffee too. Looks like you're going to need some."

I turned left out of the lounge and passed through the door of the ladies' room. At the sink, I cupped my hands under the stream of cool water and brought it up to my face. The water felt good against my skin and revived me. I finger tossed my messy hair and rinsed my dry mouth several times. With a deep sigh, I walked out of the lavatory and followed the corridor to the conference room. The room was abuzz with conversation, laptop computers, and people grabbing sandwiches.

Spelling looked at me as I entered the room. "Welcome back to the world, Monroe. Grab a sandwich and dig in. We're calling all of the companies in a fifty-mile radius that do vehicle window tinting. Meanwhile, Joe is trying to locate every vacant building in the area that's in a remote location or grouped with similar buildings without active neighbors. He should have that list complete soon." He looked from person to person. "Everyone, put down your work for a half hour and eat your lunch. We'll pick up after we finish our meal."

I sat next to Cam as I chowed down my turkey sub. "Anything new since I've been napping?"

"Nothing has come in on the tip line about the dark-colored panel van. I'm sure it's because there weren't identifiable markings in the description."

"Yeah." I nodded as I bit into my sandwich and swallowed a quick bite. "What we put out there is pretty vague. Anything to check out as far as the window tint companies?"

"Not yet, but we've just started on Milwaukee County. We have a lot of places to call."

"After lunch, I'll take over where you left off. You need a power nap."

Cam nodded and continued eating.

By one o'clock, Cam was napping, the sandwich wrappers had been cleaned off the table, and everyone was hard at work. I took Washburn County window tint businesses just because I was familiar with the area and knew how to get to most of those places quickly if needed. Most of my calls lasted a few short minutes. I asked whether anyone had installed limousine tint on a gold Mercedes sedan, possibly an E-Class, in the last year, but it hadn't rung any bells so far in Washburn County.

Bill Lewis, Val, and Maria concentrated on Milwaukee County because the business side of that area was so much larger. Bill hung up and jotted some notes.

"Did you get something?" Maria asked.

"Maybe. The person who answered at"—he looked at the business name he had written down—"Tony's Tint and Trim said according to their records, a gold Mercedes was brought in four months ago for a limousine tint. I asked if they had video surveillance and he said no, but he did remember a little about the man who brought in the car. He said he seemed like an odd duck."

"In what way?" Spelling asked as he placed his reading glasses on the table.

"Like the customer was trying to camouflage his appearance just in case there were cameras in the area. Tony said the guy acted sketchy and paid in cash."

I huffed. "Of course he did. No paper trail."

Hopkins jerked his head toward the door. "Head out and get a full description of the customer to the best of the owner's recollection. Have him make you a copy of the work order too."

Lewis stood. "You got it, boss."

I completed the list for Washburn County without a hit, but only fourteen places specialized in window tint in the entire county, anyway.

"Sir?"

Spelling looked up. "Yes, Jade."

"Is it okay if I go back to working on the rants from the notecards?"

"Sure, go ahead."

I studied the sheet of paper I had temporarily set aside and reread the messages. The first one mentioned a job they were about to do with J.T.'s help and a threat that if we interfered, Julie would pay the price. To me, that meant they were about to commit a crime. What I didn't understand was why they needed J.T.'s help. Maybe they meant that they needed his resources. I scribbled notes to myself in the margins.

The FBI didn't have a handbook on how to foil crimes before they happened—not to my knowledge, anyway. I thought back to the type of situations handled in the Violent Crimes Division. They included bank robberies, online child predators, gang threats, active shooters, gem and jewelry thefts, and Indian country crimes. I thought about the note cards and the eye-for-an-eye quote, revenge, and the mention of family. This kidnapper had a family member who was either incarcerated or killed. I was leaning toward the latter. The rants sounded too angry to be talking about someone in prison. The mention of payback being long overdue took me back to the three case files where somebody had died in gunfire.

I opened the folders for 2011, 2013, and 2014 where deaths had occurred during shoot-outs between the FBI and criminals. I glanced back at the categories that were considered violent crimes and eliminated the ones that didn't fit our current situation. I crossed out Indian country crimes and the online predators. Why would they need help or information from J.T.? I looked again and crossed out gang activities and active shooters. Those were dealt with on a day-to-day basis. That left bank robberies and gem and jewelry thefts. With the folders open in front of me, I cross-referenced those three years with bank robberies or jewelry heists. One armored transport robbery occurred in 2014 after the final pickup of the day. The truck was full of money, and according to witness statements, a U-Haul cube van barreled through a stop sign and sideswiped the armored truck on the passenger side, caving in the wheel well and disabling the vehicle. Four men wearing masks jumped out of the U-Haul, commando style, and shot up the vehicle, killing the guard in the passenger seat and wounding two guards in the back as they got out to return fire. That bold stunt netted the thieves a cool nine hundred thousand dollars. It took two months of studying numerous videotapes from the neighborhood and the correct U-Haul agency before the FBI apprehended them. There were witness accounts of the attack on the armored truck, and several people stated they saw identifiable tattoos on the person who seemed to be in charge. With three matching witness descriptions of the tattoos on the back of the hand and wrist of that person, the FBI tracked down the artist who inked the man.

I took a five-minute break to stretch, wake up, and get a fresh cup of coffee from the lunchroom. Back in my chair, I turned the page and dug in again.

The tattoo artist, when finally located, was a young man who worked at a shop along the freeway north of Germantown. According to the report, he had just left a well-known tattoo parlor in Milwaukee and started working at that smaller, less-known establishment in Washburn County. The investigators missed him in Milwaukee by days. He admitted to being the artist and mentioned that the tattoo was a particular design requested by the customer. I flipped the page to the photograph and studied it. The tattoo was simple enough and had only two colors—black and red. The photograph showed two black ovals entwined with a large red *V* over the top of them. That was it— nothing intricate—and I didn't understand the significance. I turned the page back to the report and continued reading.

Once the FBI connected the tattoo to a name and found where that man and the rest of the robbers were holed up, they conducted a surprise attack on the house just before sunrise that morning in 2014. J.T. and Curt were the agents in charge. Three of the four robbers were captured unharmed, and one was killed during a heated exchange of gunfire. J.T. happened to be the agent who fired the kill shot.

"You look like you've got something, Jade," Spelling said. "You've had your nose in that file for almost an hour."

"Maybe, but I'm not quite there yet. I still have to connect the dots." I continued to read. The robber who had been killed—a Samuel Lee Dunbar—had been adopted as a youth by a Martin and Phyllis Dunbar. Mr. and Mrs. Dunbar were in their sixties at that time and lived in Oregon, according to the report written by J.T. and Curt. Our perp's rants, especially about family, didn't fit the profile for Sam Dunbar. I was still in the dark, and none of it was making sense. I closed my eyes for a few minutes to refocus.

"Dead end?" Spelling asked.

"I'm not sure. I thought I had something, but now I have my doubts. I have to dig deeper"—I glanced at the clock—"but for now I'm going to wake up Cam. I need his help."

Spelling tipped his left wrist toward him and looked at his watch. "Yeah, he's slept long enough. None of us need more than an hour of sleep a day." He gave me a thoughtful smile. "You're very dedicated, Jade, all of you are, and I appreciate the effort everyone is putting in to help find J.T. and Julie."

I thanked him and headed to the lounge.

Chapter 25

Bill Lewis returned at two thirty with an update on the customer at Tony's Tint and Trim. He took a seat and pulled out his notepad.

"Okay, here we go. This may or may not be our guy, the one who's calling the shots for the Pirelli brothers, but it's all we have at the moment." Bill waited as everyone took out their notepads. "According to what Tony remembered, he said the guy looked to be about forty, average build, right around six foot, and knocking on the door of two hundred pounds."

I tapped the pen against my open palm. "Why would he remember such details from an average customer?"

"I asked that very question. Tony said he remembered the part about the build because the customer was about the same size as he was. He said he didn't have to adjust the seat or mirrors when he moved the car into the work bay."

Spelling nodded. "What else?"

"The man's appearance is what Tony remembered the most. He said it was like the customer was trying to look the part of a wealthy man because he brought in that expensive car."

"In what way?" Cam asked.

"He wore a suit, but Tony noticed a missing button on the jacket's sleeve. He also said it looked too big for him, like it wasn't tailored to fit properly."

"Weird that he'd pay attention to those details," I said. "I'd understand a woman noticing that, but a man in a window tint shop?"

"According to Tony, he grew up in an Italian household, and his mother and grandmother made sure the kids dressed properly. He told me looking at the way people presented themselves was ingrained in him at an early age. Anyway, the man also wore a black felt fedora and mirrored aviator shades."

I smirked at the image in my mind. "That would attract even more attention."

"I assume that's why Tony remembered him. Because the guy paid in cash, he only had a handwritten receipt. The man signed for the services at the bottom of the slip." Bill passed the copy around the table. "Of course, the signature is illegible."

Maria looked up from the receipt. "What about his hair and eye color?"

"No good. The guy never took off the sunglasses or hat."

"Doesn't applying window tint take a while? The guy just sat there the entire time without taking off the hat or sunglasses?" Hopkins asked.

"No, he left on foot and came back three hours later."

"That's definitely weird. He probably had someone pick him up a few blocks away. Sounds like the man was being overly cautious, which begs the question—why? He didn't mention his name, even when setting up the appointment?"

"Sure, but it's likely fake. He called himself C.V. Loomis. I've already looked up the name but didn't get any hits."

Hopkins leaned back in his chair and scratched his expanding stomach. "Okay, get that information added to the news description of the Mercedes. We need more tips coming in. The way that man dressed had to have raised a few eyebrows. It could spark memories in people once they hear about it on the tip line. Right now, we need all the help we can get."

I propped my fist against the side of my cheek and rested my head on it. I went back over the files I had been reading. I would start again with the 2011 case and read it thoroughly. If I went through that folder without finding anything I could connect the abduction to, I'd move on to 2013. I'd eliminate one case at a time, but something within the Sam Dunbar file stuck in my craw. I closed the folder for 2011 and went back to 2014. According to the notes and the FBI's agent investigation with Internal Affairs, J.T. was actually the shooter in that case. He fired the shot that killed Sam Dunbar.

I quickly flipped back to 2011 and 2013 and opened the tabs at the agent investigation interviews. Curt and J.T. were the lead agents in those cases as well, but neither of them shot anyone. Other FBI agents and local police officers aided in those takedowns. The criminals were shot and killed by Agent Whitney out of Racine County in the 2011 case, and a patrol officer got off a lucky round as the 2013 bank robbery unfolded.

There had to be a connection. J.T. and Curt were the only two agents who had been kidnapped, and they both had a hand in cases where deaths occurred between 2011 and 2014. Curt was murdered and tossed out of a moving van, and J.T. was being held prisoner along with Julie. If the abduction was all about the 2014 case where J.T. killed Sam Dunbar, then J.T.'s life was in serious jeopardy. I had to find the connection between the fictitious C.V. Loomis and Samuel Dunbar right away.

Chapter 26

"Hmm… your face looks a bit swollen, Agent Harper. You wouldn't happen to have a broken jaw, would you?"

"Ask your goons. By their size and attitude, they must have roid rage. Talking doesn't feel the best."

"I bet not. Eating is going to be difficult as well. Anyway, I've studied your case files for 2014 and found exactly what I was looking for. I'll be exacting my revenge on you and the city of Milwaukee on Saturday."

J.T. spoke cautiously. His lower left jaw felt as if it was about to snap. "Yeah, what's so special about Saturday?"

The man across the room chuckled. "I was hoping you'd ask. That's the day we're taking down the transport of the entire inventory of Rosemond Diamonds. I'm sure you've read that they're moving from that small downtown store to Brookfield and setting up shop in their brand-new, swanky building. They think moving their inventory is safer on the weekend. Yeah"—he laughed—"safer for us. You see, a little bird told me the route and time that transport is going down. Imagine their surprise"—he chuckled again, and Anthony and Antonio joined in—"when they don't have one piece of inventory to display in their glass cases. We're stealing all of it."

J.T. huffed at the thought. "This isn't the Wild West, you know. Robbing an armored vehicle and actually getting away with it is nearly impossible in this day and age."

"Really? Sam Dunbar and his gang got away with it in 2014, at least for a few months. I've studied everything about this upcoming transport and know exactly what we're going to do. I've learned from Sam's mistakes."

"Oh yeah, and what did you learn, Carden? Why the interest in Sam Dunbar? He was a low-life crook that had his fifteen minutes of fame until he got a bullet to the head. He was forgotten about once the ink dried on the newspaper article. My case files that you were so interested in don't explain how we knew where he and his clan were holed up."

Carden stood and paced while making sure his face remained in the shadows. "For an FBI agent, you're pretty stupid. I'm not interested in how you found Sam. I wanted to know who killed him. It was you, and that's what I wanted to know all along. The man *you* shot and killed—Sam Dunbar—was my brother."

"You're full of shit and delusional. Sam Dunbar was adopted and didn't have any siblings."

"Think what you want, Agent Harper. This isn't my first rodeo. Saturday, you're taking an active part in the armored truck robbery, and just to make sure you do as you're told, Julie is tagging along for good measure."

Chapter 27

Bill Lewis returned to the conference room and leaned against the doorframe. "Okay, the news stations are all updated. We have a description of our mystery man, at least the way he dresses on occasion and his height, approximate weight, and age range. I also forwarded photos and descriptions of the Pirelli brothers and said they were armed and dangerous. Now it's going to be a waiting game in hopes that somebody calls in a tip."

"Where is Joe with the abandoned building search?" Hopkins asked.

I stood and stretched. "I'll go find out. I need to get the blood flowing through my limbs again, anyway. I think my butt has already gone numb."

I walked to the end of the corridor and turned left. The tech department was at the end of that second hallway. Inside, I found everyone hard at work. I was sure every agent and department was helping in the search for J.T. "Hey, Joe."

He glanced over his shoulder at me. "Jade. Crazy few days, right?"

"You know it. How's it coming with the building search?" I grabbed a roller stool and wheeled it over to his cubicle then took a seat.

"I just wish we had a better idea of what we're looking for. There are dozens of empty buildings in Milwaukee County, if that's even where J.T. and his sister are being held."

I sucked in a long breath. "You've eliminated houses and places within easy earshot of gunfire, right?"

He nodded. "Absolutely, and I still have twenty-nine vacant buildings throughout the county. Mind you, that's *only* Milwaukee County."

"Got it. You can pull up a bird's-eye view for every building and print them out, right?"

"Yeah, that isn't a problem."

"Does it also give us info on the address, size of the building, and how long it's been abandoned?"

"Not automatically, but I can enter those parameters into the database so that information is attached to each photo."

I stood and gave him a pat on the shoulder. "You're the man, Joe. How soon can you get us that information for all twenty-nine buildings?"

"Wow. It's going to take a while. I'll get Jamie to help me."

"Thanks, and call us when it's ready. You know where we'll be."

I made a stop in the ladies' room and splashed more water on my face. Then I leaned against the sink and fired off a short text to Amber. I hadn't seen her since yesterday morning when I left to have breakfast with J.T. Back then, a short thirty-five hours ago, I thought everything was fine with the world. Now, I had no idea if my partner and his sister were even alive. I scooped up another handful of water, drank it, and patted my cheeks with my wet hands. I dried my face and headed back to the conference room.

With an exhausted breath, I took my seat and began jotting down every idea as it popped into my mind. "Where exactly is that tint shop, Bill?" I asked.

He stood and went to the Milwaukee County map on the back wall. "Let's see. Here we go." He stuck a red pushpin into the map.

"Something on your mind, Jade?" Spelling asked.

"Not sure. Is there any kind of statistic that tracks how far a perp normally conducts business from their ground zero point?"

"That's a tough one," Hopkins said. "Each case and situation is different, depending on the size of the city and its demographics. If someone wants to feel safe, they're going to do everything away from their home base."

"Even if it's a one-time shot, like getting his windows tinted?"

Spelling raised his brows. "I see where you're going with this, and that one-time incident might be an exception to the rule. The perp wouldn't likely run into the shop owner again, especially if most of the daily activities he conducts are in the opposite direction of the tint shop. Let's go with fifteen blocks in each direction. Give me a second." Spelling got on the phone and called Joe. He ran that information past him and hung up. "Joe is having Erin map out a fifteen-block circumference around the tint shop. We'll have the printout in a few minutes. Everyone grab a snack, use the facilities, and stretch. Be back here in ten minutes."

I joined our team in the lunchroom and stood in line as we plugged change into the vending machines. With our sandwiches and sodas in hand, we headed back and took our seats.

Erin followed at our backs and passed out a dozen copies of the fifteen-block circumference she put together using the tint shop as the center point.

"Fifteen blocks out is a pretty wide perimeter," she said, "but if there are vacant buildings within that area, you may be on to something."

Spelling thanked her and she left, closing the door behind her. "Okay, everyone, keep busy until Joe has the information on the vacant buildings."

I had been in my chair for only five minutes before I stood again. The group looked up at me.

"I have an idea that could be more useful than us sitting here without a plan. I'll be right back."

Chapter 28

J.T. heard footsteps walking back and forth through the building. The men hadn't left earlier as he had thought, and he wondered what they were up to.

They're likely making plans for Saturday.

Julie had been dragged away earlier, and J.T. didn't know what room or area in the building they had taken her to. He hadn't heard a peep from her since then.

He listened closely but couldn't make out their words from across the building. Laughter rang out between the men, infuriating him. There was nothing J.T. could do to help his sister or himself.

The click clack of shoes on the cement floor was getting louder. J.T. looked up and saw Anthony coming toward him. He carried a paper plate of food and a plastic water bottle.

J.T. glanced to his left at the broken-out second-story window. The night sky was as dark as ink.

Guess it's dinnertime.

Anthony set the plate and water bottle on a skid and

approached J.T. "Boss says you need to eat."

"Have you ever formed a complete sentence in your life, Neanderthal?"

Anthony delivered a swift kick to the right side of J.T.'s knee. "I'd kill you in a heartbeat if Mr. Vetcher would let me, but he thinks you'll come in handy during the heist. I have my doubts, and if I accidentally shoot you"—he laughed at J.T.'s pain-filled grimace—"well, shit happens, you know."

Anthony went to the left chain and unlocked it from the pillar. J.T.'s outstretched arm and the chain dropped to the floor. Anthony took the plate of food and set it in front of J.T. He cracked the plastic lid of the water bottle and placed it next to the plate. "Don't move until I tell you to." He stepped back and took a seat on the skid. "All right, eat."

"I have to use the bathroom."

Anthony rose and walked away. He returned moments later with a rusty bucket and pushed it with his foot. It slid across the floor and rattled to a stop next to J.T. "There, problem solved. Now eat."

"Did my sister have dinner?"

"Yes. You have ten minutes. I'd suggest shutting up and eating. You aren't getting anything else until tomorrow."

"What's the plan for tomorrow?"

Anthony grinned. "Wouldn't you like to know?" His cell phone rang, and he pulled it out of his pocket. "Yes, sir, I'll be right there."

J.T. yelled out as Anthony walked away. "What's in it

for you to be his trained monkey? Are you and Antonio each getting a third of the take?"

Anthony's middle finger shot up as he rounded the corner and disappeared from sight.

Chapter 29

"Sorry, Joe. I hate to interrupt, but I have an idea."

Joe leaned back in his chair and entwined his fingers behind his head. "Not a problem. We all have our roles, right? I could use a few minutes to rest my eyes and brain, anyway. What can I help you with, Jade?"

"I know how hard you're working on those vacant building maps. As you know, Erin brought us that mapped-out fifteen-block perimeter around the tint shop."

"Yep, that's correct."

"Are any of those vacant buildings within that fifteen-block circumference?"

"Great question. The fastest way to find out is to drop the map image of the circumference around the tint shop over the aerial view of the vacant buildings. Otherwise we'd have to check it by street names. Let's see what we get."

With a few keystrokes and after moving layered images around, Joe placed the circumference map on top of the aerial-view map of the vacant buildings in that quadrant. He lined up the tint shop address as the center point on both maps.

I leaned over his shoulder and looked at the composite image. "Son of a gun, it worked. There's three empty buildings within that perimeter."

Joe smirked. "I swear, you're a genius, Jade."

"Nah, just practical and Type A—I need to stay busy, or I'll go crazy. Pull up the addresses of each building and the square footage we're looking at. Can you get me a satellite image of each one that shows the doorways, the parking lot, and any nearby buildings that we may need to use as cover?"

"Sure thing, but keep in mind that Google satellite images are dated. They only update them every five years or so. What we see now may not look the same as in real time."

I nodded. "Yeah, but it's a start. Call me when that's done, please. Nobody knows why I wandered off."

Joe gave me a nod and got back to work, and I headed to the conference room. I took my seat again and asked for everyone's attention.

"Go ahead, Agent Monroe," Hopkins said.

"Okay, I had an idea that I needed Joe to test. With overlapping transparencies, he was able to place the perimeter map over the aerial-view map of the vacant buildings. It turns out that three of those buildings are in that fifteen-block circumference around Tony's Tint and Trim. He's getting us satellite images of each of those buildings with entry and exit points and so on. He should be done with that in a few minutes."

"Great work, Jade," Spelling said. "Let's get a plan in motion."

Hopkins's phone vibrated on the table. He picked it up

and glanced at the screen. "The ME is calling." He excused himself and walked out into the hallway.

I watched his expression as he talked on the other side of the glass wall. Hopkins paced as he scratched his head and dragged his fingers through his hair. The air in the conference room had become thick with sadness as everyone stole a glance at their anxious supervisor.

He returned and blew out a deep sigh as he sat. "Well, I'm sure you all know what that was about."

We kept quiet out of respect and gave SSA Hopkins a moment to regroup. Curt was one of the top agents in the downtown headquarters, and we all knew how much he'd be missed.

"The ME said Curt had three gunshot wounds in his body. One was about ten hours older than the others, meaning he suffered and lost a good quantity of blood before he was killed."

I saw the pain and sadness in SSA Hopkins's eyes as he relayed the information he had just received from the ME. His lower lip began to quiver. I looked down at the table and kept quiet. I was the newbie in the department and had never met Curt. The looks in everyone's eyes told me how much he was cared for, though. Now it appeared my own partner might end up with the same fate.

Hopkins continued. "Curt's first bullet wound was to his shoulder, and the others were to his back and head. He had suffered a broken nose and jaw, likely from earlier beatings. The ME says those injuries are the oldest. I'm under the assumption the abductors wanted information and thought beating it out of Curt would work. Apparently it didn't, or they wouldn't have needed J.T." He glanced at each face at the table. "Tomorrow you're on your own while I take that drive to Waukegan and explain to Mrs. Belmont that her son died in the line of duty. Find J.T. and his sister and get them home safely."

Joe knocked and pushed open the door. "I have the satellite images and information on those first few empty buildings."

Spelling waved him in.

Joe placed a stack of copies on the table. "I should have information on the rest of the empty buildings within the hour."

"Thanks, Joe." Spelling gave him a nod. "We appreciate you moving so quickly on this."

I leaned across the table and reached for the copies. I took one for myself and passed the stack to my right. "We need to check out these buildings tonight, sir. The cover of darkness will be a big help."

Spelling turned to Hopkins. "I'd like to hear your opinion, Tom."

"Do it. Get those maniacs before somebody else we care about dies."

We studied the images of the three vacant buildings and memorized the entrances and exits. I noticed how nothing blocked the rooftops in the aerial views.

"May I make a suggestion? I know it sounds farfetched, but it could be a real time-saver."

"Go ahead, Agent Monroe," Hopkins said.

"I'm wondering if we can call in favors."

"What organization are you talking about, Jade?" Cam asked.

"How about the Milwaukee County Sheriff's Department Search and Rescue team? They have drones that can detect humans by their body heat. I'm sure from these satellite images that they can be successful, even at night. There isn't anything over these buildings that would block the heat-seeking signal. That could speed everything up exponentially. We've helped them in the past when they needed our resources, and we've also sponsored their fundraising events for more equipment. They owe us a little help."

Spelling jerked his head toward the door. "Maria, get on the horn to them right now. We need the deputy sheriff, or whoever makes the decisions on that, and their best drone controller here, immediately."

Maria left the room to make the call.

"Sir, that's only three buildings out of twenty-nine. I wonder what the chances are of using their help to clear all of those buildings."

"I don't know, Jade, but I intend to find out as soon as they show up."

By eight o'clock, we had Sergeant Kyle Saunders and an SAR expert, Deputy Mark Spence from the sheriff's department, entering the building to meet with our group. Maureen showed them to our third-floor conference room. Hopkins and Spelling stood, shook their hands, and made the introductions down the line of agents at the table.

Hopkins explained the situation and the dire need for their immediate help. Time wasn't on our side, and we feared J.T. and Julie's lives were in jeopardy.

Sergeant Saunders spoke up after reviewing the images and consulting with Mark Spence. "Mark is confident we can get the drone over these three buildings. He needs to have plenty of unobstructed space in order to maneuver the drone over the rooftops, and he needs to be in visual contact with it at all times. We can clear the other buildings tomorrow with the help of a second drone."

Hopkins slapped the table with his open hands. "Then let's get these three done tonight. We have to know if anyone is inside so we can plan our course of action. I want four agents to escort Sergeant Saunders and Deputy Spence to each site. If nothing pops at one, move on to the next. If any of them show signs of human inhabitants, get back here immediately so we can plan our method of breaching the building. We'll catch them by surprise, under the cover of darkness."

"May I go along?" I looked from Spelling to Hopkins.

Spelling responded, "This was your suggestion, so hop aboard and keep your eyes peeled. Bill, Cam, and Val go along too. The rest of us will review the other images as soon as Joe is finished with them. Monroe?"

I stopped at the doorway. "Yes, sir?"

"Report back here immediately if there are people in any of the buildings. You're the lead agent tonight."

"Absolutely, sir, and thank you."

Chapter 30

"I think something is brewing, Mr. Vetcher."

"I'm sure you aren't talking about coffee. What's going on, Antonio?" Carden bit into the Red Delicious apple he held between his fingers then dabbed the corners of his mouth with a cloth napkin. He set down the mapped-out armored truck route he had been studying for days.

"I heard chatter over the airwaves about thirty minutes ago. Several people from the sheriff's department were summoned to the FBI headquarters downtown."

"Interesting bit of information, and I wonder why." Carden scratched his chin as if in thought. "The cops are looking for the van, according to earlier news reports. Take the Mercedes and sit outside the FBI parking structure but stay in the shadows. Surveil the situation and follow anyone who leaves the building, just stay far enough back so you aren't noticed. Call me immediately with an update if there's movement. Do you understand everything I just said?"

"Yes, Mr. Vetcher."

"Good, now go quickly before you miss something."

Antonio disappeared out the side of the building. The heavy steel door slammed with a loud thud at his back. Carden rose from the folding table and crossed the warehouse to the stairs. On the second floor, a large locked cabinet stood against the wall in a room that once served as office space. Carden dug through his front pocket until he felt the padlock key. He twisted the key in the slot, removed the lock, then temporarily set it on the floor. He pulled open the double cabinet doors wide and smiled at the contents.

Inside was an array of weapons including seven handguns, two AK-47 assault rifles, an AR-22, two shotguns, magnetic IED explosives, tear gas canisters, masks, Kevlar vests, hundreds of rounds of ammunition, and zip ties. Carden ran his fingertips over the smooth wooden stocks of the rifles. Saturday, the weapons would be put to good use. The armored truck driver and guards wouldn't know what hit them until it was far too late.

Chapter 31

The plan was for Cam and me to follow in one cruiser and Val and Bill Lewis in the other. We pulled out of the parking garage and lined up behind the sheriff's department SUV. I jumped out of the passenger seat of our cruiser and approached the driver's side window. Sergeant Saunders rolled it down.

I peeked in and nodded at Deputy Spence in the passenger seat. A large tote containing several drones and the equipment that went with them sat on the folded-down back seat. "We're ready when you are, sir."

"Sure thing. Because one building doesn't stand out more than another, we'll go in order of location. There's one due west of the tint shop, another north, almost to the fifteen-block perimeter, and the final one is due south. Let's begin with the northern one, just because it's the farthest one away, and then work our way back."

"That's fine with us. Cam and I are in the first cruiser, and Val and Bill Lewis will be taking up the rear. Let's stay off the radio just as a precaution. Here's my cell number." I rattled off my phone number and watched as Sergeant Saunders programmed it into his personal phone. "Okay, are we good to go?"

"We sure are. We'll jump on Martin Luther King Drive and head north."

I slapped the doorframe before I walked away. "Yep, let's do this."

The fifteen-block trip on MLK Drive, as the locals called it, would take a good twenty minutes. The wide street with a boulevard in the center held dozens of storefronts with barred entrances and windows. We weren't in the best neighborhood and the number of abandoned buildings in that area didn't surprise any of us. The lights at every intersection seemed to turn red as soon as we reached them. I sucked in a deep sigh at every light.

"Nervous?" Cam turned toward me.

"I'd call it apprehensive since I don't know what to expect. I guess this is a process of elimination and the fastest and most efficient way of doing it. We have to find them, but what if they aren't at any of those buildings?"

"Then we keep looking, Jade. God knows, the longer it takes, the worse their chances are."

"Exactly, and that's my fear."

When we reached the next intersection, I craned my neck at the street sign. We had seven more blocks to go.

"Looks like we're almost there," Cam said as we made a few quick turns into a run-down industrial park that appeared as if it had been abandoned years earlier. The brake lights flashed on the SUV about a block away from the fenced-in group of buildings. We pulled up to the curb behind it and parked.

Sergeant Saunders and Deputy Spence climbed out of their vehicle. We exited our cruisers and met up with them at the back of their SUV. Deputy Spence pointed toward the buildings and explained why they chose that spot.

"If we get any closer, I won't have a wide field of vision. By standing back a bit, I'll be able to see the red lights flashing on the drone and get it positioned in the best possible location. It looks like there are a handful of buildings in there, so I'll just do a wide sweep over the rooflines of all of them."

"And you'll be able to see if there's body heat coming from the buildings right on the transmitter's screen?"

"That's correct, Agent Lewis," Deputy Spence said. "Shall we begin?"

We stood out of the way while Deputy Spence set up the drone. "If people are in these buildings, the heat-seeking device will kick in, and we'll see red dots indicating body heat on the screen. If they're actively moving about the building, we'll see that too."

"Okay, go ahead."

With the drone engaged and hovering in the air, we watched as the deputy maneuvered the joysticks to position it right above the first building's roofline. Deputy Spence kept his eyes on the drone as we watched the screen.

"I don't see any evidence of body heat in that building," I said. "Chances of there being electricity, as in lighting that's still connected, are slim too, correct?"

"As old and dilapidated as these buildings look, it's doubtful. I'm sure that would be a fire hazard, and the county probably doesn't want to encourage squatters, either."

"Understood."

"I'll fly it over all of the buildings in one large pass, then I'll do a second round to double-check."

"Sure, thanks." I lifted the binoculars that I'd hung over my neck when we exited our cruiser. I held them up, adjusted the focus, and watched the drone make its passes over the buildings.

"Looks like a dead end here, Agent Monroe, but I'll do another quick sweep."

Ten minutes later and with no results at that first location, Sergeant Saunders suggested we move on to the west side of the search grid. We climbed back into our vehicles and left. Our next stop, on the far side of Wauwatosa Avenue, was fifteen minutes away. I made an update call to Spelling's cell phone.

"Hey, boss, we've just cleared the first location on the north side. That complex of buildings was a bust, dead quiet, and now we're heading to the abandoned warehouse on the west side. Yes, sir, we'll keep you updated." I clicked off and stared out the window as we followed Sergeant Saunders west.

"Something on your mind, Jade?"

I shrugged. "What isn't on my mind, Cam? None of this makes sense. We have no idea what it's about. We don't have anything to go on except our hunches. So far, there's no chatter on the Pirellis' phone taps, nobody has called in about the van, and we don't have any ransom demands, because it's obvious that C.V. Loomis thinks that Curt, and now J.T., is more valuable than money. I'm not ashamed to admit I'm at a loss. I keep replaying those notes that were spread across Julie's lap. They were vindictive and full of hate. This has to be about exacting revenge on Curt and J.T. more than anything else."

Cam was quiet for a minute as he clicked his blinker and got into the far right lane. "And you checked through the folders for deaths caused by agents, right?"

"Yes, of course, and the only one that went in front of the Internal Affairs board was when J.T. shot and killed a man who was involved in an armored car robbery months earlier. I guess with the eyewitness reports and video of the heist, they were able to locate the suspects, and a gun battle ensued."

"Yeah, that case sounds familiar. That was in 2014, right?"

I nodded.

"That was about the time J.T. began thinking about transferring into a different department. The Violent Crimes Division can get pretty hairy."

My cell phone rang in the cup holder. I pulled it out and looked at the screen. "That's weird, it's Spelling again. Hello, sir, I'm putting you on speakerphone." I pressed the icon and set the phone back in the cup holder.

"Jade and Cam, listen closely. A motorist just called in a sighting of a gold Mercedes sedan heading west on

Wauwatosa Avenue near Forty-Fifth Street. They're behind the vehicle right now and said the plate number is the same as the one that aired on the news."

"What! We just passed Forty-Fifth Street two blocks back. They're absolutely positive?"

"I just hung up with them seconds ago."

"I've got to go. I'm going to have Saunders double back at the lights and get behind him. We'll keep going straight then box the car in and take them down."

"Be careful."

"We've got this, boss." I quickly called Saunders. I told him to turn right at the next set of lights, double back a block, and get behind the Mercedes. I hung up, called Bill Lewis, and told him what was going on. I asked if they could identify the car at their rear without looking back over their shoulders.

"Hang on. I'm putting you on speakerphone," Bill said.

"Val, can you tell what kind of vehicle is behind you through your side mirror? It's possible that it could even be a few cars back. A motorist just called in the sighting."

"All I can see are headlights behind us, Jade. I can't even make out the grille or see the hood emblem. There is a silhouette of the driver, though, and it looks like a large person."

"Okay, we're going to slow things down. Saunders is circling back and scooting in behind the car. We'll box them in and take them down. Be aware that the driver, if it's actually the right car, will most likely be armed. We have to wait for confirmation from Saunders that he has eyes on the vehicle before we do anything. No wrong moves here."

Bill responded, "Got it, Jade. We'll hold steady until we hear back from you."

Chapter 32

"We've just circled back and cut across on Emmer Street. As soon as the light turns, we'll be getting back onto Wauwatosa Avenue, Jade."

I tried to get a glimpse of the Mercedes in my side mirror but I couldn't identify any cars behind us, not even the cruiser at our rear bumper. "How far ahead of you are we, Sergeant Saunders?"

"I'm turning now. I'd say you're a half dozen cars in front of us. I'm sure a few cars will split off at the light. That car is sandwiched between us somewhere. I'll have eyes on it in a few seconds. Shit!"

"What happened?" I spun in my seat and caught the rear quarter panel of a gold Mercedes cutting through oncoming traffic three car lengths back. It smacked the curb, bounced over it, and disappeared down an alleyway.

"Son of a bitch, how did he know we were on to him? Hit your lights and go after him." I clicked off and yelled for Cam to cut a sharp left over the boulevard and pull a U-turn. I engaged our lights and siren. Bill Lewis did the same.

Tires squealed and brakes locked up as cars came to an abrupt stop in the street. Horns blared, and motorists cursed each other with near misses. I looked back and saw Bill's cruiser jump the boulevard and hit the ground hard. The car bounced, and with a quick correction, he fell in at our rear bumper. We flew through the alley, right behind the SUV. "Do you have eyes on him?" I yelled into my cell phone to Saunders, who was ahead of us.

"No. We're checking every cross street too. No taillights anywhere."

"Damn it. Hang a left and drive parallel to us in the next alley. I'll have Lewis do the same to our right. Call in some backup too from the nearest police department."

"Roger that."

I jerked my head left as Saunders turned off at the next cross street. A half block away, the alley ran parallel to the one we were driving through. That entire ten-block grid was riddled with alleys and short cross streets. I called Bill's phone. "Turn off as soon as you can and take the next alley to our right. Saunders and Spence are doing that on our left. We need to get the local PD to block the main intersections and sandwich him in. He's in here somewhere, but these alleys are like a maze."

"We'll flush him out. Just keep your eyes peeled."

We had to slow down at every street so we wouldn't get sideswiped by oncoming cars. Our sirens blasted out warnings, and our cars bounced over every intersection.

With my head on a swivel, I looked up and down each cross street as we passed. I had barely enough time to hope for a sighting of tail or brake lights before we were already at the next intersection. I called Bill's cell again. "Where are those local cops? We need their help!"

"I'll try again."

We had gone through roughly a half mile of alleys and over intersecting streets. The gold Mercedes was nowhere. I pounded the dash with my fist. "Where the hell did he go?"

Cam jerked his head at me. "Call Saunders again. See if they have eyes on the car. The guy couldn't get away that fast."

The phone hadn't even rung on the other end when Deputy Spence picked up. "Jade, we have the car."

"Thank God, and the driver?"

"He's in the wind. The car had been pulled into a carport, and the overhead garage door that goes to the same address is wide open."

"Check it out. Block the alley exit and clear the car. Then go bang on the door and see if the owner is home. What block are you at?"

"We're in the alley to your left, and we're just past the intersection with Franklin Street."

"Got it. Where are the local cops?"

"They just radioed that they're three minutes out."

"No help there. We're heading over." I clicked off and could feel the hot anger climbing up my neck. "Son of a bitch, Cam. He may have taken another car or, even worse, the car and the vehicle's owner.

Chapter 33

"What do you want with me? What did I do?"

"Nothing, to both questions, so shut up. Hand over your cell phone. I wouldn't want you to get any ideas."

The man reached in his pocket and dug out his phone.

Antonio tipped his head. "Put it in the cup holder. What's your name?"

"Frank Wyatt."

"Man, the timing on that was perfect for me, but I can't say the same for you. Where were you going?"

"To the store for milk, and my wife is going to worry when I'm not back in ten minutes."

"Yeah, that sucks, but I'm sure once the cops find my car, they'll explain everything to her. Tell you what."

"Yes?"

"If you behave, I won't kill you. How about that? That should improve tonight's outlook for you."

Frank nodded and dropped his chin to his chest. "May I ask where we're going and why you're wearing gloves in the summer?"

"No, just keep quiet. We'll be there in ten minutes."

Antonio merged onto I-43 South and headed back to the warehouse. Taking the interstate was risky and he didn't need the exposure, but it was the fastest way to get back to the building. The cover of night would help for that short ride.

He pulled into the crumbled concrete parking lot that belonged to the long-deserted building that had once served as a thriving manufacturing company. Now it was only a shell of what it had been a decade earlier. Weeds sprouted from every crack in the pavement, and window glass was a thing of the past.

Antonio drove the car around to the side door and parked it out of view. He turned his head toward Frank. "Don't move a muscle." He slipped Frank's phone into his inner jacket pocket and pulled out his own. He grasped the fingertips of his right-hand glove with his teeth and pulled it off so he could make the call. With a swipe of his index finger, he woke the screen, tapped in the four-digit code, and scrolled to the contact that read Loomis.

"Boss, I need Anthony to unlock the side door. We have an unexpected guest, and I had to ditch the car." Antonio pulled the phone away from his ear. Carden's words were loud and angry. He waited as the man calling the shots ranted. "I'll explain everything once I'm inside."

The outer door slammed closed at Antonio's back as he and Anthony walked across the building side by side. With a finger prod in his back every few feet, Frank inched grudgingly forward. Carden stewed in the shadows as he watched Antonio escort Frank Wyatt to an empty room away from view of Agent Harper.

Antonio gave fair warning to the shaken man as he patted him down. "I'm locking you in this room for the time being. Make one sound and you'll either be knocked out cold or tied up with your mouth gagged. It's your choice. Got it?"

"I've got it."

Antonio closed the door and locked it behind him. He gave the handle a jiggle to make certain it was secure.

"Mr. Vetcher is pissed," Anthony said as they crossed the large open space.

Antonio spoke in a low voice. "He's the one who told me to follow them to see what they were up to. I stayed far enough behind not to be noticed. Somehow, somebody knew of the car and alerted the Feds. There was nothing else I could do but dump the Mercedes and grab another vehicle."

"Stop your whispering." The tone of Carden's voice was enough to give fair warning—he wasn't happy with the situation. "Now we have someone else who has seen your face to deal with. Have a seat and explain everything to me."

Antonio and Anthony each took a seat at the card table. The chairs squeaked under their weight. Antonio tapped his fingertips on the table as he waited for instructions to go ahead. Carden took a sip of red wine from his plastic cup as he eyed the giant of a man.

"Please explain to me how you managed to be detected."

"I have no idea, sir. I was several car lengths behind the

last cruiser on a busy street and didn't do anything unusual to give myself away. Suddenly, the sheriff's department SUV turned right at the next set of lights, and the others continued going straight. That caught my attention. A few minutes later, when I checked my rearview mirror and saw that same vehicle trying to turn right and get into traffic behind me, I knew it was time to bail off. Somehow, they knew the description of the Mercedes and that I was following them."

"Where had they gone before you were detected?" Carden folded his arms over his chest and let out a puff of air.

"They're smarter than we thought, boss. They released a drone over a warehouse complex. The only thing a drone would help with at night—"

Carden interrupted, "Is body heat. So, for some reason they've concluded that we're holed up in an empty building. That means we have to vacate this warehouse. Antonio, bring all of our supplies downstairs. They're going in the van. Anthony, make a few calls to your family. We need a place to stay that isn't on anyone's radar."

Chapter 34

"What kind of car does your husband drive, ma'am?"

Sally Wyatt wiped her swollen red eyes as she sat nervously on the edge of the couch, her feet planted firmly on the floor in front of her. Cam faced her from the other side of the coffee table. As the only female agent in the room, I took the seat nearest her and rested my hand on her shoulder.

"It's our secondary car, for errands and such."

"Understood, and it's...?" I asked.

"A 2001 Ford Focus."

"Four door or two, and the color?" Cam held his pen over the notepad he'd pulled from his inner jacket pocket.

"It's a four-door. We had young kids at the time. It made things easier. Oh, and it's black."

"Okay, and Frank just happened to go out to pick up a gallon of milk, you said? Nothing more than bad timing?"

"Yes." She looked up with hopeful eyes. "You *will* find my husband, won't you, agents?"

"We're going to do everything in our power to bring

him home as soon as possible, ma'am. What we need now is a recent picture of Frank. We also need to know his height and weight, that sort of thing, to air on the news as a missing person."

"Certainly, I'll be right back."

I watched as she exited the living room and walked down a side hallway out of earshot. I whispered to Cam three feet away, "How the hell are we going to find her husband? We can't even find J.T."

When we heard her footsteps getting louder, Cam put his finger to his lips. Sally was back with a handful of photographs and took the same seat as before on the couch.

"We just got these in the mail last week from my niece's wedding. My sister sent the duplicates to us."

I took the photographs from her hand. "And the wedding was when?" I flipped through the stack of pictures.

"It was on May twenty-seventh. We had a great time, it being Memorial Day weekend, and even extended our trip by a few days. Kate and Bobby were married in Dubuque, Iowa. We took a riverboat cruise and did a little gambling too." She dabbed her cheeks with a tissue. "Anyway, there are a few close-up pictures of Frank and me together. I'm sure you can cut me out of the ones you post on the news."

I found two that would do just fine. "I'll make sure you get these back, Sally. Go ahead with your best guess of his height and weight." I brought the picture closer to my face but couldn't make out Frank's eye color. "Are his eyes brown?"

"Yes, brown eyes"—she pointed at the photos—"and

light brown hair. He weighs around one hundred eighty pounds and is five foot eleven inches. That's what it shows on his newest driver's license, anyway."

I stood and tipped my head at Cam. "Ma'am, I think that's all we need. We'll be out back with the other agents. Don't be surprised if there's a bit of commotion for the next few hours. The car left behind will be towed to the county's crime lab, and the forensic team will be here for a while. I'll make sure they lock everything up and let you know when they're about to leave." I pulled a contact card out of my pocket and handed it to her. "We'll be in touch. Thank you."

She gave us a nod goodbye, and Cam and I showed ourselves out. In the alley, we found the tow truck backing up to the abandoned Mercedes. Butch Martin and Hal Friedman were busy dusting the garage for prints and taking pictures.

"How soon will you get to the car?" Val asked. "There's likely a lot of information inside that can help us with this investigation."

Butch scratched his head. "How about I call Leah and Terry in? They can meet you guys at the evidence garage, and you can give it a look through before we start dissecting everything."

Val turned my way. "Jade, you want to join me?"

"Yeah, but we need to call Spelling and Hopkins first and let them know what's going on. Cam?"

"You and Val go ahead and follow the tow truck. I'll update Spelling and Hopkins on our way back to the department. I'll ride with Bill. We need to get the statistics and locations for all those other warehouses." Cam turned to Sergeant Saunders and Deputy Spence. "Can you guys give us a call first thing in the morning? We're going to need those drones for the other vacant buildings."

Saunders stuck out his hand and shook ours before they left. "You got it, guys. We're ready and able to help with whatever you need. There will be two more drones at your disposal first thing tomorrow. I'll check in with you then."

The tow truck driver secured the chain under the front bumper of the Mercedes, and the winch pulled the car up onto the flatbed.

"Ready to go, agents?" the driver asked.

"Yep, we'll be right behind you." I handed Cam the photographs Sally had given me. He'd make sure that information was put on the air right away. We needed more going out on the van, additional information on the man who took the Mercedes in for window tinting, and now, the description of Frank Wyatt, who had been abducted that night. We needed the BOLOs and descriptions aired on every news station during every newscast. Dangerous criminals now held three people captive, and we still didn't know their intentions. At that point, with nothing substantial to go on, we needed the public's help in locating them.

Val and I said our goodbyes then climbed into the cruiser Cam had been driving. I took the driver's seat, pulled the belt over my midsection, and adjusted the seat forward two clicks. I was taller than average for a female, but Cam still had a good four inches on me. I turned the rearview mirror just a smidge. "I'll update you guys if we find anything in the car. I'm guessing we'll be done going through the Mercedes in a few hours." I rolled up the window, shifted into Drive, and followed the tow truck out of the alley.

We arrived at the evidence garage in less than twenty minutes. With the cruiser parked between the white lines at the back of the building, we walked through the open overhead garage doors and watched as the tow truck backed in and released the winch slowly. Val and I crossed the concrete floor to the small office space and took the two seats next to the desk.

"Want a coffee?" I asked.

"Yeah, I'm about to pass out."

I plugged a half dozen quarters into the vending machine and pushed A-6 twice. With two steaming cups of coffee in my hands, I returned to the chair next to Val and handed her a cup. We'd wait there for Leah and Terry to arrive. After they made a few initial photographs in the light of the garage, they'd allow us to sift through anything the person we had been chasing had left behind. The phone rang behind the desk of the small office area where we waited. Tammy Barella answered and passed the phone to me.

"It's Leah, Agent Monroe."

"Thanks." I leaned over the desk as I spoke since the phone was a land line and the cord was badly tangled. I imagined people pacing back and forth, turning and twisting as they talked. That was the only way I could think of to reduce a six-foot phone cord to a tangled ball of eighteen inches. "Hi, Leah. What's your ETA?"

"Hello, Agent Monroe. Terry and I should be there in ten minutes. We'll take some initial pictures inside and out, pop the trunk and hood, and then you're free to go through it while we dust the outside for prints."

"Sounds like a plan. See you in a few." I handed the phone back to Tammy and sipped my coffee. My cell rang, and I set the cup on the desk. SSA Spelling was calling.

"Hello, sir."

"Jade. How soon do you think you and Val will be back?"

"I'm estimating a few hours should do the trick. There's only so much evidence that can be inside a vehicle. I'll take pictures of anything that could be of interest and leave the original behind for forensics to test. They're going to work on the outside of the car while we look through the interior."

"That sounds good. We've already updated the news stations, and now it's a waiting game in hopes of something that will spark a memory in the public's eye." Spelling clicked off.

The creak of the outer door opening made Val and I look up. Leah and Terry walked through and headed our way. We stood and met them halfway at the car.

"This is it, huh?" Terry asked.

"Yep. I hope to God we find something too. Right now we're batting a big fat zero in the leads department. If we only would have caught up to that guy before he ditched the car."

Leah nodded. "It does get frustrating, Jade. Let's glove up. We'll snap off a few photographs of the interior, and then it's yours for an hour or so."

"Thanks, guys, and we really do appreciate you coming in at this late hour."

Terry popped open his portable bag of supplies and held out the glove dispenser. Each of us pulled out two and stretched them over our fingers. He jerked his head toward the car. "Okay, just give us five minutes inside, and then the car is all yours."

Chapter 35

"What you did was unacceptable, Antonio. There were things in the car that could lead back to us. If I didn't need you, I'd—"

"Boss, please, I didn't have a choice. I followed your instructions to the letter. Somehow they knew about the Mercedes. It wasn't my fault they circled back. I stayed plenty far behind them."

Carden jerked his chin toward Anthony. "What did you find out?"

"My uncle's brother-in-law, Dante Leone, has a cabin halfway between Milwaukee and Wisconsin Dells. The guy is clean and isn't on anybody's radar. He didn't want to say much over the phone, but he texted me the address. He said the place is on five acres of pine forest off several dirt-logging roads. We should be safe there for a few nights. There's a hand-carved black bear about four feet to the left of the front door. Under it is a spare key to the door off the garage. He said to park in the garage and to keep the curtains drawn and the doors locked. Twice a week, the neighborhood watch group patrols the dirt roads with cabins on them. He doesn't want anyone to become suspicious if they see a strange vehicle parked outside."

"Okay, our only choice is to take Julie's car and the van. The only thing the news stations have is a description of a dark-colored panel van. No plate number was mentioned. Bring all of the vehicles inside. We need to wipe everything down, load the car and van, and get out. We'll torch the place when we leave. By the time anyone notices a fire, we'll be long gone."

"What about our guests?"

"The Fed and his sister go with us, and the new guy stays behind. I want J.T. hog-tied and damn good. There better not be the slightest chance of him getting loose. Hands behind his back, feet together, and tape over his mouth. He's going in the trunk of his sister's car. I don't trust him anywhere else. The sister gets tied up inside the van. Antonio, you're behind the wheel of the car, and Anthony, you drive the van. I'll keep my eye on the sister. I want her blindfolded and gagged too. Everything else remains the same. The jewelry store pickup isn't until eleven a.m. Saturday. We'll be ready and waiting for the armored truck to pass us at the halfway point. Anthony, I'll drop you off at the storage garage. You'll drive the U-Haul cube van to that designated location and wait for my instructions. The only change in plans is we'll have to head out earlier." Carden stood and slapped his hands together. "Let's go. We're leaving in an hour. I want both of you to secure the Fed. Don't leave anything to chance. He's a fighter, and if he gives you trouble, knock him out cold."

Chapter 36

Val and I began by opening all four doors of the Mercedes and pulling out the mats. We gave them a thorough shake and placed them on the floor, out of our way. I took the front seat, and Val took the back. We searched the obvious areas first, the glove box and center console. Inside the glove box, the car's registration papers indicated that the Mercedes did indeed belong to the man from Sheboygan whose car was stolen eight months prior. I sent a quick text to Cam telling him to contact Mr. Dave Burns. His missing Mercedes had finally been located. Unfortunately, he probably wouldn't get it back anytime soon.

The glove box contained the usual—repair receipts, vehicle registration, and a tire air gauge. I closed the compartment and began looking in the console. I pulled out a tin of aspirin, lip balm, gum, nail clippers, several CDs, pens, a notepad, and a folded paper map. I backed out of the car and stood upright with the notepad and map in my hand.

"Find anything yet?" I asked Val.

She glanced over her left shoulder at me and opened her hand to count the bounty. "Let's see, I have a quarter, two dimes, three pennies, and a snow scraper that was buried under the seat."

"Hop out of there for a minute. Let's take a look at this map and notepad."

"Good, I was getting claustrophobic squished between the seats like that." Val backed out of the Mercedes and stood. She rolled her neck then brushed the carpet fibers off her knees. "What have we got?"

"I haven't checked yet, but I hope we find clues between these pages." Terry and Leah busied themselves with dusting and printing the outside of the car. I tipped my head toward the two chairs we had been sitting in. "Let's get out of their way and take a look."

We returned to the small two-chair area next to the desk. I handed the map to Val, and I flipped the pages of the notepad.

"This notepad looks relatively new, and I haven't found anything that seems related to the owner in Sheboygan. There are references to street names in and around Milwaukee, though."

"Check this out, Jade." Val pointed at areas on the map that were circled in red ink.

I flipped back to the pages in the notepad with street names. "See if those circled areas match any of these streets."

"Okay, go ahead and read them off."

"I already recognize the Center Street and MLK area from the warehouse we were at earlier."

"Yep, and that neighborhood is circled. Give me some more."

"Okay, how about West Twenty-First and Vleit?"

"Hang on. No, nothing circled there. Next."

"Um, try South Second Street and Scott."

Val leaned in and took a closer look at the small print. "Damn it, I should have brought my reading glasses."

"Let me see. I think that area is around Greenfield." I looked at the red circle on the south side of Milwaukee and tried to locate the names of the cross streets. "There it is. Yep, it's circled too. How many are left?"

"Four circled areas and a star," Val said.

"What the hell would the star signify?"

"I have no idea. There's a downtown area circled, though, and it's only five blocks from our headquarters."

I looked over the half dozen street names. "That has to be the address for Plankinton and Wisconsin, but all of those businesses are retail shops. That real estate is too expensive to house vacant buildings, and there's no privacy in the area." I pulled out my own notepad and wrote a reminder to check out the shops along that block of retail stores. "Is there a circle in the western suburbs? Calhoun and Bluemound are written down."

"Yeah, that area is circled too."

"Okay, I know we're on to something—I just don't know what that something is. I want to show these addresses to the tech department. They're much faster than we are, and they can pull up the satellite images. We'll see if the rest of these street names are near vacant buildings. How well did you check under the seats?"

"The obvious areas are done. Leah and Terry will pull out the seats, anyway, and check for more."

With a short stop back at the car to show Leah and Terry the items we were taking with us, we exited the evidence garage and left.

Once we reached the freeway, I turned to Val. "Why don't you give Spelling an update call? Tell him what we have and that we'll be there in fifteen minutes."

"Sure, no problem."

Chapter 37

"Let's see that map and notepad," Hopkins said.

We had just returned from the evidence garage and joined the rest of the team in the conference room. I had made copies of the addresses in the notepad before we left the evidence garage, and I passed them out to the agents at the table. Val unfolded the map and spread it out for everyone to see.

"Did you compare all of the circled areas to the street names in the notepad?" Spelling asked.

"Not all of them, sir. The tech department can pull in the satellite imagery and tell us if any of those addresses are empty buildings. So far, all we know for sure is that we eliminated that north location on the map with the drone earlier tonight. Two circled locations seemed odd to me, though."

Spelling arched his brows. "Like how?"

"The addresses wouldn't work as a place to hide out. One is downtown at Plankinton and Wisconsin."

"Retail space?"

I nodded. "See what I mean? And the other is out in Brookfield, nearly thirty minutes west."

"That is strange," Hopkins said. "I wonder why they noted areas so spread apart. Okay, get that info to Tech and tell them to put a rush on it."

Val folded the map, picked up the notepad, and headed down the hallway with both items.

"Do we have the locations for the rest of the empty buildings in Milwaukee?" I asked.

Cam, with a handful of papers, took a seat. "I have them right here. Each image shows the square footage of the building, the layout with entrances and exits, location of the parking lot, how long the building has been vacant, and nearby structures. We'll have to cherry-pick which ones seem like the best to start with when we get the drones at sunrise."

"I'd suggest looking at all of the buildings in the vicinity of the addresses in the notepad first."

"I agree, Agent Monroe," Hopkins said. "Let's pinpoint those addresses on the wall map and see what we have."

Val shot around the corner and startled all of us. "A structural fire alarm just went out over the scanner. The address is one of the locations on the list."

"What's the address?" Spelling grabbed one of the sheets copied from the notepad.

"The fire department was dispatched to Eleventh Street and Pierce."

Spelling ran his finger down the sheet and confirmed the address. "Let's go. That can't be a coincidence. Val, get ahold of the fire department and tell them there may be a federal agent and his sister inside that building."

We raced out of our headquarters and climbed into four available cruisers. The drive would take only ten minutes going south on Sixth Street. The vacant building, according to the address, was on the northwest edge of Walker's Point.

Sirens sounded in the distance. I spun in the passenger seat and saw the fire chief's car and a fire engine coming up quickly behind us. Spelling pulled to the right side of the street to let them pass. I prayed that the building would be empty and that the fire would be put out before any valuable evidence, if there was any, was lost. But assuming it was a deliberate act, the perpetrators might have taken along everything that could incriminate them.

We reached our destination and saw the fire engines and ladder trucks in action. Water hoses were engaged, and the firemen were dousing the building with the forceful spray. The dried-out, rickety structure was engulfed in raging flames. Barrier tape was already being stretched across the driveway to keep curiosity seekers at bay. Our cruiser and the others following us screeched to a stop. I already had my badge in hand for the first person who tried to block our entry.

My heart pounded double time when I saw what stood ahead of us. "Shit, it's a three-alarm fire. That building won't last long!"

Spelling and Hopkins made a mad dash for the fire chief. Spelling yelled out over the commotion as he ran.

"There may be a federal agent and his sister inside that

building. Do you have firemen searching the interior?"

"I have men going in right now, but they have to move cautiously. It's a large, unsafe structure. Please stay back by the tape, sir. Our men need room, and we have another truck arriving any minute."

Spelling and Hopkins returned to our sides and paced nervously with the rest of us.

"Are they going to tell us anything?" I asked.

Spelling raked his fingers through his hair. "I don't know, Jade. We have to let them do their jobs. All we can do at this point is stay out of their way and be optimistic."

Radios crackled with voices from the firemen inside the burning building. I couldn't make out anything they said, but I did hear the fire chief yell for the ambulance to back in closer. He said his men were bringing somebody out.

"Oh my God, did you guys hear that? They found somebody! It has to be J.T. or Julie." I started toward the fire chief, but Spelling grabbed my arm.

"Stay right here, Jade. I don't want you to distract them from their jobs. We have to wait and hope for the best. There's nothing else we can do."

"But J.T. is my partner. I have to know if it's him."

"No you don't. You'll wait here with the rest of us."

I walked back to our cruiser and leaned against the hood with my arms crossed over my chest. Val and Maria joined me.

"Take a breath, Jade," Val said. "I've known J.T. a long time. If anyone can get out of hot water, it's him."

Headlights bounced behind us. We turned and saw a

man get out of a car and run in our direction. We stopped him before he dipped under the police tape.

"Sir," Val said, "you have to stay back, and we'd like to see some form of identification. Why are you here?"

He pointed toward the fire. "I own that building and the property beneath it."

Val jerked her head at an officer standing ten feet away. "Officer, please get this man's information and find out how he knew his building was ablaze. See if this property is insured and call the fire inspector too."

"Yes, ma'am. Sir, come with me, please."

We watched the doorway and waited for the firemen to bring out the only person they had found so far. Paramedics stood by with the gurney and oxygen.

"They're coming out," Hopkins whispered, his voice already raspy from the smoke engulfing the area.

After the victim was carried out, given oxygen, and loaded into the ambulance, the fire chief approached his men and talked with them. The chief looked over his shoulder then headed our way. I held my breath. My fingerprints were embedded in my forearms, and I was expecting the worst.

Spelling called out, "How is he?"

"He'll make it, just a lot of smoke inhalation, but that man isn't your agent. He said his name is Frank Wyatt and he was abducted several hours ago."

"Oh my God, so J.T. and Julie are still inside?" I stared at the flames lapping every inch of the building that hadn't been charred yet.

"No, ma'am. My men have cleared the building, and there's nobody else inside. All that's left to do is put out the flames. The fire inspector is on his way, and as soon as he can get in, he'll do a thorough investigation."

Spelling let out a sigh of relief. "I want everyone to go home and get some sleep. That's an order, and I don't want to hear a single word of protest."

He stared directly at me when he spoke, so I closed my mouth and kept quiet.

"We've been on the clock for over forty hours. We'll reconvene at nine a.m. with fresh eyes and clear minds. Now go home, everyone. SSA Hopkins and I will finish up here and take care of notifying Mrs. Wyatt. As soon as Frank is able, we'll get his statement."

There was nothing we could say. Spelling had made that perfectly clear. We climbed into our cruisers and left.

It was after two a.m. by the time I was back in my car and driving home to North Bend. Going home seemed useless to me. I knew my sleep would be fitful at best, and I had consumed enough caffeine to stay awake until Saturday. A hot shower and a comfortable bed did sound good, but my mind immediately went to J.T. and Julie, and what they must be going through. I wondered where they were and whether they'd been fed or even had a wink of sleep. We'd seen the video of Julie, already injured, but we had no idea of J.T.'s condition. I prayed that he was all right.

Chapter 38

"Veer left at the next dirt road. We'll see three red reflectors nailed to a tree along the driveway we're supposed to turn in to. The cabin is at the end of that driveway, according to the directions you wrote down. We're going to need a flashlight to find the house key."

Anthony tipped his head toward the glove box. "There's a flashlight in there, boss."

Carden pulled the handle and opened the van's glove box. "Ah, there we go." He pressed the button, and the light illuminated the dash. Then he turned in his seat and shined it at Julie's face. She flinched. "So you *are* awake under that blindfold, eh? Listening to everything we're saying, aren't you?" He chuckled. "That's right, your mouth is taped closed so you can't respond. We're almost to our destination, Julie, so I'm giving you fair warning. No misbehaving or your brother will be severely punished. Understand?"

Julie nodded, and a muffled sob sounded from behind the tape.

"Good."

The van bounced down the rutted drive. Julie's car followed close behind, and both sets of headlights lit the pine forest. The cabin was straight ahead.

"Humph," Carden said, "the place looks surprisingly welcoming." He pointed at the movement in the woods. "Did you see that deer? I guess we are in the wilderness, just the way I like it. This is the perfect hideout and much more inviting than an abandoned warehouse. I think you'll feel right at home here, Julie, but I don't know if I can say the same about your brother. He's always so abrupt with us. Is that just his personality, or did I do something to offend him?" Carden let out a belly laugh. "I even surprise myself at the funny quips I come up with." He punched Anthony's shoulder. "I'm funny, right?"

"You sure are, boss, damn funny."

"That's right. Now hang out here until I open the overhead. We'll get the vehicles secured in the garage and take the supplies inside. We'll come out for the Fed and his sister after we stow the weapons."

Antonio pulled up alongside the van and got out.

Carden held up his hand. "Stay put until I open the garage door, then you can give your brother a hand with the supplies. I have to find the key first." He disappeared into the darkness. Only the flashlight bobbing up and down gave away his location. Minutes later, and with a few choice words, Carden found the key under the wooden bear. He rounded the garage to the right, found the side door, and unlocked it. With groans of protest, the heavy garage door lifted and the light went on.

"Get those vehicles in here so we can shut it down. We don't need anyone nosing around."

"Where do you want the supplies, boss?"

Carden scratched his chin while he thought about his options. They could take the guns inside and risk the chance of the Fed or his sister breaking free and turning the weapons on them, or they could leave the supplies in the van and lock the doors. "Let's leave everything where it is for now. We have to decide where to secure our guests. After they're restrained, you boys can head to that grocery store we passed on the edge of town and pick up some food. I'm starving."

Chapter 39

"Is that you, Jade?"

I heard Amber walking down the hall toward the kitchen. She knotted the belt on her robe as she rounded the corner and took a seat at the breakfast bar next to me.

"Sorry I woke you, hon. I was trying to sneak in."

"Don't ever try to sneak in. I might think you're a burglar and shoot you."

"True, but a burglar doesn't know the code to the alarm."

"Humph, you're right. Give me a hug and tell me the latest. I haven't seen you in almost two days." Amber looked me up and down and wrinkled her nose.

"Yeah, I know, I smell smoky and I need a shower. I'm still wearing the same clothes I had on Wednesday morning when I left for work, for Pete's sake."

She squeezed my shoulder. "What's the word on J.T. and his sister?"

I sighed and held my throbbing head. Lack of sleep guaranteed me a pounding headache. "We don't have a damn thing other than knowing the Pirelli brothers are somehow involved."

"They're part of the Chicago mob, aren't they?"

"Damn straight they are. Of course, nobody knows anything, so we got a warrant to have their phones tapped. So far, we've got zilch. I feel bad for Hopkins. He's going on two days without sleep and he's driving to Waukegan"—I glanced at the clock—"in about five hours to tell Curt's mom that he's dead. Curt was all the poor woman had."

I got up and went to the cabinet that held the coffee cups, vitamins, and the bottle of ibuprofen. I shook four caplets into my hand, filled a water glass, and slugged them down. "I'm beat, Sis. I need a few hours of sleep." I hugged Amber and kissed her cheek. "I love you, little sister. Say a prayer for J.T. and Julie. We need to get them home safely."

"You know I will. Good night, Jade."

"Night, hon." I stumbled down the hallway with hopes that my headache would subside by the time I drifted off. Washed up and changed into my sleepwear, I climbed into bed, barely realizing how wonderful it felt, and set my alarm for seven a.m. If I was lucky, I'd get four blissful hours of sleep.

The repetitive knocking stirred me out of my slumber.

"Jade, are you getting up?" Amber yelled from the hallway.

"Huh? What?" I rolled over and looked at the clock—7:21. I hit the button on top of the clock to silence the blasting noise.

"So you're awake? Your alarm has been screeching for—"

"Yeah, I know—twenty-one minutes. Thanks, hon, I'm up. Can you make—"

Amber opened the door and walked in. "Here, I already did."

"Bless you my child." I reached for the coffee mug and took a sip, kissed Amber's cheek, and headed to the bathroom. I turned before closing the door. "Are you still going to be here when I come out?"

"What do you think? I bet you haven't had breakfast since Tuesday. Scrambled eggs and bacon?"

"Yes, please. I love you, girl."

I had thirty minutes to go from shower to breakfast to out the door. There would be no leisurely second cup of coffee that morning. I fed Polly and Porky, apologized for being such a lousy bird mom, chowed down my breakfast, and headed out the door.

"Wish me luck, Sis. Hopefully we'll catch the bad guys and get J.T. and Julie home today."

"Good luck, Jade, and keep me posted."

The traffic gods were on my side, and I made it downtown in record time. I reached the parking structure at eight fifty and crossed the footbridge at eight fifty-four. I'd worry about that second cup of coffee later.

I walked into the conference room last but still before nine a.m. The obvious empty seats in the room tugged at my heart. J.T. always sat next to me, and that morning, SSA Hopkins was on his way to Waukegan, Illinois, to give Mrs. Belmont what was probably the worst news of her life.

Spelling sat at the head of the table, looking haggard, as

if he hadn't slept for two days—and he hadn't. "Okay, people, I have some updates. First off, Frank Wyatt will be fine."

We all breathed a sigh of relief.

"He's still in the hospital but will be released after lunch. Cam, I want you to conduct a thorough interview with him."

"Yes, sir."

"Val and Maria, I want you to join Bill at the burned-out warehouse. I've been told there are a few vehicles inside. The fire inspector has already cleared the building, but he insists nobody try to get to the second floor. The floorboards aren't stable enough for that. Go over the vehicles and anything on the first level that might prove helpful and take plenty of pictures. Forensics will show up sometime today too, so make sure you don't interfere with their work. The police have already interviewed the building's owner and sent him on his way. He wasn't involved with the fire." Spelling took a sip of his coffee then turned to me. "Jade, I want you to check with Forensics before they head out. Get the report on the Mercedes. I want to see the entire list of things found in that car—I don't care if it's a gum wrapper. After that, check on the phone tap and see if there's any chatter. I'm going to go over that map and street list again. We need to know what the connection is between the downtown location and Brookfield. Those streets were written in that notepad for a reason, and we need to find out what it is. None of the buildings in a three-block radius of those intersections are vacant." Spelling pushed back his chair and stood. "Any questions?"

We muttered a "No, sir."

"Good, then let's go. I want everyone back here by noon with an update."

We filed out of the conference room, each with our own task to complete. I headed out in my personal car to the county's crime lab a few blocks away. I signed in at the front desk then continued on to the lab, where Leah and Terry normally worked the day shift. They both nodded when I entered.

"It looks like we're all going without much sleep. Working a double?" I asked.

"Yeah, we'll be here until the night shift comes in. We were told we're on call until J.T. and his sister are found." Leah let out a long yawn.

"That sounds about right." I crossed the room to their small coffee station and poured myself a cup. "Are you done with the Mercedes?"

Leah answered for both of them. "Yep, it's been gone through about as thoroughly as possible. We found a few prints but nothing that was in the system. Whoever drove that vehicle last night was definitely gloved."

I smirked. "Figured as much. Nothing comes easy these days. Find anything of interest? Spelling wants the complete list, no matter how insignificant it may seem."

"Sure, give me a sec," Terry said. "I'll print out a copy for you."

"You have everything bagged and tagged already?"

"Sure do," Leah said.

"Good. Hang on to that stuff for now but send the photo file to my email."

Terry returned with the copy and handed it to me. "There wasn't a lot, Jade, so the list is short. I think that map and notepad you found was the most significant. Everything else seemed to be a nonissue."

"Okay. Appreciate it, guys. Don't forget to email me the photo file."

Leah took a seat at her computer station. "I'll do it right now."

With the evidence sheet tucked in my purse, I left the crime lab and returned to our downtown building. Inside, I ducked into the computer lab and took a seat. I woke up a computer and logged in to my FBI email account. As promised, the photo file Leah said she'd send was waiting in my in-box. I pulled out my notepad and checked that task off my to-do list. My phone rang just as I was about to make the call to our tech department. Joe was calling.

I chuckled when I answered. "That's why my ears were burning. You were dialing me right when I was about to call you."

"You may want to hear this, Jade. There's been some activity on the wiretap."

"Give me thirty seconds. I'm on my way." I power walked down three hallways to the tech department and entered. Joe sat on the other side of the room and waved me over.

"I have everything set up. Here, give it a listen."

I pulled out my notepad and pen then gave him a nod.

Joe pressed the play button, and a back-and-forth conversation began. I heard an outgoing phone call made by Anthony Pirelli to his uncle Freddy, one of the patriarchs in the Chicago area. Anthony was looking for a place to lie low for several days. The uncle offered up his brother-in-law's cabin, hidden away on a five-acre wooded parcel between Milwaukee and Wisconsin Dells.

"Come on. Give me a name," I said as I wrote down everything I'd heard.

"It's coming, Jade, in just a second." Joe hit Pause at the two-minute mark. "Okay, he's going to give the name right now." He tapped Play again, and the uncle mentioned the brother-in-law's name—Dante Leone.

"Bingo! That's all I need. We can check the property tax bill under his name, and the location of the cabin should pop up." I pushed back my chair and stood. "You're amazing!"

Joe laughed. "It's the wiretap that's amazing. I just do the eavesdropping when an alert comes in."

I returned to the computer lab and took my seat. With a quick jiggle of the mouse, the sleeping monitor sprang to life. I'd have to do a county-by-county property tax search since I didn't have an exact address for that cabin. I typed in a search for southwest Wisconsin counties to see how many I'd have to call. I came up with six counties just to cover all possible areas. I made a call to Spelling's cell phone to tell him my plan.

"Go ahead and get started on that. Did you get the inventory list for the Mercedes?"

"Yes, but I haven't even opened the email from Leah yet. Just as I was going to, I got the call from Joe about the wiretap."

"Give me that brother-in-law's name. I'll make those calls to the county courthouses and get the address. Go ahead and review the inventory from the Mercedes. If nothing pops, we can cross that off our list."

"You got it, boss. I'll let you know at lunchtime if I found anything."

Chapter 40

Julie and J.T. had been bound in separate rooms. Blindfolded, gagged, and tied up, neither had seen or talked to the other in over twenty-four hours. The cabin was larger than Carden had imagined, and that gave him options. He liked the idea of keeping the Fed off balance. The thought of Agent Harper worrying about his sister's welfare made the entire situation much more pleasurable to Carden, and the Fed wouldn't be inclined to try the escape ploy again.

The three men sat at the table, drank coffee, and ate grocery store doughnuts as they reviewed the plans for Saturday morning. Nothing could be left to chance. Every detail needed to be ingrained in their minds to make the diamond theft go as slick as ice. They would all wear masks, including J.T., but under his mask, his mouth would be sealed with duct tape. He'd be armed like the others, yet he'd pose no real threat—his gun would be empty. He'd follow the instructions to the letter or Julie would die a slow, painful death.

J.T. would lead the ambush. If gunfire broke out, the

Fed would die. He was expendable, and he'd feel the pain of a piercing hot bullet tearing through his skin, muscle, and bone. His organs would explode, and he'd bleed out, just as Sam did the day he was shot and killed by J.T. in 2014.

Carden tapped the laptop's mouse, and the screen opened to a map he had been reviewing last night. "This is where you'll sit in the U-Haul." He pointed at a turnout, hidden in tree cover along a secondary road. "Have your phone handy and wear your Bluetooth. I'll call you when the armored transport truck is several miles from your location. That's when you'll get the agent in place. The second I yell go, you're going to gun it and T-bone the truck. The driver will likely be killed upon impact. The truck will be disabled, and I'll be right behind them. We'll all jump out of our vehicles and attack them while they're knocked senseless. It worked in 2014, and it will work again."

Anthony rubbed the two-day stubble on his chin then gave his cheek a scratch. "But your brother was killed, boss."

"Not during the robbery, idiot. It was months later. We aren't going to make that mistake twice. Once we split up the diamonds, we'll part ways and disappear. Sam and his friends stuck around too long enjoying their spoils. I was the only person with enough sense to become scarce." Carden jabbed his head with his index finger. "There's a brain inside that skull of yours, and sometimes you have to use it."

The sound of furniture scraping along the wooden floor alerted them. Carden jerked his head at Antonio. "Go shut that Fed up. Where the hell does he think he's going, anyway, when he's cuffed and tied to the bunk bed?"

Chapter 41

I propped my head against my closed fist while my elbow rested on the desk. I tried my best to fight the urge to shut my eyes, even for a minute. I knew if I did, I would be sound asleep in seconds. I reviewed the inventory list from the Mercedes a half dozen times and still couldn't remember a single thing I had read.

That's it. I need to move around for a minute.

I pushed back my chair and left the computer lab. A quick walk through the hallways might wake me up enough to concentrate on my work. Ending up in the lunchroom, I went straight for the coffee machine and dug through my pocket for change. After I plugged three quarters into the machine, a cardboard cup dropped and hot coffee poured into it.

I was overtired and cranky. I just wanted my partner returned to the fold, safe and sound. I walked back to the computer lab, pulled out my chair, and sat. Then I gave my eyes a thorough rub and dug back in. This would be the seventh time I looked at the photographs Leah sent with the list. With my index finger on the mouse, I clicked on each picture, gave it a few seconds of attention, then moved on to the next. I clicked on photograph number nine, continued on, and a memory popped into my mind. I scrolled back and enlarged the image. I was certain I was looking at a drawing torn from the notepad I took out of the center console of the Mercedes. Everything about that sheet of paper matched the notepad used by the suspect, and something about that drawing seemed very familiar. With my fingertips pressed against my forehead, I tried to rub away the brain fog.

That's it! The image is the same as the tattoo Samuel Dunbar had on the back of his hand. Two entwined ovals with a large V over the center of them.

The image I was staring at on the computer screen was drawn with a black pen and didn't have the bright red *V*, but the *V* was there nonetheless. Other than the color, the drawing was an exact match to the tattoo worn by the armored truck thief J.T. had shot and killed in 2014. There was a connection, and it involved that robbery, J.T., and the man who kidnapped him and Julie. I hit the print icon for ten copies and pushed back my chair, then powered down the computer, picked up the copies, and raced to the office Spelling had been using for the last two days.

I knocked impatiently and turned the knob before I heard him say to come in.

"Boss?"

Spelling pulled off his reading glasses and looked up. "Where's the fire, Jade?" He shook his head. "Sorry, that was in bad taste. I'm overly tired. What's going on?"

"I have something, I just don't know what it is yet."

"Okay, you have my attention. Tell me what you've learned."

I passed one of the copies across his desk. "This drawing is from the evidence list of items from the Mercedes. I haven't asked where it was found yet, but it wasn't in the glove box or the center console because I searched those areas."

"It looks like it was torn from the same notepad the addresses were on." Spelling picked up his phone and called the tech department. "Joe, do you have that notepad handy? Yeah, we need to check something on it. Thanks." Spelling hung up. "Joe will be right here with it. Call Leah quick and ask where they found it."

"I'm on it, sir." I dialed the forensic lab, and Terry answered. "Hey, Terry, it's Jade. Do you remember where that slip of paper with the design on it was found?"

"Hang on, I'll ask Leah."

I waited for a few seconds, then Leah came to the phone. "Hi, Jade. Are you asking about that piece of notepad paper?"

"Yes, with the drawing on it."

"Sure. It was between the driver's seat and the console by the seat belt clasp. It was pretty far down where nobody's hand would fit. I used the long tweezers to pull it out when I saw it with my flashlight."

"Perfect. Thanks for the info."

"One more thing before you hang up, Jade. Hal wanted

me to tell you that there weren't any usable prints on the body bag Curt was found in."

I let out a deep breath, thanked her, and hung up. I told Spelling about the body bag and where Leah said the slip of paper had been found.

Joe knocked and entered the office, the notepad in hand. "Is there something I can help you guys with?"

"Take a look at this photo. See where the edge was torn away from the notepad coils? There may still be pieces of paper stuck where that page was torn out. Let's take a look."

Joe carefully turned each page until he found an area with small shreds of paper stuck in the coils. "Look where the chads, so to speak, remain in the coils. It's exactly where that page was ripped out. We definitively know that drawing came from the fifth page of this notepad."

"Yeah, and the suspect was doodling that image, but why? The only way he would have known about it was because he saw it at some point on Samuel Dunbar's hand."

Joe raised his brows. "Do you know what it means?"

"No, but it must have been important enough to be turned into a tattoo. I need to read J.T.'s file again from that armored truck robbery. At least three witnesses had described that pattern. When Sam was shot by J.T., we confirmed Sam's connection to the robbery because of that very tattoo on his hand."

Joe paced. "How are you doing with those two questionable addresses?"

"There are a number of retail spaces on Wisconsin near Plankinton. I don't know which one has relevance in the mind of our suspect."

"And the Brookfield location?"

"There's a large strip mall on that block and a freestanding store that looks like it's in the process of being built."

"Google Images are never current. Let me see what I can find in real time. If I can't get anything online, I'll drive out there."

Spelling gave him a thank-you nod, and Joe closed the door at his back.

I turned toward the door too. "I'm going to grab that file again, sir."

"It's almost noon. Bring it into the conference room. We'll reconvene with the rest of the team and brainstorm this new discovery."

I grabbed the file folder containing J.T. and Curt's cases from 2014 and headed for the conference room. My teammates were on their way in too.

"I think we may be on to something," I said to Val and Maria as we walked the hallway together.

"Good, because we need all the help we can get," Maria said.

We took our seats around the table and waited for Spelling to arrive. He entered with Joe at his side.

"Okay, people, we have a lot of puzzle pieces to put together. Our hope is that J.T. and Julie are still alive and will be found as soon as possible. We aren't leaving this building until we figure something out. Everyone on board?"

We pulled out our notepads and were ready to dig in.

Spelling sucked in a deep breath. "Okay, everyone was sent out with a task to complete. Let's see what we have." He turned to Maria, Val, and Bill Lewis. "Was there anything in the burned warehouse that can help us?"

Bill spoke up. "There wasn't a lot in the building, sir, just because it had already been abandoned. What we did find is telling us a story, though."

Spelling nodded. "Go ahead, Agent Lewis."

"First off, we can confirm J.T.'s car was among the rubble, as well as Frank Wyatt's vehicle. Both cars were burned badly but identifiable. The VINs were still legible. Of course, we popped the trunks, and they were both empty. The room Frank was found in contained a cot, a metal table, and several metal chairs. Two other rooms were set up in a similar fashion. That's telling us the warehouse was prepared in advance of the kidnappings. We believe the suspects were staying there as well. We found remnants of two chain-link holding cells, I guess one would call them. Each had a melted padlock fused to the gate. We believe that's where J.T. and Curt were held. Julie may have been kept in one of the rooms with a cot, but there's no way to confirm any of it. It's only our best guess. According to the statement the building's owner gave the PD, he had no idea anyone was taking up residence there. He said the building had been empty for nearly ten years, and he only kept it because the land was valuable. He raced to the scene when he heard the fire report on his scanner and knew the location was somewhere in the area of his building."

Spelling jotted notes on the whiteboard behind him.

"Cam, what did you get from Frank Wyatt?"

"I want to ease everyone's mind by saying Frank will make a full recovery. His throat and lungs are sore, and he speaks in a raspy voice, but according to the doctor, he'll be back to normal within a week's time."

I heaved a sigh of relief. The last thing I wanted was for the death count to rise.

"I did get some valuable information from him, though. I showed Frank photos of the Pirelli brothers, and he identified both of them. He said it was Antonio who ditched the Mercedes and hijacked his car. Frank was taken to the warehouse where Antonio called somebody and addressed him as 'boss' and said he needed Anthony to let them in. Frank said he heard the man on the line yelling at Antonio."

"Obviously, that was our mystery man."

"I agree, Jade. Frank said he was taken to a room, the same one the firemen rescued him from, and locked inside. He never saw anyone again but did hear people talking on the other side of the door. He couldn't make out their words, though."

Maria spoke up. "So he never saw anyone except Antonio and Anthony? He had no idea if J.T. or Julie were even there?"

"Guess not."

"Okay, Jade, tell us what you know so far."

"Thanks, boss. Right now I'm trying to figure out the connection between our mystery suspect and the death of Samuel Dunbar back in 2014. We need to know what that is to understand why this man had it out for Curt and J.T. We've already seen Curt's fate, and I'm sure J.T. is running on borrowed time. I'm going to need help from all of you. I have too many fires burning"—I rolled my eyes—"sorry, bad analogy. There was chatter on the wiretap about a cabin somewhere between Milwaukee and Wisconsin Dells. The owner is a Dante Leone, and he's the brother-in-law of one of the Pirelli uncles. I'd bet my bottom dollar that's where they're holed up, and it's imperative that we find that cabin immediately."

"I've contacted the Dane and Sauk County Courthouses, and there's no record of property owned by that man," Spelling said. "Joe, can you take on that task? We still need to check with Iowa, Columbia, Richland, and Adams Counties. If nothing pops, expand the search."

"You got it, sir. Just one bit of news before I go. I have information on that building in Brookfield. Believe it or not, it's the new store for Rosemond Diamonds. I took it upon myself to contact Mr. Rosemond directly. He said all of their inventory is being moved from their old store on Wisconsin Avenue to the new Brookfield location tomorrow."

I buried my face in my hands. "Holy shit, they're going to attempt a jewelry heist, and J.T. is going to be in the middle of it. We need to know where that cabin is now!"

Chapter 42

"Go together to check on Agent Harper. Give him some food and water. He gets one free hand to eat, drink, and piss in a bucket, then he gets cuffed again. Later, we'll let him in on the plan. He has only one option and that's to cooperate and be the man who will take one for the team." Carden chuckled. "No loss there, and you know how the saying goes."

Antonio smirked and elbowed Anthony. "Tell us, boss."

"Karma is a bitch, and then you die. Looks like Agent Harper's number is up. He'll block any bullets that may come our way with his body. Unfortunately, we only have three vests, so sorry, Fed. It sucks to be you." Carden jerked his head toward the door of the room J.T. was in. "Take care of him. He's beginning to irritate me with his noise."

"What about the sister?"

"Give her a bathroom break and some food, then she gets tied up again too. I have to review the route and the map once more. Keep them quiet. I don't want to be disturbed until later. At dinnertime, you boys can go into town and get a few pizzas to bring back here. Lights out at ten o'clock tonight. Tomorrow will come soon enough, and I want everyone to be well rested. We need to be alert and on our game for the big score." Carden rubbed his hands together. "We're leaving here at seven a.m."

Chapter 43

I paged through J.T.'s file slowly and deliberately. I didn't want to miss anything. There could be clues that I hadn't realized the first time I read through it. I flipped to the tab with the agent investigation report conducted by Internal Affairs. I read it again. According to the witness statements, Sam Dunbar seemed to be the leader of that armored truck robbery. Now, our fictitious C.V. Loomis was in charge, and somehow the two men were connected. I stared at the page, and then it hit me. Dunbar was the name of an armored vehicle service, and so was Loomis. They made a joke of the names and decided their fate would be tied to robbing armored trucks for cash and now diamonds.

But C.V. Loomis isn't a real name. We've already established that. And actually Dunbar wasn't Sam's real name, either. He was adopted.

"Sir?"

"Yes, Jade."

"Is there a way we can get access to Samuel Dunbar's adoption files?"

"With a court order or subpoena, probably. Why?"

"I think I'm on to something. Dunbar and Loomis are both names of armored vehicle companies. They're mocking the system, or at least they were until Sam was shot by J.T. I want to know what Sam's birth name was, but we need those records now." I grabbed my notepad and drew the tattoo from memory. "Two entwined ovals with a large *V* over the top of them. Why a *V*?"

"Victory, maybe?" Maria grimaced. "Or possibly victims."

"How about a real last name? What if Sam and our mystery man were related, and the entwined oval means they're connected, or linked, and the *V* stands for their real last name? There has to be a reason C.V. Loomis used that as his fake name. This abduction could be all about retaliation."

Spelling nodded at Cam. "Get ahold of that information now."

Joe burst through the door. "I have it! I found out there are property tax records in Columbia County for a D. Leone. It has to be the same person."

"The location would fit," I said, "and it's between Milwaukee and Wisconsin Dells."

"I checked with the online plat book for Columbia County and found that name attached to a five-acre parcel near Portage. The property is going to be tough to find given that most of the roads around there are just logging trails or fire lanes."

"The locals know that area better. Bill, make a call to the Columbia County Sheriff's Department. Tell them to get out there now. There's a chance that a federal agent and his sister are being held hostage by three suspects. They need to go in quietly and cautiously. If these men are actually planning to rob an armored truck tomorrow, then they're armed to the teeth. Right now, our main concern is getting J.T. and Julie out of there. Get somebody else to work on the connection between Dunbar and Loomis." Spelling turned to me. "Find out how far we're talking. With any luck, we can take the Escalade and a cruiser and be there before dark."

"Got it, sir. Joe, show me where the parcel is in the plat book."

Spelling added, "We'll let the sheriff's department make the initial move on the cabin. They need to surveil the situation and see if the suspects are actually there before closing in on them. If they feel they can apprehend the suspects and get J.T. and Julie to safety, then we'll let them take lead, but be ready to move out, either way."

Bill hung up from the call and let out what sounded like a sigh of uncertainty. He explained the conversation he had with the sheriff's department. "Their county law enforcement consists of four deputies, two detectives, and the sheriff. That area is a mixed bag. Cabins in the woods, farmland, state parks, and land owned by logging companies make up most of Columbia County. They don't come across crime of any real significance. The sheriff said there's a neighborhood watch unit that patrols around the vacation cabins to make sure there aren't any vandals or suspicious looking people milling about." Bill checked

Spelling's expression before continuing. "He said he'd borrow the patrol vehicle and act like he was making a routine pass to see if he notices any activity at the cabin. I warned against it, sir, but he insisted. He said it was the only safe way to know for sure. If somebody is actually at the property, he'll knock, find out who they are, and leave, then come back with the entire department and move in on them."

"J.T. and Julie could be used as human shields. That sheriff could be opening a can of worms. It's far too risky for all of them."

"I told him that, boss, but he said he was only five minutes from the property. He'll update us after he passes by."

Spelling dropped down in his seat. "Are his deputies standing by in case the shit hits the fan?"

"He said they have radios, and he'll update them too. Apparently, he's wearing street clothes. He assured me he wouldn't do anything to raise suspicion."

"I'll give him fifteen minutes"—Spelling turned his wrist and checked the time—"and then we're calling back and moving out."

Chapter 44

"Mr. Vetcher, somebody is driving down the fire lane pretty damn slow." Anthony barely touched the curtain but moved it aside just enough to get a glimpse of the neighborhood watch vehicle crawling toward the cabin. "There's writing on the side of the car."

"Dim the lights. All of the curtains are drawn, aren't they?"

"Yes, sir, so I don't know why he's moving at a snail's pace."

"There's a neighborhood watch patrol in this area. Maybe they always drive by that slowly." Antonio jammed a handful of potato chips into his mouth. Crumbs dropped to the tabletop as he spoke. "Just keep quiet and don't let him see you moving those curtains around."

"Shit."

Carden set the newspaper down and scurried toward Anthony. "What's wrong?"

"He stopped the car, boss."

"Son of a bitch. Do we have any guns in here?"

"They're still in the van."

Carden jerked his head toward the garage door. "Go get the pistols, Antonio, and don't make a peep. Don't turn on the garage light, either. Grab the flashlight. Now hurry!"

Antonio crouched and ran across the living room, grabbed the flashlight off the counter as he passed through the kitchen, then eased the garage door open.

"What's he doing now?" Carden whispered.

"He's getting out, sir. This isn't going to end well."

"Let's wait and see, and I'll do the talking. What's your uncle's brother-in-law's name?"

"Dante Leone."

"Right. What's taking Antonio so damn long?"

"The man is coming up the sidewalk, Mr. Vetcher."

Carden craned his neck toward the kitchen. Antonio was nowhere to be seen. "Damn his slow ass. Go help him, quick."

Anthony cleared the living room right as a knock sounded. Carden rolled his neck, took in a large gulp of air, and opened the door. On the other side, a man who looked to be in his mid-sixties and wearing a T-shirt and khakis stood with a wide grin on his face. Carden gave the car in front of the garage a quick glance. An advertising magnet with the words Neighborhood Watch Group was secured to the door.

"Howdy. I'm Bob Wells, one of the volunteers for our neighborhood watch association. I just happened to notice shadows behind the drapes and thought I'd check out the situation. You are?"

"Dennis Banks." Carden stuck out his hand to shake Bob's. "Sorry to trouble you, Bob, but we aren't having a situation."

"Sure thing, Mr. Banks, so what brings you out this way?"

"Fishing."

"Fishing?" Bob chuckled as he raised his brows and scratched his chin. "The nearest fishing lake is twenty miles west of here. It seems like you could have rented a place closer to the water. By the way, who owns this cabin?"

Carden stared him down. "I'm sure you know who owns the property, Mr. Wells."

Both men jerked their heads toward the sound of a door opening. Anthony and Antonio came around the corner from the kitchen, each with a pistol tucked in his waistband.

Bob glanced from Anthony to Antonio. "I doubt if you're going to do much fishing dressed that way."

Anthony looked at Antonio's pressed slacks and starched shirt. He turned back to face Bob. "Don't like our clothes, old man?"

A noise sounded from behind a closed door down the hallway. Bob's eyes darted in that direction, and the jerk of his hand was enough to set things in motion. He reached for something at his back. In an instant, Antonio pulled the pistol from his waistband and fired into Bob's chest. A sharp crack rang out, and muzzle smoke circled above the gun's barrel. Blood spray filled the air, and a grunt came from deep within Bob as the impact launched him backward off the porch to the sidewalk three steps below.

"Son of a bitch! Antonio, why the hell did you do that? Gunfire echoes for miles around here." Carden's face twisted into an angry snarl.

"He was going to shoot you, boss. Would you rather be dead? I believe you hired us to help *and* protect you." Antonio stepped outside and rolled Bob over with his foot then pointed. "There's his gun." Bob lay dead with a pistol beneath his body. Antonio looked over his shoulder at Carden. "Need I say more?"

Carden turned to Anthony. "Help your brother put him in the van. We'll take the body deep into the woods and dump him."

"What about his vehicle, boss?" Anthony asked.

"We have to get rid of that too, and it's blocking the garage, anyway. Come on. Let's make this quick before someone sees us." Carden crossed the living room and went into the kitchen. He turned the knob on the garage door. "I'll open the overhead."

Antonio knelt over the body and fished through Bob's pockets.

"Robbing the guy?"

"I'm getting the car keys, asshole." Antonio pulled out Bob's wallet. "But we'll take the wallet too." He tossed it to Anthony.

Anthony flipped open the wallet. "Shit. Mr. Vetcher isn't going to like this."

Antonio pushed off his knees and stood. "He won't like what?"

"Nice move, idiot. That dude is the county sheriff."

The rumble of the overhead opening told the men it was time to go. Anthony jerked his head toward the garage. "Slip your hands under his armpits. I've got his legs."

Carden opened the van's back doors and moved the rifles to the side. "Throw him in. Do you have the car keys?"

Antonio wiped his bloody hands on his pants then dug in his pocket and pulled out the keys. He jangled them in the air. "Right here, boss, but we have a problem."

"Other than a dead man lying in the van?"

"Yeah, he's not only dead, he's the county sheriff."

"I swear to God, Antonio, you get one step closer to having a bullet lodged in your brain every single day. Now, let's go. Get those damn magnets off that car and move it out of my way so I can back out the van. Anthony, turn off the lights inside, lock up the house, then throw the doormat over that mess." Carden jerked his chin toward the blood smear on the sidewalk. "I don't need anyone who may come calling to see it. Neighborhood watch, huh? Something or someone set off an alert for that nosey sheriff to stop by." Carden slammed the back doors of the van and climbed into the driver's seat. He used the side mirrors to back out onto the gravel driveway. The heavy overhead came down, and Anthony exited the front of the house, dragging the doormat behind him. He tossed it over the blood that followed the sidewalk cracks, then he headed toward the van.

"You drive so I can figure out where to go." Carden climbed out of the driver's seat and walked around the van. He pulled up a local map on his cell phone. "Okay, there's no shortage of logging trails around here. Go left at the end of the road. We'll find one that's pretty remote and get rid of the sheriff and that stupid car." Carden directed Anthony deeper into the woods.

"What if we get stuck, Mr. Vetcher?"

Carden rolled his eyes. "Really? It hasn't rained in a month, so there's no reason to get stuck unless you decide to go off-roading. That would be on you, and if that happens, you might get a bullet to the brain too." He pointed to the right. "Follow that trail. We'll park a few hundred feet in. The tree cover is pretty dense back there, so it's a good place to ditch the car. Wave Antonio around us."

Anthony rolled down the window and waved Antonio by. When they were side by side, Antonio lowered the passenger window. "What?"

"Go around us and park as far in as you can, and the deeper back, the better. Make sure you wipe down everything you've touched."

Antonio nodded and continued on.

"How did your brother get so stupid?"

Anthony shrugged. "The old man put him to work at a young age. Antonio never went past the eighth grade. He's big and bulky and Pops thought he'd be good at strong-arming people."

"You're just as big as Antonio."

"Yeah, but my expertise is my brain."

Carden laughed. "If you say so."

Anthony killed the engine as they waited for Antonio.

He looked back at the body lying behind them. "Where are we going to dump him?"

"We'll find another secluded spot a few miles from here. Hopefully the coyotes will make short work of him."

Antonio opened the back door and climbed in. "Jesus, the old man's eyes are open."

"You shot him, you deal with it," Carden said. "Turn the van around, Anthony. Let's go dump this body."

Chapter 45

"Try his phone again."

"I've tried it three times, sir. If he actually approached the house, he either left it in the car or turned the volume off. The suspects would probably get suspicious if his phone rang in front of them and he didn't answer it."

Spelling looked at his watch. "It's been twenty-five minutes." He tipped his head toward Bill. "Call his deputies and see if they've talked to him."

"Right away, sir." Bill hit Redial on his contact at the sheriff's department.

"Columbia County Sheriff's Office, Renee speaking. How may I direct your call?"

"Hello, this is Agent Bill Lewis from the FBI. I called earlier. Is there a deputy I can speak with?"

"One moment, sir."

"Hello, this is Deputy Reese. How can I help you, Agent Lewis?"

"Where is your sheriff, Deputy Reese? Isn't anyone keeping tabs on his whereabouts?"

"Sure thing, Agent Lewis. Sheriff Wells gave me a call about fifteen minutes ago. He said he was almost to the property."

"And you haven't spoken to him since?"

"No, sir. We're standing by."

"Get out to that property now! Your sheriff may have just gotten himself, our agent, and his civilian sister in trouble."

"Yes, sir. I'll round up everyone and head out."

"Deputy Reese, no sirens and no lights. Go in quietly and call me back the second you arrive." Bill hung up and pounded the table with his fists. "Damn Podunk crew. I don't think they're taking this seriously. I'm sure that neck of the woods has never dealt with anything worse than someone poaching a deer."

Spelling stood. "Everyone, suit up in your vests and grab your weapons and extra magazines. We're taking the chopper. Cam, get on the horn with our hangar at Mitchell Field and tell the crew we need our helicopter ready to go in thirty minutes. Have them clear our arrival with the airport in Portage. I want vehicles at our disposal and somebody waiting there who will lead us to that cabin. Have a SWAT team get out there as soon as they can."

Thirty minutes later, six of us climbed into the waiting chopper, the blades spun, and the helicopter began to lift. The flight to the Portage airport would take just under an hour, and we still hadn't heard a word from the deputies.

Chapter 46

"Shit! What do you want me to do, boss?" Anthony slammed on the brakes when he saw three sheriff's department cruisers sitting along the fire lane.

"The cars are empty, which means they're trying a sneak attack on the cabin. Let me think. Okay, Anthony, you and I will move ahead in the van, and Antonio, you'll come in from behind. They'll be surrounded with no place to hide." Carden jerked his head at Anthony. "Roll down the windows." He turned to Antonio at the back of the van. "Hand me one of the AK-47s and a pistol. Arm yourself with the other AK. We're here to hit our targets, so keep it in semi mode. These idiots aren't going to ruin our plans for tomorrow." Carden reached over his shoulder and took the assault rifle from Antonio. "I see movement in the woods, so they haven't reached the cabin yet. Get out and find cover behind a tree. Take out as many of those deputies as you can, and for God's sake, don't get shot. I'll let them have it from the road. Ready?"

Antonio opened the rear doors and looked over his

shoulder at Carden before he jumped out. "Ready, boss."

Carden gave Anthony a nod. "Gun it."

The van's wheel spun in the loose gravel and caused rocks to fly like small missiles. Carden looked back and caught a glimpse of Antonio as he disappeared into the tree cover. With his window down and the rifle aimed at the woods, Carden braced the AK against his shoulder and began firing. He saw three men hit the ground. The ping of return fire glancing off trees and ricocheting down on the van was too close for comfort. The sound was like rain pelting the vehicle's exterior.

"Those sons of bitches are done." Carden took aim again, but the sudden blast of Antonio's rifle in full auto sent men running for their lives. Trees exploded into shredded bark from the force of bullets hitting them. The deputies didn't have a chance against two rapid-fire AK-47s. They were outgunned and, one by one, fell to their death. The woods went quiet as the echo of gunfire drifted away with the breeze.

"Get to the cabin," Carden yelled as Anthony floored the gas pedal and barreled down the path. "We have to get the agent and his sister out of there before we're surrounded. This racket is going to attract every law enforcement agency in a twenty-mile radius."

The van skidded to a stop in front of the cabin. Carden lurched forward so hard he almost hit the dash. He jumped out, ran to the door, and kicked it in.

"Get Antonio over here quick. We need his help." Carden ran through the cabin and grabbed the zip ties off the coffee table as he passed through the living room. With a second forceful kick, the bedroom door broke free of its frame.

Julie coiled back against the headboard and tried to scream through the duct tape on her mouth. Fear covered her face.

"We're leaving now, so get up! You do one thing to piss me off and you die, got it?"

She nodded.

Carden yanked her by the hair and pulled her off the bed. He stretched the zip ties around her wrists then released the ropes that bound her. "Move!" He jammed the pistol into her back and pushed her out the door.

Antonio and Anthony were in charge of getting J.T. out. "How do you want us to do this?" Anthony asked.

"Knock him out. We don't have time for resistance."

Anthony shoved the door open so fast it bounced off the back wall. J.T. jumped off the bed, but his efforts were useless. He had only a foot of chain allowing him movement, and with his hands cuffed behind his back, there wasn't anything he could do. Both Anthony and Antonio had an easy fifty pounds on him. J.T. braced for it as a grapefruit-sized fist was about to nail him between the eyes.

"Grab an arm. Let's go." Anthony jerked his head toward the door. He and Antonio dragged the agent out and threw him in the trunk of Julie's car. "Antonio, put some fresh tape over the agent's mouth and double-check those cuffs. We've got to get the hell out of here." Anthony ran to the van to help Carden secure Julie. "We'll be ready to go in five minutes, boss."

"We're leaving in two minutes. Get that trunk closed up and torch the cabin."

A frown furrowed Anthony's forehead. "Dante is going to be pissed."

"I don't give a shit about Dante, and we don't have time to grab what we brought in or wipe the place down. That's why people have insurance. Now torch it." Carden jumped in the driver's seat and started the van. He laid on the horn and pounded the dash with his fist. "Let's go!"

Antonio pulled Julie's car out of the garage and started down the driveway. Thick black smoke began to seep out of the cabin's seams and chimney. The crack of hot window glass told Carden the house would go up in flames any second.

Anthony closed the overhead, ran out the front door, and jumped in the van. "We're good to go, sir, and not a minute too soon." He looked back over his shoulder as Carden barreled down the driveway, a foot behind the bumper of Julie's car. Orange flames licked the cabin's log exterior, and the windows exploded outward.

Chapter 47

Spelling wrung his hands. "This doesn't feel right. We haven't heard a word from anyone." He pulled his sleeve back and looked at his watch for the fifth time in ten minutes. "Check your phone, Bill. Maybe you missed the call from Deputy Reese."

Bill Lewis pulled his phone out of his vest pocket. "No calls, sir."

"We've been in this bird for nearly a half hour. The deputies should have called with an update. Where is the SWAT team? They should be at the cabin too."

"I'll try the number for the unit commander in Portage. I'm sure he went to the site with the team." Bill pulled up the direct number for Corey Franklin, the SRT commander of the Portage team for the last nine years. He covered the microphone with his hand as it rang on the other end. "Just an FYI, sir. Portage has an SRT unit, not a SWAT team. All in all, they fulfill the same type of requirements and duties." Spelling nodded and stared out the chopper's window.

"Hello, is this Commander Franklin? Yes, it's Agent Bill

Lewis calling from the FBI. Our chopper should be landing at the Portage airport in about fifteen minutes. Does anyone have eyes on the cabin? Is there activity on that property?" Bill waited quietly as Commander Franklin spoke. "What? You're sure, and it's the right address?" Bill clenched his fist. "Yes, we'll be there as soon as possible. Please get the coroner and a forensic team to the site." Bill hung up from the call. "I don't believe this shit!"

"Please tell me it isn't J.T. and Julie." I stared at my feet and felt hot tears welling up in my eyes. Maria squeezed my hand.

"They haven't seen anyone except dead deputies in the woods. The cabin is in flames, the fire trucks just arrived, and there aren't any vehicles at the scene except three sheriff's department cruisers along the road. They've requested law enforcement's help from as far away as Madison."

"Oh my God," Val said. "What happened to the sheriff, and where the hell are they headed now?"

"The sheriff may be another hostage. It's possible they're driving his vehicle. We need to get a BOLO on that car. Jade, call the Columbia County sheriff's dispatch and find out who operates the neighborhood watch near those cabins. That's the car we need to look for." Spelling tapped the pilot on the shoulder. "How long before we land?"

The pilot pointed ahead. "We're coming up on the Portage airport right now, sir. We'll be on the ground in five minutes."

"Bill, call the airport and make sure there are vehicles

and a guide waiting on the tarmac for us. We'll take a minute to use the facilities, and then we're off."

"I'm on it, sir."

We landed and had to wait a minute for the blades to slow their rotation before we could exit the helicopter safely. Spelling jumped out and approached a man who stood alongside two black SUVs fifty feet away. They exchanged a few words, then Spelling turned toward us.

"Everyone, we're leaving in those SUVs in five minutes. Bill, you can drive one, and this man, Dave Conway, will drive the lead vehicle. All right, do what you need to do and be back here in"—he checked his watch—"four minutes."

We climbed in the Explorers a few minutes later. Dave, Spelling, Maria, and I were in the lead vehicle. Bill, Cam, and Val took up the rear.

"The location of the property in question is a ten-minute drive from here, Agent Spelling."

"Thanks, Dave. Are you in law enforcement?"

"No, sir, I work for the airport. My job is to arrange transportation for people coming in or act as the driver. I know this area like the back of my hand. Born and raised in Portage, so any side road, logging path, or fire lane you need to find, I'm your man."

"Good to know." Spelling pulled out two contact cards and handed one to Dave. "May I have your phone number? We may need to call on you again if we're here longer than today."

"Sure thing." Dave rattled off his phone number, and Spelling wrote it on the back of the second card then tucked it into his pocket. "Two more dirt roads and we'll be at the property."

Spelling pointed out the windshield. "I can see the smoke from here. We must be close."

Dave pulled in behind the SRT vehicle and parked. Bill tucked his SUV in tight behind ours.

"I'll wait here, sir," Dave said.

Spelling nodded.

A navy blue van with Coroner written in white block letters sat empty along the ditch, and the forensics van was parked out of the way, nearer the woods. A half dozen Portage patrol cars, even out of their jurisdiction of the city limits, were parked along the road. We exited the vehicles and headed toward the firemen. Two water trucks were stationed within feet of what used to be the cabin, and eight firefighters manned the hoses. Smoke billowed, and what remained of the fire hissed against the force of the water. Charred logs, a caved-in roof, and remnants of a stone fireplace stood in front of us.

"Stay back, folks. This fire isn't contained yet," the firefighter nearest us said.

Spelling jerked his head toward the woods. "Looks like most everyone is out there. Let's go introduce ourselves."

The six of us headed into the heavy pinewoods, where we found the coroner and his assistant, the forensic team of three, city police officers there to help, and the SRT unit that consisted of Commander Franklin and six specially trained officers in tactical gear. Spelling took the lead and made the introductions to Commander Franklin.

"What did you come in on, Commander?"

"Call me Corey, please. I'm not the formal type. My unit and I arrived forty-five minutes ago after a short briefing at our headquarters. My men needed to know in advance what we might be walking in on—a possible hostage situation, sir."

"Understood. Then what?"

"A few miles out, we noticed smoke above the tree line. I called the Portage fire department to see if they had been dispatched to any location in this area, which they hadn't. I requested one water truck at the time since we didn't know exactly where the fire was or its intensity. When we arrived at the scene, we came upon three cruisers parked along the ditch on the secondary road just west of the fire lane that leads to the cabin. The firefighters got here ten minutes later. The structure was totally engulfed in flames, and we feared the worst—that the deputies were inside. That's when one of our men happened to notice the carnage out here in the woods."

"You're referring to the deputies?"

"Yes, sir."

"And all three deputies were deceased when you came upon them?"

"That's correct, Agent Spelling, and a few minutes later I received the call from Agent Lewis. Coroner McFadden and his assistant, Jack Demler, along with the forensic team, got here about twenty minutes ago. They're in the preliminary stages of assessing the bodies."

My cell phone rang, and I excused myself. "FBI Agent Jade Monroe speaking."

"Agent Monroe, this is the Columbia County Sheriff's Office dispatch operator calling back with the information you requested. Ma'am, what's going on, and what happened to our deputies? Where is Sheriff Wells? It sounds like all hell is breaking loose. I've seen patrol cars speeding through town with their sirens blaring and lights flashing. They were heading out in that direction. I can't reach anybody in our squad, Agent Monroe."

"I'm sorry, but we don't have detailed information yet. We just arrived at the scene. It's going to be awhile before we have answers. Your name is?"

"Trisha Moorehead, ma'am."

I heard her sniffle before she continued.

"The vehicle in question belongs to Billy Sommers. He does the neighborhood watch route twice a week. He said Sheriff Wells stopped by a few hours back and borrowed the car and left his cruiser at Billy's house. When it's in use, Billy attaches door magnets that show he's with the neighborhood watch group. The car is a 2009 white Chevy Caprice. He bought it at the police car auction in 2011."

"And what are the plate numbers, Trisha?"

"Wisconsin endangered resources plate number TLP-502. The gray wolf design is on the left."

"Got it." I pocketed my notepad and pen, thanked Trisha, then contacted the state patrol and issued a statewide BOLO for that vehicle.

After rejoining my team, which was gathered at the coroner's back, I pulled Spelling aside so I wouldn't interrupt the ongoing conversation. "Sir, the dispatch officer said the car is a four-door 2009 white Chevrolet Caprice. It has magnets on both front doors showing it's the neighborhood watch vehicle. The car has the endangered resources plates, in this case, the gray wolf. Tag number is TLP-502. I've already put a BOLO out on it with the state patrol."

"Good work, Jade. We can assume the magnets have been thrown away, and the tags could have been swapped out by now. Find out from the firefighters if there are any vehicles in the garage. If not, we have to assume Julie's car or that dark van may be transporting our criminals too."

"I'd doubt if the Pirelli brothers could fit in a Ford Fiesta. I'm guessing they're using the Caprice and the van, where there's more room for five people and the guns they're carrying. Keep in mind, they somehow need a way to restrain J.T. and Julie. That leads me to think they're in the van."

"Good point, but nothing has hit on the BOLO for the van yet, has it?"

"I'm afraid not, sir. I'm sure the description was too vague, and we didn't have a plate number, either."

Spelling tipped his head toward the group. "Come on. Let's go hear what the coroner has to say." He craned his neck toward the fire trucks. "It looks like the fire is almost out. We'll give them a few more minutes."

"Agents." The coroner pushed off his knee, stood, and glanced at his sticky gloves that were coated with sap, dirt, and pine needles. He pulled them off and rolled them into a ball, then he jammed them into his pocket and put on a clean pair. With a few words between them, the coroner pointed toward the van and the assistant headed in that direction. "Sorry. I asked Jack to get a few tarps to cover the deceased. It's a real shame, you know. These men, whose job it is to protect the public, were gunned down without a chance in hell against something like an assault rifle. They got off a few shots"—he pointed at the weapons lying near the deputies—"but they were sitting ducks." He looked up at the trees. "This woods is thick with pine trees, but they're still relatively young. Their trunks aren't strong enough or wide enough to take safe cover behind. "He pointed out the damage to the bark on the trees. "See how they exploded during the gunfire? That amount of damage comes from semi or fully automatic weapons, primarily assault rifles like the AK-47 or AR-15. Forensics concurred with my assessment." He shook his head as he helped Jack spread the tarp over Deputy Reese's bloody body. "The only saving grace that came out of today's savage assault is that these men were dead before they hit the ground."

I glanced through the trees at what was left of the cabin. It looked as though the firefighters had extinguished the fire, and only smoldering embers and wet, soggy logs remained. I whispered to Spelling that I'd check on the possibility of vehicles in the garage.

I walked away from the group and headed toward the fire trucks. "Excuse me, sir?"

The nearest firefighter turned around. I realized it was a woman when she removed her helmet. She smiled. "I get that a lot."

I stuttered out the question mixed with an apology for my mistake. "I'm Agent Jade Monroe with the FBI. I realize the dwelling was fully engulfed in flames when your department arrived and there was nothing you could do but extinguish it, but do you have any idea if there are vehicles in the garage?"

"I'd venture to say that's a negative, Agent Monroe, but we'll check that out real soon. I'm pretty sure the entire county would have heard gas explosions if cars were in there."

I nodded. "Good point. I hadn't thought of that."

"Give us fifteen minutes. I'll come and get you when we open up the place."

"Good enough." I stuck out my hand and shook hers. "Thanks for your service and bravery."

"My pleasure, ma'am. Following in my pop's footsteps." She pointed over her shoulder. "That's my old man right there. He's the captain."

I grinned with familiarity and felt her pride. I missed my own dad so much. "What's your name?"

"Rosie Fredrick, ma'am."

"We really appreciate everything you do, Rosie. I'll be over there with my team when you're ready to go in."

"You bet. I'll come and get you."

The group of people had moved farther into the woods and stood near the second body. Two men from Forensics were snapping pictures of the bullets lodged in tree trunks and of the deceased deputy on the ground. We didn't need to identify each victim. Their name tags told us who they were.

I stood next to Spelling. "The firefighter said they'd open up the garage in fifteen minutes. She seemed certain the garage would be empty since we didn't hear any gas explosions."

"She?"

"Yeah, my mistake. I called her sir. So it is likely there are three vehicle possibilities after all. The chances of them being out of the area by now are pretty high. Everyone in law enforcement is here helping out or—"

Spelling nodded. "Understood."

Chapter 48

"How do you think they figured out where we were, boss?" Anthony stared out the windshield at Julie's car in front of them.

"I wasn't sure at first, but when we found out that guy was the sheriff, there was no other explanation."

"Yeah?" Anthony raised two thick, questioning brows. "What's the explanation?"

Carden couldn't hold back the insult. "Didn't you mention something earlier about having brains? The phones were tapped, idiot. It's the only thing that makes sense. When you called your uncle, the Feds were listening in. I guess we're on our own and we need to find a secluded place to hunker down, at least until dark. We can't be out in broad daylight with these vehicles. Tomorrow is going forward like we've planned. We just have to get our wits about us, swap out these cars with something else, and get back to Milwaukee. Everything will be fine as soon as we have different vehicles." Carden went silent for a minute as he thought. "We can't hijack someone's car unless we kill them. They would report it, plus they'd see our faces. We have to stay off the interstates and state highways. Plate readers are everywhere these days."

"We're close to the Dells, Mr. Vetcher, and people from all over the country vacation there. We can cherry-pick license plates from different states."

"Hmm, not a bad idea. Look on your phone for campgrounds or state parks nearby. We need to stay out of sight until dark. After that, we'll help ourselves to a few out-of-state license plates and make our way back to Milwaukee. Staying at my apartment would make the most sense, but getting two gagged, blindfolded, and cuffed people inside without being noticed is an entirely different thing."

Anthony browsed campground locations on his phone. "I found a campground with openings about five miles east of the Dells. Apparently nobody actually works there. It's all done over their website, which is good for us. We pay online, and right at the gate we can scan the barcode they send to my phone. The payment confirmation tells us which campsites are ours."

"Can you see the available sites?"

"One second. I think there's a map. Okay, yeah, we can pick our choices and then see if they confirm the ones we want."

Carden clicked the blinker and moved to the far-right lane. He laid on the horn, and finally Antonio moved over too.

"I swear that brother of yours is in his own world. Okay, book two spots and choose the ones farthest away from anybody else. We don't need that pissed-off agent kicking the inside of the trunk and attracting attention."

"According to the map, you continue north on this road, and then a mile south of the Dells, you'll turn right on Bonners Road. It looks pretty secluded according to the satellite image. It's a two-lane road and pretty shaded. That will take us to the campground."

"What's it called?"

"Stone River Campground. Should I call Antonio and tell him to get behind us?"

"Yeah, but first reserve the spaces." Carden looked in the rearview mirror at the blindfolded Julie in the far back of the van. "You did jam the plugs in her ears, didn't you?"

"Yeah, boss, it's all good."

Chapter 49

Val pulled a pine needle out of her hair as we made our way to the charred ruins of the cabin. "Now what, sir?" she asked. "They set the place up in flames just like they did to the warehouse and, once again, are in the wind."

"Let's see what's going on at the garage."

Rosie waved us toward her. "Agents, we had to open the side door of the garage with the battering ram. It was a steel door that melted against the framework, but go ahead and take a look for yourself. It's wet, stinky, and smoldering inside but empty."

We didn't have to step in. Peeking through the opening where the door once stood confirmed it was an empty garage. I sucked in a deep breath of rancid, smoky air and instantly coughed it out.

Spelling tipped his head toward a clearing. "Let's talk over here out of the smoke. We came here in hopes of rescuing J.T. and Julie. The suspects were one step ahead of us and, from the looks of it, well prepared. I think the best thing to do right now is fly back to Milwaukee. If this armored vehicle robbery is actually going to take place tomorrow, we need to alert Rosemond Diamonds, get all the facts, the name of the transport company, and the time and route they're taking to Brookfield. I'm sure the suspects know everything already, and I'm beginning to wonder how they acquired that information."

I crossed my arms and gave that some thought. "Inside job, maybe?"

"Possibly, but from the jewelry store itself or the transport company? Either way, this may be our last chance to save J.T. and take down those criminals. From the devastation that went down today"—Spelling stared into the woods—"nothing is going to stop them except a kill shot. At least this time we'll be one step ahead of them."

"Agents?"

We turned and saw the captain heading our way. He stuck out his hand and introduced himself as Al Fredrick, Portage County fire captain.

"I wanted to make all of you aware that we did do an initial sweep of the dwelling. It's a total loss and completely vacant—no humans, dead or alive. No one was in the residence at the time the home went up in flames, other than the person who started the fire, and they left unharmed. The investigator will be out here tomorrow to go over the dwelling and to file his initial report. Will you be staying in Portage?"

Spelling responded. "We're heading back to Milwaukee, Captain Fredrick. We had hoped to find our missing agent and his sister here, but as you said, the dwelling was empty.

We're sorry for the loss your county has suffered today." Spelling handed him his card. "If you wouldn't mind having the investigator send me a copy of his findings, I'd really appreciate it."

"Sure thing, sir." He shook our hands before returning to his duties. "Have a safe trip to Milwaukee."

We walked the fire lane back to the vehicles. Dave was sound asleep in the driver's seat of the first SUV. He woke with a start as Spelling opened the passenger door and climbed in. Bill got into the backseat with me, and Maria followed Cam and Val to the second SUV.

Spelling tapped Dave's shoulder. "We're ready to head back to the airport, Dave."

"You got it, sir." Dave rubbed his eyes, rolled the kinks out of his neck, and turned the key in the ignition.

"Can you call the airport and make sure the chopper is ready for us? We'll be leaving for Milwaukee immediately."

"Not a problem, Agent Spelling. I'll take care of that right now."

"Sir?"

Spelling looked over his shoulder at Bill. "Agent Lewis?"

"We need to contact the store in Milwaukee and tell them to expect us."

I knew Bill couldn't say much in front of a civilian, but we understood what he meant. Rosemond Diamonds needed to be told immediately what was in the works and what we planned to do about it. We needed a sit-down with the people in charge, and it had to be done that night.

"Make the call as soon as we get to the airport, Bill. Speak with the owner, identify yourself, and tell them"—Spelling glanced at his watch—"to expect our team at their downtown location at six o'clock. I want all of the people in charge present, including the transport company manager and the drivers who are scheduled to run that errand tomorrow." Spelling gave Bill a nod of understanding. They had to speak in vague terms in front of Dave.

Twenty minutes later, we were seat belted in the chopper and on our way back to Milwaukee. Bill had already made the arrangements over the phone with Rosemond Diamonds. They said they would organize everything necessary on their end, and the people involved in the transport would be present for the meeting too.

The helicopter landed in front of the FBI's Milwaukee hangar at 5:22 p.m. Our vehicles sat on the west side of the building, right where we left them almost five hours earlier.

We climbed into the cruisers and headed for the downtown jewelry store with time to spare. I was thankful for the few extra minutes since we were smack in the middle of rush hour traffic. I sat in the passenger seat and checked messages while Spelling drove.

"Hmm… Joe sent me a document attached to an email."

Spelling's forehead furrowed. "See what it says."

I tapped on the attachment and saw a copy of some adoption papers. I had totally forgotten about where I was going with that potential lead as soon as we left for Portage. "Wow, it looks like somebody from the tech department was able to finagle the adoption records for Sam Dunbar."

"Maybe the documents weren't sealed anymore because

he was an adult and now deceased. What was his birth parents' last name?"

"Would you believe Vetcher, as in the large *V* centered over the entwined links on the back of his hand? He was named Orly James Vetcher according to the original birth certificate, and there isn't a father listed. The address for the mother was a street in Soddy-Daisy, Tennessee. What kind of name is that? It can't be too far from Chattanooga since that's the hospital on record. According to the birth certificate, he would have been thirty-five years old when he died."

Spelling clicked his blinker to merge onto the freeway. "That information doesn't match what his death certificate showed. According to that, he was thirty-nine when he died. Chances are, his adoption may have been under the table, or a little shady at best."

"Have you ever heard of that last name, sir?"

"Vetcher, as in a criminal I'm familiar with?"

I nodded.

"Nobody comes to mind." Spelling scratched his chin and pulled into the center lane. "A single mother in a small Tennessee town that probably couldn't afford to raise that child could have had several babies that she gave up, or I hate to say it, possibly sold. There could be other criminals out there who once had the last name of Vetcher."

"Agreed, but all I know is somebody was linked to Sam Dunbar, and he goes by C.V. Loomis. I'd bet my career that the *V* stands for Vetcher." I glanced through my side mirror and saw our second cruiser right behind us. We'd be at

Rosemond Diamonds in less than ten minutes. I knew the night would be a long one of planning how we'd foil the robbery attempt of the armored truck tomorrow.

Spelling slipped into a parallel parking space a block from the store. Cam pulled in directly behind him. I opened my purse and dug out my FBI credit card. Val did the same for their numbered parking space, and we both paid parking fees that would cover us until midnight.

Bill pulled out his phone and called the jewelry store as we walked. "Mr. Rosemond, this is Agent Bill Lewis from the FBI. We've parked and are heading to your building. Our team will be there in a few minutes." He clicked off the call. "We're good to go. It sounds like everyone who needs to be part of this is there."

The jewelry store had been a Wisconsin Avenue landmark for thirty years. Although the interior of the building was beautiful, the rent had increased tenfold over time, and that intersection of Plankinton and Wisconsin had fallen into disrepair. Most of the retailers couldn't keep up with the exorbitant rent or the maintenance on the buildings.

After being buzzed through the revolving security door, we entered the store single file. Most of the glass display cases had already been emptied of their treasures and were being loaded into a semi in the alley behind the building. Mr. Rosemond ushered us in and led us to a well-appointed office at the back of the store. Once inside, we were introduced to his business partners as well as the district manager and drivers of the armored transport company that had been hired to make the move tomorrow. We took seats around a large walnut-and-chrome conference table.

Mr. Rosemond began with the most obvious question—why did we assume a robbery of the truck was planned at all? Spelling went on to explain our lengthy but guarded bit of intelligence that led us to that conclusion.

"We knew of a previous armored truck heist that netted the criminals a large sum of money, nearly a million dollars to be precise. The main player in that robbery was shot and killed several months later by the very FBI agent who was just kidnapped. There once was a very close connection between the robber in the first heist and the person who kidnapped our agent, but we haven't figured out what that connection is yet. The location of this jewelry store on Wisconsin Avenue and the new store in Brookfield was found in a stolen car among the kidnapper's notes."

Bill Lewis picked up where Spelling left off. "Two of our top agents were part of the FBI's Violent Crimes Division in 2014 when that armored truck robbery took place. One of them was my current partner until this kidnapper murdered him several nights ago."

The room fell silent, and people brushed away invisible bits of dust from the table. Their expressions told me their hearts were heavy for our loss.

"This kidnapper has been silent for nearly three years until now, so it begs the question—what is the common thread? We believe he's surfaced because he's learned of another armored truck transport worth millions of dollars that is scheduled to take place tomorrow. The fact that the agent he just kidnapped was the one who shot and killed the robber in 2014 is more than a coincidence." Bill poured himself a glass of water and placed the pitcher back on the table. He took a sip before continuing. "Because this unidentified man had a close relationship of some kind to the robber who was killed by our agent, we feel this is a crime of greed, opportunity, and revenge. The kidnapper not only killed one of our agents and kidnapped another, but he also kidnapped our agent's sister. We can only assume she was taken to be used as leverage so our agent will assist them in this heist."

The manager of Trident Armored Transport, John Bentley, spoke up. "If they pull this robbery off, we'll lose our franchise. We won't be able to afford the insurance coverage anymore."

"We feel the same way, agents," Mr. Rosemond said. "We've put a ton of money into this new store. We need our inventory. Why can't we just do the move tonight when the crooks aren't expecting it?"

Murmurs began among the people around the table. They were all in agreement that it would make the most sense to transport the diamonds that night. It would be the smartest time to make the move.

"We understand your logic," Spelling said, "but doing that guarantees the deaths of our agent and his sister. We'll never see them again and will likely never find their remains, either. These men are vicious, cunning, and deadly. Earlier today they massacred three deputies and the Portage County sheriff."

Gasps sounded among the group.

John spoke up. "I'm sorry, but I won't expose my drivers to that kind of risk, Agent Spelling. I'd never forgive myself if something happened to these good men."

"We understand, and we have an alternative plan. What we need right now is all of the information you can give us about the time, route, and security measures you have in place for the diamond transport." Spelling's phone rang. "Take five minutes, everyone. I have to get this call."

Chapter 50

They sat in the vehicles in the most secluded campsites of Stone River Campground. The van and Julie's car were backed against a grove of trees. The campground map showed those spots as some of the best for privacy and beauty, usually chosen as the perfect location to set up a campsite, although farthest from the campground amenities. The men didn't care about that. They weren't planning to stick around once the sun dipped beneath the horizon. They chose those spots because they were the farthest away from other people. Behind that grove of trees was a rushing river, great for muffling the sounds of the agent in the trunk. They'd wait it out until dark then head back to Milwaukee on quiet country roads.

Carden, Anthony, and Antonio huddled in the van and reviewed the armored truck's route map for the umpteenth time.

"What time are you picking up the U-Haul?" Carden asked, testing Anthony.

"At ten o'clock, boss. It's already reserved and paid for,

you're dropping me off, and I go inside and get the keys. I drive to that turnout and wait for your instructions."

"Good, very good. Hold on. That isn't going to work. Shit!"

Antonio ripped apart a piece of beef jerky and popped half of it into his mouth. "What's wrong, Mr. Vetcher?"

"We have to change the plans a bit." He turned toward Anthony. "I'll drop you off at the U-Haul place, and then we'll wait for you at the turnout. When you get there, we'll transfer Julie to the trunk of her car, and J.T. will be tied up to the cube van. I'll drive the car back a few miles and watch for the armored truck. J.T. has to be ready to go when I tell you the vehicle is a mile out. His mouth will already be taped closed. We'll have on our Kevlar vests and masks. He only gets a mask. We'll toss him out first with an empty AK-47. Whoever isn't knocked senseless when you smash the cube van into the armored truck will naturally shoot at J.T. That's when we'll kill everyone, grab the diamonds, and disappear in the car. We'll ditch it when we're safely out of the area and catch a ride on the Freeway Flyer to Chicago." Carden watched as two RVs pulled in and turned right at the first fork in the road. He rubbed his forehead and let out an audible breath before continuing. "We'll lay low for a while, then you boys can figure out something with your family. I'll head for parts unknown with a lot of diamonds to fence."

Antonio swallowed the jerky with a hard gulp. "What about the sister?"

"Collateral damage. She gets a bullet to the head, and

we'll toss her in the brush. The agent gets what's coming to him for killing Sam." Carden grinned widely. "Poetic justice, you know. The Fed shot my brother, the guards are going to shoot him, and I'll have the pleasure of killing his sister."

Anthony smiled at Antonio then at Carden. He rubbed his hands together briskly. "I can't wait until tomorrow, boss. Everything is going to go exactly how we've planned, and we'll all be rich."

Carden's enthusiasm was evident. "I'm counting on that along with some much overdue revenge."

Chapter 51

We waited for SSA Hopkins to arrive after his phone call to Spelling. He had just gotten back to Milwaukee after delivering the bad news of Curt's death to his mother in Waukegan. Hopkins told Spelling he was on his way and would join our meeting at Rosemond Diamonds in ten minutes.

Fifteen minutes later, John Bentley leaned over the large map that was rolled out across the conference table. Coffee cups held the corners down. Hopkins had just taken his seat, and we were about to begin the meeting.

"Everyone ready?" John asked.

Our nods confirmed that we were.

He pointed at the route he had planned for his driver to take from Milwaukee to Brookfield. "I may have to reconsider the back way I had originally planned and have the guys take the freeway instead. I wanted them to stay under the radar by driving the country roads, but in hindsight, that could be setting ourselves up for disaster. The freeway is the only route I'll have my guys take if we go through with this move. I doubt if anyone would try to take down a Trident Armored Transport truck on a busy freeway while driving seventy miles an hour."

When John finished voicing his idea, I spoke up. "How did these criminals know when your company was doing the move and the route you planned to take?"

Mr. Rosemond raised a brow and looked from face to face as he tapped a pen on the table. "Good question. I'd like to know that myself."

First, the color drained out of John's face, then it went bright red. "Are you people insinuating that this is an inside job? My company has been in business without a single mark against us for nearly thirty years."

"Sir," I said, "nobody is accusing you personally. How many employees does your company have on staff?"

"Trident is a nationwide company located in seven major cities. I don't know how many people are employed overall. Transfers happen, and people get hired and fired. The number of employees changes all the time."

"How many people are staffed in Milwaukee?" Spelling asked.

John pounded the table with his closed fist. "I resent this type of questioning. Maybe there's somebody employed at the jewelry store who needs a raise and this is how they plan to get it. Why aren't you grilling them?"

Mr. Rosemond stood. "We're a family-owned company, John, located in one town, at the same storefront all along. We too have been in business for thirty years."

"And every employee is a family member?" John asked,

appearing to grow angrier by the second.

SSA Hopkins spoke up. "Okay, guys, this bickering is getting us nowhere. Somebody, somehow, has a connection with these criminals. I realize there was a press release on the opening of the new store, but the transport date, time, and route was never shared publicly. We can figure out the connection later, but right now we all need to work together."

Spelling walked around the table to the whiteboard perched on an easel in the corner of the office. He picked up the red dry-erase marker and held it against the board. He started by drawing a number one. "We're going to need the time this is supposed to go down tomorrow and exactly what the driver and guards normally do during a pickup and delivery." He paused as if he had something else on his mind. "But before I get ahead of myself, let's take a minute and review that map again." With the red marker in hand, Spelling drew a line along the designated route then set the marker down. He studied the map.

"What are you thinking, boss?" I asked.

"We need a street view of the most secluded part of this route. I want a group consensus on the most likely area for an ambush to take place, and why. Let's go."

Mr. Rosemond said he was going to get his laptop computer and stepped away.

John huffed his anxiety and stood. "Like I said, Agent Spelling, I'm not subjecting my driver and guards to a planned attack on their lives. This is a waste of time, and the transport isn't worth the danger. Rosemond Diamonds can find somebody else to do the move. My men aren't going in like sheep to the slaughterhouse. I'm calling it off."

"No you aren't, now sit down. We're going to review the most vulnerable spots along the route first, then you're going to explain to us everything that's involved in a transport, the normal precautions taken, and what your men do in a worst-case-scenario situation. I'm sure all of your drivers and guards had that type of training before they were hired, didn't they?"

"Well, yes, but I'm standing firm on this."

"Don't worry, John. Your men will be fine because they aren't transporting anything in that truck. My team and I are taking over. Our agent and his sister's lives are at risk, and I intend to bring them home safely. We'll be making the transport in an empty truck." Spelling turned to address Mr. Rosemond, who sat down with his laptop in hand. "Tomorrow is about apprehending those criminals and rescuing J.T. and his sister. Your diamonds, Mr. Rosemond, can be delivered a different way, and I have the perfect idea."

"But—"

Spelling shot him a stern look. "But what? Do you want all of your inventory stolen, possible deaths on your hands, and a lot of exposure, or would you rather have your diamonds moved quietly without any press?"

Mr. Rosemond hung his head. "You're right, Agent Spelling. Go ahead and take over. I'll do whatever you suggest. The Google street view is ready whenever you are."

Chapter 52

"It's almost dark, Mr. Vetcher. Should we head out?" Anthony stared at the evening sky. A crescent moon and a few twinkling stars had taken over for the setting sun.

Carden opened the driver's side door. "I have to make a phone call first. Be ready to leave in ten minutes no matter what. We'll get to Milwaukee by nine o'clock, eat something, and firm up the plans. Tomorrow we have to be on top of our game." He climbed out of the van and walked down the path. Carden scrolled through his contact list until he found the number he needed. He pressed the call button and waited while the phone rang.

"Hello."

"It's me, and we're in a jam. We need a place to sleep tonight."

"You can't go to your apartment?"

"Not with two extra guests who are bound, blindfolded, and gagged. They would be hard to explain to the neighbors." Noticing a camper and his dog heading their way, Carden turned down a different trail.

"Are they going to pose a problem for me?"

"I guarantee you they won't. My go-to guys, Anthony and Antonio Pirelli, are with me. They'll make sure the guests remain quiet."

The man chuckled on the other end of the phone line. "How many vehicles do you have?"

"Two—a van and a small car."

"Okay, I'll move my cars out to the driveway. Both vehicles need to go in the garage. When should I expect you?"

"We'll be there at nine o'clock. Oh, and can you order four large pepperoni pizzas and two loaves of garlic bread for delivery? I'll pay you when we get there. Beer sounds good too."

"Everything will be ready when you arrive."

"Thanks, dude, and remember, tomorrow you'll be a rich man."

"Good, because I'm counting on it. I've put my freedom on the line for this payday."

"Not a problem, and nobody can connect you to us, anyway. Your hands are clean. Hell, you can even keep that shitty job at Trident Armored Transport if you want. You'll just be thirty thousand dollars richer, that's all." Carden ended the call and pocketed his phone. He took the path back to the van and climbed in behind the wheel. "Anthony, you can drive the car back to Milwaukee. Stay close behind me. We aren't going to the apartment, we're going to my old buddy Zack Kenny's house instead." Carden pulled out his phone again and clicked on Google

Maps. He needed a good way to get there that didn't involve interstates or well-traveled freeways. "Okay, it looks like we're taking Highway 16 until it trails off, and then we'll veer south. If I can find a less-used alternate route, I'll take it. I don't need you getting lost."

Anthony opened the passenger door and got out. "I'll be right behind you, boss."

Carden watched over his shoulder as Anthony got into the driver's seat of the Fiesta. He chuckled at the sight then turned to Antonio. "That can't be comfortable. Weren't your knees hitting the steering wheel?"

"Yeah, they were, and the seat was pushed back as far as it goes."

Carden turned the key in the ignition and clicked on the fog lamps. He creeped along the gravel path and took his time as he made his way to the campground exit. He didn't want to attract unnecessary attention to the vehicles. When he reached the blacktop, he turned southeast toward Milwaukee and clicked on the headlights. If everything went according to plan, they'd arrive at Zack's house in ninety minutes.

"How much did you say the haul is worth, boss?" Antonio asked as he reclined the seat and got comfortable. He turned toward Carden with a wide smile then popped a handful of sunflower seeds in his mouth.

Carden did a double take. "Where'd you get those?"

"They've been in my pocket for a while."

"Do you ever stop eating?"

"Not when you're my size. I need a lot of food to look this good."

Carden shrugged and continued talking. "I'm estimating there to be at least three million dollars' worth of stones. When I browsed Rosemond's store last month, they had quite the inventory building up. I imagine their intention was to fill every display case in their new digs. From the looks of it, that new building in Brookfield is twice the size of the downtown location." Carden pointed his thumb over his shoulder.

Antonio looked back and shook his head. "She's either sleeping or faking it, but no matter what, she can't hear us with those earplugs jammed deep in her ears."

Carden raised the volume on the radio and opened his window several inches. "Fencing the diamonds is going to reduce that number somewhat, but we're going our separate ways after the hit. I'm getting rid of my take little by little so it doesn't raise suspicion. Zack got his ten grand advance, and now we just owe him twenty more. After that, we'll still net over half a million dollars each."

Antonio jerked his head then opened the window and looked back. "What's he doing?"

Carden peered out his side mirror and saw the headlights behind them flash on and off. "Son of a bitch, now what?" He clicked his blinker and turned down a secluded country road. He drove another mile before stopping.

Anthony pulled to the gravel shoulder ahead of him, backed up to the van's front bumper, and killed the engine. He climbed out and walked back to the van.

Carden lowered the window even farther and stuck out his head. "What's the problem?"

"I'm sick of this asshole kicking the hell out of the trunk, and I don't fit in that vehicle. I feel like I'm driving a bumper car."

Carden got out of the van and slammed the door so hard the window rattled. "Fine, I'll take over, but first shut him up."

"Gladly." Anthony returned to the car, reached under the dash, and popped the trunk.

"Don't overdo it, either. We need him tomorrow." Carden climbed into the driver's seat of the Fiesta and felt the car bounce several times. Muffled grunts and thuds sounded from the trunk area for a few seconds, then everything fell silent.

Anthony approached the driver's side window. He rubbed his knuckles and grinned. "It's all good, sir. I think he'll be napping for a while."

Carden jerked his head toward the van. "No more stops. Follow me and don't lag behind. If you need to say something, use your phone, not your headlights."

"Got it."

Carden watched through the rearview mirror as Anthony walked to the van and climbed in behind the wheel. Satisfied for now, Carden started the car and checked the mirror one more time. The van's headlights went on, and Anthony backed up. Gravel crunched under the Fiesta's tires as Carden pulled out, turned around, and took to the road again. He adjusted the seat forward, tapped the radio buttons until he found a smooth jazz station, and continued the drive to Milwaukee for the next hour without interruption. He picked up his phone at 8:55 p.m. and thumbed the screen to his contact list. He tapped Zack's name.

"We'll be there in ten minutes. I had an unexpected disturbance to take care of earlier."

"Not a problem. The garage door is open, so pull both vehicles inside. Close it behind you and come in through the mudroom. The pizzas are on the table."

Chapter 53

"Where should we put them?" Carden asked as he pulled the handle and lowered the overhead.

Zack swiped the air as if to brush the comment away. He leaned against the mudroom's doorframe, raised his brow, and stared at the trunk of the car. "You had to listen to that all the way here?"

Anthony chuckled. "Not all the way. I helped the agent with a much-needed nap about an hour back."

Zack glanced at Carden and winked. "I take it that was the disturbance you mentioned?" He opened the van door and peeked in. "What about her?"

"She isn't half as bad as her brother," Antonio said. "We'll keep them under control. Don't worry."

"Good, then let's go inside. We'll deal with them later." Zack held the door open, and the three men entered the house ahead of him. "Sit down and take a load off. We'll eat, and then you can tell me how tomorrow is going to play out. Anthony and Antonio can escort the guests to the basement after dinner. I'm sure they can find something useful downstairs to act as restraints."

Carden tipped his head toward the table. "Have a seat, boys. It looks like there's plenty of food for all of us." He pulled out four twenty-dollar bills and handed them to Zack. "Appreciate your help, man."

Zack opened the cardboard boxes and passed a plate to each man. Steam wafted from the pizzas. "Help yourselves while they're hot. There's plenty of beer in the fridge too."

Anthony crossed the room and opened the refrigerator. He pulled out a six-pack by its plastic sleeve, set it on the table, and returned to his seat.

Zack dropped a slice of pizza onto his plate. He pulled off a round of pepperoni and popped it into his mouth. "So how do you intend to breach the truck?"

"We have semi and fully automatic assault rifles. If the guns and our threats don't do the trick, we'll use the magnetic IED. That'll bust open the back door without any problem. I doubt if anyone inside will live through it, though." Carden bit into a piece of pizza and burned the roof of his mouth. "Son of a bitch, that's hot." With a snap, he popped the beer tab, gulped a mouthful, and swished it around before swallowing. "Damn cheese. Anyway, we're better prepared than we were in 2014, and we got away with it then. This should be a piece of cake, and having the agent as a decoy will help too. Let's take a look at that basement. I'd still like to get a good night's sleep once we have them squared away."

"Sure thing. I forgot, you haven't been to this house yet. Right this way." Zack pushed back his chair and rose from the table. He munched on a piece of garlic bread as the three men followed at his back.

The lower level of the rented house had been used as office space at one time. Two rooms separated by dated paneling filled the left half of the basement. One large room, devoid of anything except the cement floor and the beams holding up the first story, filled the right side.

"This is perfect. The sister can go in the first room, and Mr. Macho can be chained to the beam farthest away from her in that wide-open space. Let's bring them down," Carden said.

Zack cracked his knuckles then grasped the handrail as he climbed the stairs. "He's blindfolded too, right?"

"Absolutely. He doesn't need to see either of our faces. Boys, bring the sister in first. We'll give her some garlic bread, she can use the facilities, and then she's going downstairs. J.T. will be a problem, as usual. He may have to get knocked out again to keep the transition to the basement easier."

Julie's muffled cries got louder as they led her through the door and into the house.

"Keep it down unless you want a broken jaw like your brother. That makes eating far more difficult." Antonio pressed his mouth against her plugged ear. "Hold out your hand. I'm going to give you a piece of garlic bread to eat."

She stuck out her bound, shaking hands. Antonio wedged a piece of bread between her palms then ripped the duct tape off her mouth. She winced and moaned as blood droplets formed on her lower lip.

"Suck it up and eat that bread." Antonio pushed her down on a wooden kitchen chair and leaned against the table as he waited for her to finish it. "Okay, let's go." He took two steps, slipped his hand under her armpit, and pulled her off the chair. "The bathroom is over here. You get three minutes, then I'm coming in after you." He entered the room, lifted the toilet lid, and walked her to it. "I'll be right outside, and don't even think of pulling that blindfold off." He left the bathroom and closed the door behind him.

"How's it going?" Carden asked. He threw the smashed beer can into the recycling bin and took a seat on a chair in the living room.

"She'll be done in a minute, sir, and then we'll get her secured downstairs." Antonio studied his fists. "J.T. might have to get a knuckle sandwich, though."

"Do whatever you need to do to get him in the basement with as little drama as possible. I'm growing tired of his resistance."

Antonio banged on the bathroom door. "I'm coming in." He turned the knob and pushed, then he looked at Anthony and laughed. "The bitch locked the door." Antonio shouldered the door with a hard thrust and snapped it off the hinges. "What the hell did you think that was going to accomplish?" He grabbed Julie by the hair and yanked her to the basement stairs. She screamed with each downward step. Once she was tied to a beam in the first room, Antonio stretched a fresh length of duct tape across her mouth and tightened the blindfold. "Enjoy your last night alive, Julie." He jammed the earplugs deeper in her ears then closed the door and returned to the living room. "Let's get the agent, brother. I'm on a roll." He stared at his large, somewhat unscathed hands. "Guess it's time to scrape up these knuckles." Antonio led the way out to the garage. With the driver's side door open and his hand on the trunk lever, Antonio gave Anthony a quick glance. "Got the gun?"

"I've got it."

"Okay, I'm opening it, but he's not going to come out willingly." Antonio jerked his head toward a baseball bat that leaned against the wall. "That should convince him to behave. Grab it."

With the bat in hand, Anthony gave his brother a nod. "Pop the trunk."

Chapter 54

Spelling checked the time on the analog clock above the office door. It read eleven thirty.

"Does anyone have questions before we call it a night?" He looked from one tired face to the next. "We all know the plan and the areas on the route where we need to be on high alert?"

My colleagues and I nodded that we understood.

Mr. Rosemond seemed to want reaffirmation of his own. "So the safest time to move the diamonds is tomorrow when the fake transport is scheduled to take place?"

"That's correct, sir. The criminals will be too busy watching us to even think a bait-and-switch has happened. You'll have the moving service show up and load the truck, and then the Trident driver and guards will take over. Everyone wins. The downtown police department will escort you to the city limits, and the sheriff's department will take it from there. They'll follow a few car lengths behind on the freeway, then the Brookfield Police Department will take over on the surface streets and escort you to the back of the store, where the truck will be unloaded. You'll never see the criminals, and they'll have no idea what's really taking place. We're going to accomplish two goals at the same time. We'll be the decoy while the actual transport is under way. Tomorrow, we're taking down the bad guys once and for all. We'll get them off the street, rescue our agent and his sister, and you'll have your inventory delivered safely."

John Bentley stood. "I hope there are no hard feelings, Andrew. We'll still make the delivery like we agreed on, just not in our own truck and not by risking my employees' lives. Under the circumstances—"

Mr. Rosemond interrupted with a nod. "I understand. Just find out who leaked the transport details and turn them in. The police can decide what to do with that person."

"Okay, agents, we're meeting at the downtown headquarters at eight a.m. We'll review everything one more time in-house, and then we'll gather here at ten o'clock and wait for the Trident armored truck to arrive. That's when we're going to change into their uniforms and take over the show. We know the areas on the route where we need to be on our highest alert. Everyone will be wearing their vests, we'll have radio contact at all times, and backup will be dispatched if needed." Spelling cracked his knuckles before addressing the store owner. "Just one more thing before we call it a night. Mr. Rosemond, make sure your transport truck doesn't arrive until we've left the store. I'd say once we pull out with the Trident armored truck, have the moving truck come in ten minutes later, load up your inventory, and let the Trident driver and guards take over. Okay, people, go home, get some rest, and I'll see you in the morning."

Back at the FBI parking garage, I parted ways with the other agents. The drive home to North Bend was long and lonely, and my mind was filled with what-ifs. I thought about J.T. and Julie as I drove. A million silent prayers passed between my lips for a positive outcome tomorrow. I knew what bad timing, bad luck, and bad results were all about and had experienced enough of them to last a lifetime. I wanted tomorrow to be a good day—I prayed for it—and whether he knew it or not, J.T.'s life depended on it.

If I was lucky I'd get five hours of sleep at most, but it was more than I'd had at any one time in the last few days. I pulled into my garage just before midnight. The thought of sleeping on the sofa in our agents' lounge had crossed my mind, but my need for a shower, a comfortable bed, a clothing change, and a decent breakfast won out in the end. I quietly tiptoed into the house and down the hallway to my bedroom. As I passed Amber's room, I heard the TV playing but knew that at that hour, she likely had the alarm set and was sound asleep. I peeked under the birdcage cover and smiled at Porky and Polly. They too, side by side on the perch, were fast asleep. I slipped on my pajamas, brushed my teeth, and fell into bed. Morning, and hopefully a successful rescue and apprehension, would come soon enough.

I didn't remember anything beyond my head hitting the

pillow last night, but at six o'clock, my phone alarm buzzed obnoxiously on the nightstand. The delicious scent of coffee wafted down the hallway and was enough to coax me out of bed. Amber was apparently up and likely making breakfast. I was sure my purse hanging over the back of the barstool had told her I was home. I slipped on my bathrobe and headed toward the kitchen.

"Hey, big sis. It's nice to see you again." Amber poured coffee into two waiting cups and placed them on the breakfast bar then embraced me with a tight squeeze. "We've missed you."

"You and the menagerie?" I covered my yawn with my fist. "Today is going to be intense." I sat at the bar and sipped my coffee.

"I hope you got enough sleep." Amber rested her hand on my shoulder. "Do you think it's going to turn out okay?"

I shrugged. "We've gone over our procedure a dozen times. We know the likely area they'll strike within a couple of miles. All we can do is be prepared for the worst and hope for the best."

"How do you think J.T. and Julie come into play?"

I shook my head and watched as Amber got up and pulled two bowls out of the cupboard.

"Is this okay?" She turned toward me and held up a package of apple cinnamon instant oatmeal.

"It's fine. My stomach is doing flip-flops, anyway. We don't know exactly how anything is going down. All we know is that they kidnapped J.T. and Curt, and both of them were involved in the takedown of the bank robbers in

2014. J.T. was the one who happened to shoot Sam Dunbar, though. Once they realized that, they killed Curt."

"Why not just let him go?" Amber got up and pulled the bowls out of the microwave.

"You know they couldn't do that—no witnesses left behind. That's why we need to be one step ahead of them. I'm guessing this heist is about financial reward and revenge. We already know there's a connection between Sam Dunbar and the guy who's calling the shots. Those notecards placed on Julie's lap in the video they sent us confirm that. The whole 'eye for an eye' and 'family is everything' rant leads us to believe that."

"You mean like a blood relative?"

"It has to be. The last name Vetcher came up as Sam Dunbar's surname at birth. He was given up for adoption as a baby, which makes tracking down family members even more difficult. The man running the show goes by C.V. Loomis. The *V* probably stands for Vetcher, and don't you think the Loomis and Dunbar names are a mockery of the armored car companies?"

"Absolutely. So why can't you guys just stake out the transport company and arrest the kidnappers when they show up?"

"That's the problem." I thanked Amber for the bowl of oatmeal she placed in front of me. "We think they'll blitz attack the truck during the drive. We don't know if J.T. and Julie will be with them or not. If we swoop in prematurely, we may be putting them in even more danger. We're going to turn the tables and be ready and waiting for the ambush.

Right now, in their opinion, J.T. is the pawn and Julie is the leverage, but we're about to change that."

Amber gave me a concerned stare. "This really worries me, Jade."

"Honey, I've been involved in plenty of bad situations. There are two people's lives at risk, and one of them happens to be my partner. We have to get them out safely."

I finished my breakfast, gave Amber a tight squeeze and a kiss on the cheek, then headed out. Today, the nightmare would end, one way or another.

Chapter 55

"Wake up, Fed, it's time to go." The hard kick to J.T.'s leg stirred him back into consciousness.

He winced as he grabbed his shin. "What good am I going to be to you? You guys did a number on me."

"Were we too rough on you last night, Agent Harper? I thought you were tougher than that. Julie doesn't even piss and moan as much as you do." Anthony laughed as J.T. tried to swat at him and missed. "Yeah, I guess Antonio's knuckles were sort of banged up now that I think of it. Anyway, it's all superficial wounds. We didn't break any bones. Now, roll over and lock your hands so I can cuff you."

The sound of heavy footsteps descending the stairs alerted them that Antonio was heading down. "Ready to bring him up?"

"Yeah, in a minute. I've got to cuff his hands together first. Is the girl in the van?"

"Yep, she's good to go." Antonio looked down at J.T. and chuckled. "Damn, your face looks like shit. Can you even see out of your right eye?"

"Go to hell, moron."

"Soon enough, but right now we have a job to do. It looks like you'll be taking one for the team, so to speak."

Carden yelled down the stairs, "Enough chitchat. Let's go."

Anthony gave Antonio a nod. "He's set. Go ahead and unlock the chain." Anthony yanked J.T. up, but his legs folded beneath him. "Stand up. There's nothing wrong with your legs, and we don't have time for your crap. Pull yourself together or Julie dies."

J.T. leaned against the beam and stood. "Give me a second to get my bearings."

"We're leaving now. You can get your bearings in the trunk."

With a brother on each side of him, J.T. was pushed up the stairs and out to Julie's car.

Carden stood in the shadows of the covered porch and watched as the brothers loaded J.T. into the trunk. Once the lid was closed, he walked out to the driveway. "Son of a bitch, Antonio, his face looks like hamburger."

"He'll be fine, sir. He's just putting on a show. He may have a few bruises and scuffs, but there isn't anything seriously wrong with him. He'll be wearing a mask, anyway."

Carden sneered. "He better be able to walk under his own power when this ambush takes place."

"He will or Julie dies. I made sure he knew that."

"Get in the car and go to the turnout. Wait there while I drop off Anthony at the U-Haul facility. We'll catch up with you fifteen minutes later and transfer J.T. and our weapons to the cube van and Julie into the trunk. Do you understand?"

"Yes, boss, I understand."

"Good. This better go exactly like I had planned. Now move!"

Carden climbed into the driver's seat of the van. Anthony took his seat on the passenger side, and Antonio drove away in the Fiesta.

"Your brother is going to be the death of me, Anthony."

"Boss, you shouldn't say that. You might jinx yourself."

Carden heaved a deep sigh while he drove the back roads to the U-Haul location. "I can't wait until this day is done. I'm leaving town as soon as possible."

At 9:55 a.m., Anthony stepped out of the van at the U-Haul building. "I should be at the turnout soon, boss."

"Good, but call me if anything goes to shit."

Anthony gave the windowsill of the passenger side a slap as confirmation before he walked away. "I will, I promise."

Carden turned left at the end of the parking lot and arrived at the designated spot seven minutes later. He backed into the weeded pea gravel turnout that occupied a space once used as a small parking lot. Ten years earlier, that spot led into a nature preserve filled with trails, bridges, and ponds. Now, all that remained was gravel hidden beneath weeds and brush. The trails had been overgrown and abandoned for years. Most motorists would drive by and never notice its existence. The van and car were well hidden from anyone passing by—the perfect place for an ambush.

Julie and J.T. were held captive, side by side, one bound in the trunk and the other restrained in the van. The blindfolds and earplugs kept them from knowing what was going on or where they were.

Carden lowered his window and motioned for Antonio to do the same. With the van backed in and the Fiesta facing forward, the driver's side windows were next to each other. "Any trouble or suspicious looking characters on your drive over here?"

"No, sir. The morning seemed as normal as any other."

"Good to know. Anthony should be here soon, then we'll swap out our guests." Carden's cell phone vibrated. He dipped his hand in his pocket and pulled it out. "It's Anthony." He apprehensively hit Talk. "What's wrong?"

"Nothing, boss, I just wanted to give you a heads-up. I'm coming around the last curve and will be there in under a minute."

"Okay, make sure you back in against the front of the car." Carden hung up and jerked his chin toward Antonio as he climbed out of the van. "Let's roll. It's time to move our guests."

Chapter 56

As we entered the diamond store, we heard voices echo down the hallway. Mr. Rosemond buzzed us through and ushered our group to the conference room, where ten anxious looking people sat around the table. John Bentley, his driver and guards, and the Rosemond family were all there. The armored truck we'd soon use as a decoy was in place behind the building and ready to be loaded with empty jewelry containers meant to fool the cast of criminals in case they were watching.

A half dozen guard uniforms, intended for our use, hung on the coatrack just inside the back door. For our plan to succeed, we needed to assume the places of the driver and guards who would have been in the Trident Armored Transport truck that morning.

"Good morning, everyone," Spelling said. He glanced at the clock before continuing. "We have forty minutes before we put everything in motion. As of now, the plans we discussed last night still stand. Our agents will change into the uniforms in a few minutes and load the back of the truck. We have no idea if the store is being watched or not, so we have to play this as if we were actually transporting millions of dollars' worth of diamonds."

SSA Hopkins picked up where Spelling left off. "Once our people leave the area in the truck, the Trident guards will load the real merchandise in the moving van and leave for the Brookfield store. Agent Spelling and I will follow from a distance, but rest assured, there will be some division of law enforcement present at all times, watching your vehicle. The transport will go smoothly, and the rest"—he scratched his chin—"we have no clue, but our people are well prepared for any scenario." He checked the time. "You're loading the truck and leaving in a half hour. Cam is the designated driver, and Jade will be the eyes and ears for all of you, so keep those radios on and clear of any chatter. Bill, Maria, and Val will be in the back, ready to act on command. We don't want anyone getting trigger happy, either. Remember, our mission is to bring J.T. and Julie home safely. The criminals are secondary to that. They'll be captured or killed, but either way, they'll be in custody when this ordeal is over." Hopkins gave us a nod of encouragement. "All right, agents, go ahead and change into those uniforms and make sure your vests are under the shirts and concealed. Let's get this show on the road."

Val, Maria, and I entered the ladies' room to change clothes.

"Are you nervous, Jade?" Maria asked.

"Of course I am, and I'd be lying if I said I wasn't. The truth is, I'm more worried about J.T. and Julie than I am about the rest of us. At least we're armed." I patted Maria's shoulder. "It'll be okay. It has to be. I have faith in our team."

Twenty minutes later and after loading forty empty containers, we were ready to head out. I shielded my eyes and panned the area from one end of the alley to the other. Everything appeared as normal and quiet as we would expect on a Saturday morning. The downtown area was always at its busiest on weekdays. Spelling and Hopkins gave us the thumbs-up and reminded me to update them every few miles, especially when we reached the target area.

"Will do, boss." I gave Cam a nod, and he climbed in behind the wheel. I grabbed the handle above the side mirror and pulled myself into the passenger seat. With a quick mic check to make sure the agents in the back could hear me, we were off and heading west.

"What's your gut telling you, Jade?" Cam gave me a look of concern as he drove out of the downtown area.

"I spent a good amount of time going over the 2014 armored truck robbery involving Sam Dunbar when I was trying to learn what the connection was between J.T., Curt, and their kidnapper. When we received that video of Julie holding the cards with the rants about family, and how blood is everything, I knew the Sam Dunbar case and this one had to be connected. That was especially true when we found out our mystery man went by the last name Loomis, as in Dunbar and Loomis."

"Yeah, those two were real comedians. They must have worked together on that first robbery."

"That's the part that doesn't make sense. The eyewitnesses said there were four men involved. Months later, three were arrested, and Sam was shot and killed while trying to escape."

Cam turned toward me and sighed. "By J.T."

"Yep, by J.T., and I'm afraid this heist is about revenge."

"And millions of dollars' worth of diamonds. So, do you think today will be a repeat of 2014?" Cam stopped at the red light and checked his mirrors.

"If the method worked in the past, why wouldn't it work again? You have to create a distraction to slow down or stop the truck altogether or somehow disable it. In the Dunbar case, they rammed the side of the armored truck with a large U-Haul cube van. The hit was hard enough to disable the truck and disorient the guards inside. They were sitting ducks. The scary part was, they did the hit in front of witnesses and still got away with it."

"Only temporarily."

"True, and they did pay the piper when it was all said and done. You know, that might have been an inside job too. I'm making a quick call to Joe."

Cam tapped the side of his head. "Think about it. It's Saturday, remember? Joe is at home, where normal people unwind from a grueling workweek. What were you going to ask him?"

"I need to know if any employee who works at Trident used to work at Branded Armor in 2014. Chances are, if there is a common person, they may be the insider. Who's working the tech department today?"

"I think Penny's in charge. Go ahead and make the call and I'll update Spelling."

I called Penny and gave her the bits and pieces of information I had. She said she'd let me know when, and if, she found a common thread.

Cam hung up right after I did.

I cracked open my bottle of water and took a sip. "Are they loaded up and on the road?"

"Yeah, Spelling said they're almost to the freeway entrance. No problems so far. Check out your mirror. How does it look on your side?"

"Everything is dead quiet—not a vehicle in sight."

Cam smirked. "Humph."

"What does that mean?"

"What you said sounds ominous. I'm sure a dead-quiet road was what those crooks were hoping for. We must be getting close. Keep your head on a swivel, and let the guys in the back know to be ready for anything."

Chapter 57

Carden watched as Antonio and Anthony pulled J.T. out of the trunk and walked him to the back of the cube van.

"Cuff him to the door latch for the time being. Get his mouth taped up good so there's no chance of him yelling out. Take his blindfold off and put the mask over his head after I have mine in place. He has no reason to see my face." Carden slipped on his mask, opened the back doors of the van, and untied Julie. With a hard yank of her hair, he jerked her out and led her to the car. "Move it!"

Her muffled scream as she was thrown into the trunk sent J.T. into a fit of rage. The cuffs dug into his wrists as he twisted and pulled while witnessing Julie's abuse.

"Aw, did that piss you off, Agent Harper?" Carden slammed the trunk lid and checked the time on his phone. "Okay, get a move on. They're going to be here in fifteen minutes. Anthony, get me one of the AK-47s. I need to go. Do not screw this up!" Carden secured his Kevlar vest and slung the rifle strap over his shoulder. He approached J.T. and stood within a foot of him. "Just so you know, Fed, you do one thing wrong and your sister will endure a slow, painful death. Do you understand? She dies inch by inch, minute by minute, but you—you'll get a bullet to the brain, just like Curt did." With a fast thrust of his fist, Carden delivered a hard gut punch and knocked the wind out of the agent.

J.T. groaned through the tape as he doubled over, his knees ready to buckle.

"I asked if you understood what I said."

J.T. nodded.

"Good." Carden turned toward the brothers with a stern warning. "I'll call you when they're two miles out. That's when you'll take off his cuffs and push him to the end of the turnout. When they're a mile away, you give the agent one of the assault rifles and position him in the middle of the road with the gun facing the oncoming transport truck. Anthony, you'll be behind the wheel and ready to T-bone them. Antonio, you'll be hiding in the brush with your AK pointed at J.T. the entire time. If he does anything off script, blow him away."

Antonio chuckled as he wiggled his hand. "My pleasure, boss, and this trigger finger is already feeling itchy."

Carden grinned. "Just don't get carried away. I'll be a quarter mile behind the transport vehicle. Once you've incapacitated them, I'll start shooting into the cargo hold. If I can't break through with the assault rifle, I'll use the magnetic IED. You two take out the driver and the guard up front. By that time, Mr. Agent Man will likely be dead from their shots. Any questions?"

Anthony stared at J.T. with piercing dark eyes as his upper lip curled into a sneer. "Nope, we're good to go, Mr. Vetcher. You can count on us."

"You better hope I can, and stay out of sight. Keep your phone glued to your ear. You'll be getting a call from me within the next ten minutes." Carden climbed into the Fiesta and sped away.

The overgrowth of brush hid them well as Anthony and Antonio waited out of sight and leaned against several available trees. J.T. grunted and writhed at the back of the van.

"Keep still. You're distracting me, and those cuffs aren't coming off until Mr. Vetcher says so," Antonio yelled out.

Anthony swatted Antonio's arm. "Keep it down, bro. I have to listen for the phone call." The buzz caused them both to look toward Anthony's front pants pocket. "It's showtime." He reached in and pulled out his cell. "What's the word, sir?"

"The truck just passed by, and it's what we anticipated. Two people were sitting up front. It's the standard setup. Take the cuffs off the agent and watch every move he makes. If he's going to try anything, it'll be when his hands are free."

"He's no match against Antonio and me."

"I'm sure that's true, but have Antonio get him out to the road, and you wait inside the truck. You'll be sideswiping the transport soon. Tell Antonio to give Agent Harper the second AK. I'll call you back in one minute. Now hurry."

Anthony ended the call and released J.T.'s restraints. "Get him out to the road. Here's the unloaded AK for him and the AR-22 for you. Keep your gun on his head at all times. They'll be here in a few minutes." Anthony jogged back to the cube van and stepped up on the running board. He climbed in, turned the key in the ignition, and sucked in a deep breath through his nose. Any minute now he'd get the second call, and there would be no turning back. He'd gun the cube van between the driver's door and the front wheel well. The truck would be unable to move. The diamonds would be theirs within minutes of everything taking place. The agent, driver, and every guard inside the truck would be dead, and he and his co-conspirators would disappear with three million dollars' worth of cool, icy diamonds.

The phone rang again. Anthony picked up.

"Start the truck. They're thirty seconds out. Tell Antonio to place the agent in the center of the road and then have him back away. It's time to move, now!" Carden hung up, and Anthony yelled out the window.

"Get him out there. The truck is coming around the curve." Anthony snapped his seat belt, placed the pistol between his legs, and turned the key in the ignition. He pressed the gas pedal to the floorboards and gunned it. Gravel sprayed around the vehicle, and the cube van lurched forward.

Chapter 58

"So far, so good." I took a quick look in my side mirror and saw nothing behind us, and as I looked out the windshield, everything was clear. "We're halfway there. I hope we didn't get this wrong." I turned to Cam. I'm sure he noticed the disappointment covering my face. "It's not that I want to be in a firefight, but if the kidnappers don't show themselves, we'll never find J.T. and Julie."

"Chin up, agent." Cam gave me a thoughtful smile. "We still have twelve miles to go."

The road was thick with a lush green canopy overhead. One lane in each direction took us around gentle curves where slits of sunlight broke through the shade. As much as I wanted to take in the beauty of the rustic road, I knew I had to be on high alert. I'd enjoy that route another time, maybe on a relaxing Sunday when Amber and I had nothing else to do that required our attention.

Cam hugged the *S* curve and came out on the other side in the rays of sun that bounced on the pavement between the foliage. He lowered his visor then leaned forward and stared. "What the hell? Son of a bitch, here we go!"

Cam slammed on the brakes, and we were jerked forward against our seat belts. The truck began to skid. I radioed to the crew in the back. "Heads-up! There's someone standing in the road with an assault rifle pointing at us. Get ready for the ambush!" I whipped out my gun from my shoulder holster and took aim. "Why isn't he firing on us?"

Cam yelled as he tried to get the truck under control. It teetered from the overcorrection, and we were headed for the ditch. The sudden impact caused the right side of my head to bounce off the window, and we were hit hard on the driver's side. Our truck was pushed against a tree, making it impossible to open my door fully. Glass exploded through the windshield of the vehicle that rammed us, and bullets pelted the armored skin and windows of our transport truck. I couldn't find my mic to call for help, and my cell phone had fallen. I had no idea where it was. A flash of movement caught my eye as the driver exited the truck and ran toward our rear gun ports.

"Cam, are you okay?" I looked down at my empty hand. "Shit!" My pistol lay somewhere on the floor.

Cam moaned from the impact, and his left arm was bleeding badly. "Jade, I think my ribs are broken."

"Hang tight, partner." I grabbed his gun out of the shoulder holster, but my efforts were in vain. There wasn't a gun port that could help me. The driver's side door was blocked by the truck that rammed us, and mine was against a tree. I had a six-inch space to squeeze out of my door if I needed to, and I'd use that to my advantage when the opportunity arose. I had no idea what condition Bill, Val, and Maria were in. If they weren't able to shoot out from the back, they could be sitting ducks. I looked toward the road again and saw two masked men standing there. Their positioning told me they knew where every gun port was and assumed they weren't in any danger. A vehicle flew past the smashed trucks and came to a stop in front of us.

Oh no—that's Julie's car.

Another masked man exited the vehicle, pulled out an assault rifle, and slung it over his shoulder as he approached the two in the road. That made four men in total—two huge and two of average height. It made no sense.

The large man in the front yelled toward us. "Open the back of the truck or he dies." He ripped the mask off the man's head, and I saw a horribly beaten man standing in front of me. My breath caught in my throat—I couldn't even swallow. "Cam, that has to be J.T. Look what they've done to him."

Cam swore at the sight of our colleague. "Jade, you have to rescue him, but I'm no good to you. You have to find out if the guys in the cargo hold are okay. We need their help, and you have to call Spelling. He'll get back up here right away."

I looked out to the road again and stared at J.T.'s injured face and the tape that covered his mouth. Anger filled my mind, but I knew I had to keep my wits about me. "I can't find my phone or the damn mic."

"Reach in my right front pocket. My phone should be

in there. Call Bill first and find out their condition, then call Spelling. Lean down and don't let them see what you're doing."

The large man yelled again that they were growing impatient.

I scrolled to Bill's name and hit Call. I prayed that somebody would answer it, and he did.

"Cam, are you all right?"

"It's Jade. Cam is injured. Are you guys okay?"

"I am. Val and Maria are banged up a bit. We're lying on the floor near the rear door. There's a rifle barrel sticking through the gun port above our heads. This is the only safe place to be unless the maniac starts firing and bullets ricochet off the interior walls."

I peeked over the dash and saw that they forced J.T. down on his knees. "Oh my God, Bill, I have to call Spelling."

"I already did, Jade. They're fifteen minutes away, but the Brookfield police are en route."

"Bill, these men have full auto assault rifles and who knows what else. They have J.T. too, and he's beaten badly."

"Shit! Have you seen Julie?"

"No, I have no idea where she is. Cam's side of the truck is disabled, and I have about a six-inch clearance that I can squeeze out of when I need to. They're yelling for you to get out of the cargo hold or they'll kill J.T."

"I'll tell whoever is holding that rifle above us that we're coming out. We need to buy J.T. some time. We can't let on that we're FBI agents. That'll put all of us in more danger."

"I know, but as soon as they realize there aren't any diamonds in the truck, it won't matter who we are, we'll all be dead. I just hope the police get here fast."

I heard the man at the back of the truck call to the ones holding J.T.

"They're coming out."

The sound of the rear door opening told me that Bill, Val, and Maria were about to put themselves in danger.

The man standing at the back of the truck called out, "Don't try to be a hero. You won't win. If any of you are carrying a weapon, put it down now or you'll get a bullet to the head the second your feet touch the pavement."

I heard a short commotion. Then I saw Val, Maria, and Bill being pushed with the barrel of a rifle toward the other two assailants standing in the road with J.T. I knew which masked man was the person in charge. The Pirelli brothers could hide their faces, but they couldn't hide their size. I'd keep my focus on the man standing next to J.T. and wearing tan pants.

After a brief conversation between them, one of the brothers walked back to the cargo hold.

"Cam, he's going after the diamonds. This is going to get very dangerous in about sixty seconds."

"You'll have to get their attention, Jade. Tell them we have the diamonds inside the cab. The cops should be here any minute."

I looked around frantically. "We don't have any type of container in here."

Seconds later I felt the weight of someone moving around in the back. I knew he was searching the cargo hold. I held my breath as I heard containers crashing and the man yelling.

"There's nothing back there, boss. The containers are all empty."

The man in the tan pants put his rifle to J.T.'s head. I pressed on the horn to get his attention. We needed to buy some time. They looked up, and the man in charge sent one of the brothers to the front of the truck.

"What do you want, lady?"

"I have what you're looking for inside the cab, but we're stuck in here. We can't get out."

He waved his rifle in the air. "Show me."

Cam tipped his head to the passenger side footwell. "Lift your purse. They may think it's an attaché case."

"Yeah, that might work." I lifted it and found my pistol on the floor beneath it. I whispered to Cam. "I found my gun. Do you think you're capable of shooting if you have to?"

"Yeah, pass my pistol back to me. I'll try to roll down my window without them noticing. I have a four-inch clearance."

"But that's your left hand, and it's injured."

"I'll make it work. As long as there are bullets buzzing past their heads, they'll take cover."

"They're wearing Kevlar vests. We'll have to aim for specific areas. Try to blow their shooting hand off. If that doesn't work, nail them in the heads." I slid Cam's gun across the seat then lifted my purse to the windshield. The sudden shriek of sirens behind them made the men spin in their shoes.

"Now!" I pushed my door open and took aim as I squeezed my body to a standing position on the running board. Cam fired out of the small opening between the smashed vehicles. I yelled out to my unarmed colleagues. "Take cover! Hit the ditch!"

Bill and Val grabbed J.T.'s arms and leapt into the nearest ditch. Maria was at their side. With rapid fire at the brothers, I covered my colleagues as they took shelter.

Cam hit one of the brothers in the shoulder. "I slowed one of them down."

"Good work, Cam." I took aim and kept firing.

The police cars blocked the road on both sides as gunfire rang out from all directions. The officers took cover behind their car doors as bullets from automatic rifles whizzed by them. Bill and Maria scurried along the ditch on my right.

I yelled, "Can you guys get to your weapons?"

"We're trying to, Jade. Val is watching over J.T. Cover us. We have to run to the cargo hold."

"I've got your backs!" I ejected the magazine, loaded the second one, and began firing again. Out of the corner of my eye, I saw the man in the tan pants slip away into the tree cover. "I don't think so. I'm going after him, Cam, so he doesn't get away. Have Bill and Maria take up the rear behind me."

"Be careful, Jade. His gun is much more deadly than yours."

"Any gun is deadly if you hit your target. I'm not going to let him get a bead on me." I tapped my shirt. "I have on Kevlar too."

Chapter 59

Branches snapped in the distance. I knew I couldn't be too far behind him, but I had to stay out of the sights of his high-powered rifle. It had a lot more distance than my sidearm. I inched forward, following the sound even though I couldn't see him in the thick brush. I stopped and listened. Then I turned and saw Maria and Bill coming up behind me.

I motioned them over. With my voice just above a whisper, I told them my thoughts. "He's probably fifty yards ahead of us in that direction." I pointed slightly to my right. "Don't forget, he's carrying an AK-47. We're no match against him. If he sees or hears us, he'll take down this entire woods."

"The only thing that will work is if we have a direct visual on him," Bill said.

I nodded. "Keep your heads on a swivel and stay low. Let's spread out a bit."

We used the larger trees as cover and stopped every few yards to scan for movement. When nothing caught our eye, we forged ahead.

A sudden round of gunfire lit up the woods. Branches cracked and dirt sprayed around us.

"Get down!" I hit the ground and tried to see where the shots were coming from.

"He's straight ahead," Bill yelled as he returned fire.

Maria screamed. "Son of a bitch, I'm hit."

"Where?" I scrambled to her side as fast as I could.

"I think he got my calf. It burns like hell."

I called out to Bill. "I hope you're covering us. How much ammo do you have?"

"Two more magazines. See how bad Maria's leg is."

I pulled up her pant leg and took a look. "It's a hard graze, Maria, but luckily he only caught the outer part of the muscle." I tore the sleeve off my guard uniform and wrapped it around her leg. "Keep yourself behind this tree and stay small. No exposed body parts. Got enough ammo if you need it?"

She checked her supply and gave me a nod.

"Okay, call for backup. Tell them we're a quarter mile in and heading due south." I belly crawled to Bill. "See him?"

"I don't see shit, and I don't hear him anymore, either. I have no idea how deep this woods is, so he could be pretty far ahead of us now."

"Shh… listen." I cocked my ear to the right. I cupped my hand over my mouth and whispered. "I hear something over there."

"It could be a squirrel for all we know. Do you want to push ahead?"

"I don't know. That man is no joke, and Maria needs medical attention. Five more minutes and we're calling it off." I crawled another twenty feet forward and stationed myself behind every large tree I could find. I stood and peeked around an enormous prairie oak. Bullets zinged past my head. "Son of a bitch!" I pulled back and took a deep breath.

"Jade, he isn't worth it. We'll get the Pirelli brothers to talk. I'm sure between the police force and the FBI, those two are already in custody."

"You're right. Let's back out of here." I jerked my head toward the sound of a car door and a female voice screaming. I knelt to the ground and cautiously looked over a downed tree. In the distance I saw a clearing and a car speeding away. "That maniac just carjacked someone!" I ran through the woods in that direction and heard Bill yelling at my back. I cleared the tree cover and spotted a woman who looked to be in her fifties lying on the pavement. Her knees were scuffed and bleeding. I spun in every direction to see if I'd get a visual on our suspect, but he was gone. "Ma'am, are you okay? Let me help you up. What is this place?"

She jumped at my voice, but the guard uniform I wore must have calmed her.

"It's the old Calumet Park. This is the only area where people still go for walks. That man came out of the woods with a huge gun right as I was getting out of my car."

"Consider yourself lucky he only took the car. Let me help you back to my group. We're going to walk through the woods. Can you manage that?"

"Yes, I'm just shaken up, that's all."

"Understood. What's your name?"

"Janet Cooper."

"Okay, Janet, I'm Jade. Take my hand, and I'll lead you out of here."

We reached Bill and Maria five minutes later. Spelling and Val were already at their side.

"The coast is clear, sir. He took off in this woman's car."

"Are you all right, ma'am?" Spelling asked.

"That maniac ripped me out of my car and tossed me across the pavement. I'm scuffed up, but I'll be okay." She held out her hand. "I'm Janet Cooper."

"And I'm SSA Spelling with the FBI. Let's get you looked at. Bill, give me a hand with Maria. Jade and Val, help Janet back."

"You got it, boss. How's J.T.?" I asked.

"He'll be okay after a few days of hospital food—Julie too." Spelling looked over his shoulder and gave me a grin.

"You found Julie? Is she all right? Where was she?"

Val spoke up. "Would you believe in the trunk of her car?"

"Oh my God, and there were bullets flying everywhere. She wasn't hit?"

"Luckily, no." Val stepped over a log and reached out to help Janet. "They're both banged up. J.T. got it the worst. He may have a broken jaw and a few cracked ribs. We aren't sure yet. The EMTs are getting them ready to transport to St. Mary's."

"What about the Pirellis?"

Spelling smirked. "We've got them in custody. They aren't going to see the light of day for a while. Now we need them to start singing about the mystery man."

"I'd be happy to pit one against the other. We'll get in their heads, sir, and somebody will tell us what we need to know."

We reached the turnout and road. Backed into the brush was that dark van we had a BOLO out for. Spelling said Forensics was on their way. Valuable information was likely inside the vehicle. Janet gave us a thorough description of her car as we exited the woods, and Spelling put out an APB for it. Cautious apprehension was advised. The driver was most assuredly armed and dangerous.

I looked out at the people, vehicles, and mayhem that had been spread over that seemingly quiet, pristine road just ninety minutes earlier. A makeshift triage area had been set up to get J.T., Julie, Cam, and Maria stabilized. They were loaded in the ambulances and taken away. The last EMT on site cleaned and bandaged Janet's scuffed knees before he left.

Spelling, Hopkins, and the rest of the agents were huddled against the hood of Spelling's cruiser, and I walked over. "So, did the package arrive at Rosemond Diamonds safe and secure?" I managed an exhausted smile.

Hopkins spoke up. "We're happy to say it did, and without a single problem. All that's left to do"—he jerked his head at several cruisers where the Pirelli brothers were cuffed in the backseats—"is to get those oversized monkeys to the holding cells and begin the interrogations."

Spelling waved an officer over. "Jade, have that officer take Janet's statement, then he can drive her home. We'll do our best to get her car back to her as soon as possible."

"Yes, sir, and then is it okay if I head to St. Mary's to check on J.T. and Julie? I haven't had a word with him in so long. I need to know how they are." The gravity of the week was setting in and my eyes teared up.

Spelling squeezed my shoulder. "You bet." He looked at all of us standing in the road. "I couldn't be more proud of the group of agents we have here in Milwaukee. You guys go over and above what is expected of you."

"We're family, sir."

Spelling grinned. "Damn straight, Monroe."

Chapter 60

He paced behind the liquor store on North Twenty-Seventh Street. His ride showed up a half hour later. Carden opened the passenger door and climbed in.

"Thanks, man, I owe you one."

"No, you owe me twenty thousand more to be exact." Zack chuckled. "The scanner has been going nonstop. You must have created quite a commotion near Brookfield. Sounds like a handful of people are being transported to St. Mary's, including Antonio. That idiot got himself winged."

"Yeah, I know, but there's a bigger problem than Antonio."

"Really, what? You got away. That's a positive thing. You mean because the brothers got nabbed?"

"No, because it was a setup. Every container in that armored transport was empty. They knew we were coming."

"That's just awesome, dude. How the hell am I supposed to get paid?" Zack pounded his fist against the steering wheel.

"You've gotten the advance. I'll come up with the rest

somehow. We've worked how many robberies together? Payment has never been an issue."

"Yeah, until there isn't one. What are you going to do now?"

"I need a day to think this over, but there's one thing I know for sure."

Zack jerked his head. "Yeah? What's that, genius?"

"Agent Harper hasn't paid for his crime against Sam yet. My brother's death needs to be avenged, and I know exactly how to do it."

Chapter 61

I stood in the ladies' room of St. Mary's Hospital and splashed water on my face. I stared at my reflection in the mirror, surprised at how rough I looked. Rutting around and belly crawling in the woods had left its mark on my skin and on my torn guard uniform.

I'd take only a few minutes to check on J.T. and Julie, peek in on Maria and Cam, then I'd head back to the downtown location, clean up a bit, and see what Spelling needed me to do next.

The woman at the reception counter tapped a few keys on her computer and told me J.T. and Julie were on the third floor. I thanked her and rode the elevator up while getting my fair share of stares from visitors and staff alike.

At the nurses' station, I inquired about all of my injured colleagues and Julie and whether I was able to check on them. Libby Jacobsen wore a name tag showing she was the charge nurse. If anyone, she could tell me the most. I directed my questions at her.

"Agent Harper and Agent Jenkins are still in X-ray. Agent

Jenkins probably has a few cracked ribs from that hard impact, and we're hoping Agent Harper's jaw is only dislocated. With some manipulation, we may get it back in its proper place. Having a broken jaw is quite an inconvenience. Of course, we're waiting on X-ray confirmation of that."

I nodded with relief. "And his ribs?"

"Same situation as with Agent Jenkins. The X-rays will tell us more. Give me one second, please. She rounded the counter and, with a few taps on the computer keyboard, looked up and smiled. "Julie Harper is resting comfortably in her room. Would you like to see her?"

"I sure would."

"Okay, right this way."

Libby led me down two hallways to room 317. She knocked then pushed the door open and peeked around the curtain. "Julie, you have a visitor. Agent Monroe is here to see you."

I heard Julie cough and clear her throat. "Sure, she can come in."

Libby gave me the go-ahead and walked out. She closed the door behind her. I stepped around the curtain and saw Julie's haggard looking face. My heart instantly broke for her. I was sure the ordeal she had been through would scar her for years.

"Julie?"

"Jade, please come and sit by me."

I didn't know Julie well, barely at all, now that I thought about it. We had met just once at our Christmas party. J.T. had spilled his cocktail all over his dress shirt, and Julie was kind enough to bring him a clean shirt from home. She stayed for an hour at most, had a glass of wine with us, and left. Because her brother was an FBI agent, Julie had endured the wrath of those evil people who wanted to punish J.T. and take down an armored truck. She ended up tangled in the mess of revenge that we still didn't know that much about.

Julie tapped the bed and pointed at the chair on her left. "Sit here. I'd like you close to me."

I took a seat and let out a deep sigh.

She chuckled at my appearance. "It kind of sucks to live far from your job. There's no time to clean up, right?"

I had already forgotten how badly I looked. I felt my face flush, but I smiled, anyway. "Yeah, sorry, I didn't have time to dress up. In all honesty, I was worried about both of you." I squeezed her hand when she seemed to have gone back to that dark place for a moment. "Julie, I'm not here to ask you questions today. You need time to calm down and regroup. I only came to see if you were all right."

"I am physically, save a few cuts and bruises. How's J.T.?"

"I haven't seen him yet. The nurse said he was down in X-ray, and they're hopeful that nothing is broken."

Julie looked away. The blinds were open, and her focus went toward the window. "It looks like a nice day after all. There's no time to appreciate the sun when you're held prisoner. Jade—"

I knew where her question was going. "The Pirelli brothers are already in custody. They'll never hurt anyone again."

"What about Carden Vetcher? Did you get him?"

"Carden Vetcher? That's his name?"

"Yes. I heard the brothers call his name many times. J.T. did too, but we never saw the man's face. He was either in the shadows or had a hat and dark glasses on. Today it was the mask."

"It's urgent that I update Agent Spelling." I pushed back the chair and stood. "I'm sorry I have to leave so abruptly, but we didn't have his full name before, only a hint that the last name Vetcher was somehow involved."

She looked worried. "So, you haven't captured him?"

"No, not yet, but ask me again tomorrow." I drew the curtain by the door and left the room.

At the nurses' station, I spoke to Libby again. "Are Agents Harper and Jenkins still in X-ray?"

"Sorry, but yes." She gave me a gentle smile. "You need to go home and take a hot bath, Agent Monroe." She looked me up and down. "A clean set of clothes will make you feel better too."

"Thanks, I will. How about Agent Delgado?"

"I'm afraid she's in the surgical suite getting stitched up."

"Okay, I'll check on all of them tomorrow. Please tell Agent Harper I was here."

"Will do."

I hit the button for the down elevator and left the hospital. In the car, I called Spelling as I drove. "Boss, Julie told me the mystery man's full name. It's Carden Vetcher."

"So Vetcher did come into play. Sam Dunlap and C.V.

Loomis were related after all, and now the C.V. makes sense. It stands for Carden Vetcher. Good work, agent. I'll get somebody in Tech on that name right away. Oh, and the APB came back on Janet's car."

I was surprised to hear that they found the car so quickly. "Go ahead and tell me. It was abandoned, right?"

"Of course it was. I imagine there were far too many law enforcement agencies looking for it. It was left along the street off Hampton in a less than desirable neighborhood. He must have had somebody pick him up."

"Sure, that makes sense. At least with his name, we can pull up his last known address and check out his associates."

"Okay, I'll get that started. Go home, Jade, and get some rest. I've already called in the second shift weekend agents. I've sent everyone else home too."

"Are you sure, sir?"

"Absolutely. All of you deserve it."

Chapter 62

My cell phone rang on the bathroom counter as I stepped out of the tub and slipped on my robe. I looked at the screen. Spelling was calling. "Hey, boss, what's up?"

"I hope you're relaxing."

"You mean by scrubbing the embedded dirt and twigs off my body? Yeah, that was done as soon as the tub was full of bath salts and hot water."

Spelling chuckled. "Anyway, I just got an update from Portage County on Sheriff Wells."

"I hope he was found wandering aimlessly in a nearby county."

"Unfortunately, he wasn't that lucky. A couple of hikers found his body early today. He was shot point blank."

"Those bastards. I hope none of them ever see the light of day again."

"I doubt if they will, but we have to apprehend Carden Vetcher first."

"I know, and we will. I'm sure of it."

"Okay, that's all I had. Go relax. Tomorrow I'll keep you plenty busy."

"Thank you, sir. Good night."

"Night, Jade."

I stepped from the bathroom into my bedroom and dressed. I couldn't help thinking of J.T. I'd make sure to call him after dinner and see how he was doing.

Amber grabbed the remote and clicked off the TV. She lifted the sleepy, limp Spaz off her lap and set him on the couch. "How are you doing, Sis? I'll admit, you look more human than you did forty minutes ago."

"I feel more human too. How about a pizza for dinner? I'm too lazy to sit at the table and eat, and I'd rather relax and catch up with you than watch you cook."

"Works for me. Pepperoni?"

I grinned. "Of course, and I'm buying."

"Good, then I'll order an extra-large."

After our order arrived and Amber and I had stuffed ourselves with pizza, I made a call to Bill. "Hey, Bill, nice work today."

"Back at you, agent. What's up?"

"I was wondering if you've heard anything about the likelihood of the same employee working at Trident now and Branded Armor back in 2014."

"Nobody has said anything to me. Let it go for the night, Jade. Turn that gerbil wheel off. The bad guys will still be around tomorrow."

I let out a long breath. "You're right. Have you spoken to J.T.?"

"Nah, but I thought you knew."

My heart began to pound double-time. "Knew what?"

"His left jaw was broken, and he's in surgery right now. He's going to be out for the night."

"Damn it. He'll have to endure six weeks of pure hell with protein shakes and vitamin drinks."

Bill sighed. "It could have been worse, Jade. We'll catch up with him and Julie tomorrow. We need their statements."

"Yeah, you're right. Okay, good night." I hung up and dropped down on the couch next to Amber. Spaz squeezed between us, curled up, and fell back asleep.

"Jade… Jade?"

"Huh?" I cracked open my eyes and saw Amber leaning over me with Spaz in her arms.

"It's ten o'clock. We're going to bed. I think you need a good night's sleep and not on the couch. Come on. I'm shutting down the house."

"Okay, I'm up." I stumbled to my bedroom. "Night, Sis. I love you."

Amber hugged me before she closed her bedroom door. "I love you too."

I crawled into bed, fluffed my pillow, and drifted off.

What seemed like minutes later, the summer sun pierced through the slit in my blackout curtains and caught me square in the eyes. I rolled over and stared at my cell phone screen—6:27. My alarm was set for six thirty. I stretched and gave myself three more luxurious minutes to lie in bed.

I thought about the day—Sunday. A day normal people enjoyed their yard, had a barbecue, or went to brunch with their parents and grandparents. I was headed to work to do my best to track down a vicious killer and a potential armed robber. I needed to learn the connection between Sam Dunbar, named Orly James Vetcher at birth, and Carden Vetcher. I grabbed my phone while the thought was fresh in my mind. Using the memo app, I tapped out a message to myself to have the tech department try to access Carden's birth records. I'd have them look up Chattanooga, Tennessee, first. That might tell us if he and Sam were actually brothers.

I showered, dressed, and followed the scent of freshly brewed coffee wafting down the hallway. Amber was still in bed, but thanks to the auto-start on the coffeemaker, I didn't have to bother preparing it that morning. It was ready to go, and I poured myself a cup. Back in my bedroom, I fed Polly and Porky, promised I'd give them more attention that evening, and returned to the bathroom to dry my hair.

I quietly left the house at eight o'clock. Amber hadn't awakened yet, and she deserved a good night's sleep. The drive to our downtown headquarters would take thirty-five minutes, and Sunday mornings were traffic-free.

At 8:45 a.m., we met in the large conference room upstairs, and every chair had an occupant. Spelling and Hopkins were seated at the head of the table.

Spelling began. "What we thought would be a slam dunk in locating Carden Vetcher's home and known accomplices has hit a snag."

A group moan sounded throughout the room.

Spelling raised his hands as if to tell us to pump the brakes. He continued. "We did confirm his birth name is

Carden Vetcher through hospital records in Tennessee." He looked at me. "Good call on that one, Monroe. As far as anything else, there is nothing in the entire state showing home ownership, a rental, or even a bank account under his name. He has to be using a second identity, or a third."

I cleared my throat and raised my brows at Spelling.

"Go ahead, Jade. I can see you're chomping at the bit."

"Well, sir, it's only my personal theory. Carden Vetcher is his real name, and according to Julie when I spoke to her last night, he didn't object to the Pirelli brothers using it. Julie overheard that name mentioned many times. Even though it's his real name, he likely doesn't attach it to anything important that can be tracked. He's definitely using an alias for everything that is tied to a permanent record."

"I agree, Jade," Hopkins said. "And C.V. Loomis was probably one of his aliases."

I caught movement through the glass conference room wall. Penny from the tech department was heading in our direction. There could be only one reason she would be entering our meeting—she'd found something about the insider.

Hopkins waved her in just as she raised her fist to knock. "What have you got, Penny?"

I crossed my fingers that it was something we could use.

"Good morning, everyone." She scanned each face at the table. "I'll get to the point since you look knee deep in this case. I believe I've found the insider."

"Go ahead," Spelling said.

"A man who goes by the name Zack Kenny used to work at Branded Armor from 2012 to 2014, when he abruptly quit his job without notice. Coincidentally, he disappeared shortly after that armored truck heist." She grinned. "The best part is, he's been working at Trident for seven months. I went ahead and took the liberty of entering his name in the system to see if he had any priors, but he doesn't—he's squeaky clean."

My enthusiasm deflated, and my rigid shoulders dropped.

Penny noticed and continued. "But that's exactly what would be expected from anyone who works at an armored transport company. Those types of places are very stringent and won't hire somebody with a record. It's typical, and a criminal who has enlisted his help would want him to stay under the radar and gather as much intel as possible. He could be your guy."

"Did you pull up an address for him?" Hopkins asked.

"Sure did. He seems to move around often and only rents."

"Good way to make a quick exit if he needs to," Bill said.

Penny continued. "He currently lives in Wauwatosa. Google satellite images show the house is somewhat secluded and perfect for somebody who wants to stay under the radar. There's a lot of tree cover around it in the summer."

"The Pirelli brothers could tell us more," I said.

Hopkins snickered. "They're as tight-lipped as they come. We thought for sure they'd roll on Vetcher or, worst-case scenario, each other. So far, we've got nothing."

I glanced up at the clock. "J.T. and Julie might know something. They had to be hidden somewhere after they left Portage. What better place than a secluded house not far from the route the armored truck was scheduled to take? And don't forget, Carden abandoned Janet's car and somebody picked him up."

"True enough, Jade." Spelling cocked his head toward the door. "Go talk to J.T. and Julie. I know you're itching to see your partner, anyway. Find out what you can about Friday night into Saturday morning and where they were held. If Zack Kenny is the accomplice, and Carden is laying low there, there's a chance that we can apprehend both of them today."

Bill spoke up. "Has anyone actually seen this man other than a freaked-out older woman, for a half second, and the guy at the window-tinting place who saw a man wearing a fedora and dark sunglasses?"

Spelling shrugged. "Other than the Pirelli brothers and probably Zack Kenny, I'm sure there's dozens of people. Problem is, they know him under a different identity."

I pushed back my chair and stood. "Okay, I'm heading out."

"Keep us posted," Spelling said. "We'll be here brainstorming our approach into Zack Kenny's house, just in case."

Chapter 63

I reached St. Mary's Hospital on the east side of Milwaukee at nine thirty. I was told during a phone call to the nurses' station that J.T. had just finished his breakfast of a vitamin shake. I was sure he had gone through four days of pure hell, and now he'd have that reminder for weeks to come. I rode the elevator to the third floor and walked the glistening white halls to room 302. I felt nervous for J.T. I didn't know what he had gone through, only that it was bad, but we needed to start that conversation so we could capture Carden Vetcher.

I knocked on J.T.'s door. I heard the TV volume go down then a muffled "Come in." I pushed the door open and slowly slid the privacy curtain to the side. With no idea what to expect, I hoped I'd be able to contain my emotions. J.T. was the toughest guy I knew, other than my old partner, Jack, and my dad, before his death. I was afraid of what I'd see on the other side of the curtain.

"Hey, partner, it's me." With a brave face, I slid the curtain completely open.

J.T. was unrecognizable, and I'm sure my expression showed my shock. His face was so swollen that it looked as if it would burst. He was also cut, scuffed, and black and blue. Stitches covered a two-inch space above his left brow. I took in a deep breath and sat on the chair next to his bed.

"J.T., my God. I can't imagine." I wiped my eyes with the back of my hand.

He tried to force a smile but couldn't—his face was too swollen.

"Does it hurt to talk?"

"No. Nothing moves except my lips. Can you understand me?"

"Yeah, well enough. What did they say about your ribs?"

"Bruised but not broken."

"That's a relief."

He reached out and squeezed my hand. "Have you seen Julie yet?"

I nodded. "I stopped in her room yesterday when you and Cam were getting X-rays. She's scuffed up but physically okay. I don't know what kind of emotional toll this will have on her, J.T. This isn't what she deals with on a daily basis. She's a caregiver, for Pete's sake."

"I'm worried about her, Jade."

"I know. She may need counseling. Maria is here too. She caught a rifle graze to the calf. I haven't seen her yet."

"Damn it. The team is going to be down three agents."

"Don't worry about that right now. We can report to the downtown office until all of you are back to work. We need your statement, J.T. Sorry it's so soon, but we have to apprehend Carden Vetcher."

"He got away?"

"We did our best to catch him, but he carjacked a woman and sped off while we were still trudging through the woods after him. We were no match against his AK. What was going on with that, anyway?"

"The part where I was standing in the road?"

"Yeah, with an assault rifle pointed at us."

"It was empty. I didn't have a vest on, either, and this huge goon, Antonio, was hiding in the brush with his AR-22 pointed at my head."

"The Pirelli brothers, Anthony and Antonio."

"Pirelli? As in the crime family based in Chicago?"

"None other."

J.T. reached for the cup of ice water and pressed the straw against his teeth. He took in an awkward suck and dribbled water down the sides of his mouth. "Damn wired teeth."

I handed him a tissue. "Were you guys transported Friday night?"

"I think so, but I lost track of the day of the week. We were either traveling or handcuffed in rooms by ourselves. For a while, I was in a cage of sorts next to Curt—"

"We know about Curt, and Hopkins took care of going to Waukegan to inform his mom. His brother is flying in from Omaha to help with the arrangements." I shook my head. "I'm so sorry, J.T." I paused to think of the sadness that had to be taking over the hearts of the Belmont family.

I continued. "At any time were you in a house?"

"Yeah, that much I remember. I was chained to a beam in the basement, and it was definitely a house, but I have no idea of who it belonged to or where we were."

"Do you remember how long it took to get from Portage to that house?"

"We stopped for a while, maybe an hour or two, then continued on. I know we pulled into a garage that was big enough for the van Julie was in and her car. I heard one voice I didn't recognize, so it must have been the homeowner."

"Good." I wrote down everything J.T. said. "Do you remember hearing anybody say the name Zack?"

"Not that I recall, but I don't recall a lot, anyway."

"Okay, I'm going to step out for a minute, update Spelling, and grab a coffee in the cafeteria. I'd offer to get you something, but you're on a liquid diet."

"Yeah, but I'll take a chocolate milk."

I grinned. "At least your humor is intact. I'll be back in ten minutes with two chocolate milks. That sounds way better than coffee." I peeked out the door and saw the guard enter the men's room at the end of the hall. I turned back to J.T. "The officer at the door should be back any minute. Looks like he just went to relieve himself." I handed J.T. the remote. "I think your favorite soap is on." I gave him a wink and walked out.

Chapter 64

He sat inconspicuously in one of the visitors' chairs lining the wall. He flipped the pages of a magazine and kept his head low. He heard the door close to room 302, the one he'd been eyeing, and cautiously looked that way. A woman walked out and turned left toward the bank of elevators. He listened for the ding and the sound of the doors parting. There it was.

The nurses' station stood thirty feet away, and several lab coats hung from the coatrack next to the counter. He waited for the right moment and looked down the hall. The officer was still in the men's room. His eyes followed the only nurse in the area when she rose from her chair, walked away, and entered a patient's room at the end of the hall. The moment she was out of sight, he sprang from his chair and removed one of the lab coats from the rack. He slipped it on, entered room 302, and made sure to close the door behind him.

The agent lay in bed, his eyes focused on the television. He briefly glanced at the male nurse who had entered his room then went back to watching TV.

The man approached J.T. and moved the roller cart out of the way. He closed in and leaned over the bed.

"How are the ribs today, Agent Harper?"

J.T.'s eyes darted back to the man. The voice alarmed him, and his face was vaguely familiar. "Do I know you?"

The man grinned. "You certainly do." The crunch of his fist against J.T.'s cheekbone knocked the agent senseless. Carden ripped the pillow out from behind J.T.'s head and covered his face with it.

J.T. thrashed, and his arms flailed wildly as he tried to find the call button. Carden pushed the pillow down harder and held his weight against it as he suffocated the agent.

The door swung open, and the woman's voice on the other side of the curtain called out.

"I bought you two chocolate milks since I knew one wouldn't be enough." She chuckled and pulled the curtain aside. The milk cartons fell to the floor.

Jade was on Carden in two strides and jerked him backward. Carden stumbled and hit the roller cart as he fell to the floor. The hard kick to his midsection knocked the wind out of him and gave Jade just enough time to draw her weapon.

"You make one move and I'll shoot your head off." She yelled for help as she reached across the bed and pulled the pillow off J.T.'s face.

The commotion alerted everyone, and within seconds the room was filled with nurses and security personnel.

"Hurry, Agent Harper needs help! This man was smothering

him with the pillow." After she jammed her knee into Carden's back and secured him, Jade holstered her gun. She held his wrists together and looked over her shoulder at the security guard behind her. "I need some cuffs and the hospital police right away."

"Yes, ma'am."

Jade looked up. Two nurses were tending to J.T. and checking his vitals. "Is he going to be all right?"

"He's breathing on his own, but we need to get him out of this room so the doctor can examine him. The stitched areas have come apart. He's bleeding again."

Jade leaned in against Carden's ear as he lay on the floor. "You're going down, asshole, and you'll never see daylight again. Consider this your lucky day—you lived through it." When the hospital police entered the room, she turned and looked over her shoulder.

"What's going on in here?"

"I'm FBI Agent Jade Monroe. This man just tried to kill a federal agent and is already wanted for murder and kidnapping. Get him the hell out of my sight."

Carden was pulled to his feet and taken away. Jade stood and brushed off her knees.

"J.T., can you hear me?"

He nodded weakly.

"You're going to be okay, partner. The doctor will make sure of it." She looked at the nurses who were wheeling J.T.'s bed out of the room. "Where are you taking him?"

Libby, the charge nurse, spoke up. "He's going back downstairs to the emergency wing, Agent Monroe. Dr.

Franklin will give him a thorough examination and secure those broken stitches."

Jade left the room and took a seat in the hallway. She scrolled to Spelling's number and hit Call.

"Hey, Jade, what's the latest?"

"I got him, boss. Carden Vetcher is finally in custody."

Chapter 65

J.T. remained in the hospital the longest—five days in all—and was scheduled to be released that day. Julie, Cam, and Maria had gone home on Monday, and both agents were on a two-week medical leave. Julie decided to take time off too.

For now, our group would be stationed downtown, and we'd work with that division until our entire team was healthy again and able to go back to work at our Glendale office.

With some digging, we were able to go back to 2014 and pull up Zack Kenny's bank records. We found a large cash deposit had been made to his account at the time of the armored truck robbery. His current statement also showed a larger than normal deposit, likely an advance on the diamond heist Carden and the Pirelli brothers thought they would get away with. With a warrant in hand, our agents searched Zack Kenny's house. They found a map showing the truck route for the diamond transport and the time it would take place. He was arrested and taken into custody, where he spilled the beans on Carden Vetcher for a reduced sentence. He and Vetcher had worked together—along with Sam Dunbar, Carden's brother—in four bank and armored truck robberies in the past.

We sat around the conference table, finishing up our paperwork on the case.

"So, Carden and Sam had been estranged for nearly thirty years before they found each other and got reacquainted?" I asked.

Hopkins nodded. "It appears that way. Years back, the mother admitted to Carden in a deathbed confession that he had three siblings she gave up for adoption. Orly James Vetcher, or Sam Dunbar, as he was known when he was adopted, was the only sibling Carden ever found. It turned out they both had records for robbery. That's when they began conspiring in their crimes and brought in Zack Kenny too. That's about the time Carden began using the name C.V. Loomis, an apparent joke between the brothers."

"And Zack Kenny told you all of this?" Bill asked.

"Yeah, for a lesser sentence. He was the lightweight in the bunch, but we told him he would be charged with serious crimes as an accomplice to kidnapping, murder, and robbery if he didn't cooperate."

I took a sip of water before speaking. "I bet Cam's wife was happy to return Ralph to Julie." I grinned. "Liza said he slobbered everywhere. Kaden was probably getting too attached to Ralph, anyway. This entire case amazes me, though."

Spelling tapped his pen against the table. "In what way?"

"That J.T. recognized Carden after three years. They were actually face-to-face in 2014 when J.T. interviewed him as the driver of the Branded Armor Transport truck that day. He was in on that heist all along."

"True, using the name Jeff Peterman back then. I'll admit, the man is clever."

I smirked. "He isn't that clever, boss. Sneaking into a hospital room to try to kill a federal agent because you didn't succeed the first time—well, that's just stupid."

"Agreed." Spelling looked at the clock. "Isn't it about time you go pick up your partner."

"It sure is, and I think the nurses are going to miss him. Even though his teeth are wired shut, they say he constantly gives them the raspberries."

Bill nodded. "That sounds like J.T., and I'm sure he's happy to be alive."

Val agreed. "Amen to that."

"Just a reminder, everyone. Curt's service begins at two o'clock. Do you think J.T. will be up for it?" Spelling asked.

"He insists, and I'll be doing the driving. He'll be fine," I said.

Spelling cocked his head toward the door. "Okay, go bail out your partner from that hospital."

"With pleasure, sir."

It was only a ten-minute drive to St. Mary's, but I still had time to relive the past week. It seemed like an eternity ago that I'd sat at the window table at Café Central and waited for J.T. to show up for breakfast—but he never did.

I knew our days would go on as they always had, save a few more bumps and bruises. With heavy hearts, we'd mourn the loss of a good agent, but three violent criminals had been taken off the street and would be caged in six-by-eight-foot cells for the rest of their lives. Another, Zack Kenny, would serve a five-year sentence. It was karma at its best.

I entered the hospital and rode the elevator to the third floor, where I walked the hallway to room 302. J.T. sat in the guest chair next to the bed, looking terrible, yet he wore a smile. I mirrored his grin.

"Ready to get the hell out of Dodge, partner?"

He muttered through his wired teeth, "Sure am."

I took a seat on the edge of the bed. "You know, J.T., I've been doing some serious thinking."

It looked as if he tried to furrow his brows, but his swollen face couldn't manage it. "Really? About what?"

"You may not have given this any thought because of the mess you've been through. Maybe you aren't even aware of it."

"Go on."

"Your Corolla got torched in the warehouse." I smiled.

J.T. tried to laugh but couldn't. "I bet that makes you happy."

"Actually, it does. You can't use the lame excuse anymore that you drive a girly car because it gets good gas mileage."

"I imagine you have something better in mind?" J.T. gingerly stood and pulled the curtain aside.

"Oh boy, do I ever." I helped him into the wheelchair and pushed it out the door. "This weekend, I'm taking you car shopping."

THE END

Thank you for reading *Leverage*, Book 4 in the new Agent Jade Monroe FBI Thriller Series. I hope you enjoyed it!

Follow the complete Jade Monroe saga starting with the **Detective Jade Monroe Crime Thriller Series**. The books are listed in order below:

Maniacal
Captive
Fallacy
Premonition
Exposed

The Agent Jade Monroe FBI Thriller Series follows on the heels of *Exposed*, Book 5 in the Detective Jade Monroe Crime Thriller Series. Currently available books are listed in order below:

Snapped
Justified
Donors

Stay abreast of my new releases by signing up for my VIP email list at: http://cmsutter.com/newsletter/

You'll be one of the first to get a glimpse of the cover reveals and release dates, and you'll have a chance at exciting raffles and freebies offered throughout the series.

Posting a review will help other readers find my books. I appreciate every review, whether positive or negative, and if you have a second to spare, a review is truly appreciated.

Again, thank you for reading!

Visit my author website at: http://cmsutter.com/

See all of my available titles at:
http://cmsutter.com/available-books/

Printed in Great Britain
by Amazon